PENGUIN CRIME FICTION

THE SHORTEST WAY TO HADES

Sarah Caudwell (a pseudonym) studied law at St. Anne's College, Oxford, was called to the Chancery Bar, and practiced law for several years at Lincoln's Inn. She is now a member of the legal section of the Trust Division of Lloyds Bank, Ltd., London. Her first novel was *Thus Was Adonis Murdered.*

THE SHORTEST WAY TO HADES

Sarah Caudwell

PENGUIN BOOKS

PENGUIN BOOKS
Viking Penguin Inc., 40 West 23rd Street,
New York, New York 10010, U.S.A.
Penguin Books Ltd, Harmondsworth,
Middlesex, England
Penguin Books Australia Ltd, Ringwood,
Victoria, Australia
Penguin Books Canada Limited, 2801 John Street,
Markham, Ontario, Canada L3R 1B4
Penguin Books (N.Z.) Ltd, 182–190 Wairau Road,
Auckland 10, New Zealand

First published in Great Britain by Century Publishers 1984
First published in the United States of America
by Charles Scribner's Sons 1985
Published in Penguin Books 1986

The characters and events described in this book are
entirely fictitious. Any resemblance to any actual person or
event is pure coincidence.

LIBRARY OF CONGRESS CATALOGING IN PUBLICATION DATA
Caudwell, Sarah.
The shortest way to Hades.
(Penguin crime fiction)
I. Title.
PR6053.A855S5   1986   823′.914   86-2459
ISBN 0 14 00.9401 6

Printed in the United States of America by
Offset Paperback Mfrs., Inc., Dallas, Pennsylvania
Set in Baskerville

This page is an exception to the rule that my friends J. T. and J. B. never appear on the same side of anything. Those that follow are dedicated to them jointly, in gratitude for their kindness and encouragement and innumerable drinks in the Corkscrew.

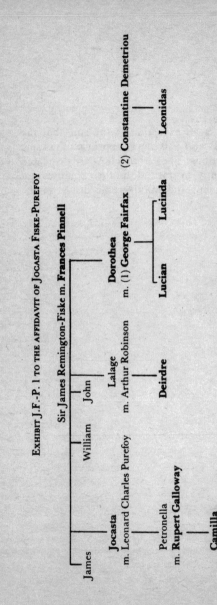

EXHIBIT J.F.-P. 1 TO THE AFFIDAVIT OF JOCASTA FISKE-PUREFOY

Sir James Remington-Fiske m. Frances Pinnell

James

William

John

Jocasta
m. Leonard Charles Purefoy

Petronella
m. Rupert Galloway

Camilla

Lalage
m. Arthur Robinson

Deirdre

Dorothea
m. (1) George Fairfax   (2) Constantine Demetriou

Lucian   Lucinda

Leonidas

Persons living at the date of swearing of the affidavit are indicated in bold type.

PROLOGUE

Cost candour what it may, I will not deceive my readers. By some whim of the publishers, and despite my own protests, the ensuing narrative is to be offered to the public in the guise of a work of fiction. Well, I will have no part in so gross an imposture: what follows is not some ingenious invention, but a plain, unembellished account of actual events, of interest, I fear, only to the more scholarly. Some of my readers, perhaps many, having expected to find in these pages diversion rather than instruction, will now hasten back to their booksellers to demand indignantly, it may be with threats of legal action, reimbursement of the sum so ill-advisedly expended. So be it: such readers will give me credit, I hope, for having enabled them by my prompt confession to return the volume unread and in almost pristine condition; and I for my part (for publisher and bookseller I cannot speak) would rather forgo the modest sum which would accrue to me from a sale—very modest, meagre might be a better word, one might almost say paltry—would infinitely rather forgo that sum than think it obtained by deception.

Ah, dear reader, would that I could indeed bring to my task the skills not merely of the Scholar but of the novelist. Would that the historian might be permitted to have regard to Art rather than Truth, and so enliven the narrative with descriptions of scenes known only by hearsay or speculation. Would above all that I could begin my story, as the writer of fiction might so easily do, at the true starting-point of the strange and tragic events which I propose to relate: the execution, on a March day in 1934, at the offices in Lincoln's Inn Fields of Messrs Tancred & Co., Solicitors, of the last Will and Testament of Sir James Remington-Fiske.

How admirably, and with what profusion of persuasive detail, would a novelist convey the scene: the dark old-fashioned office, its walls lined with Law Reports and Encyclopaedias of Conveyancing Precedents; the window looking

7

out on the green rectangle of Lincoln's Inn Fields; the weary-eyed, sober-suited clerk, perched on his stool to prepare the engrossment of the Will, copying the draft on to parchment in laborious black copperplate. (So shortly before the client arrived to sign it? Yes, I think so—it may be supposed, since Sir James died within the month, that he already knew the mortality of his condition, and that the Will was a matter of haste and urgency.) Outside, the pale sunbeams play a coquettish hide-and-seek with the springtime clouds; purple crocuses brighten the grass at the foot of the plane trees; a girl in a pretty dress walks past, the breeze ruffling her hair; the clerk, looking up and seeing her, smiles and returns with a lighter heart to his labours.

A motor-car—a Rolls-Royce, I suppose—draws to a purring halt outside the office. The man who steps from it has at first sight the large, looseknit physique which seems designed for walking grouse moors, and the high complexion that comes from doing so; but his flesh, when one looks more closely, is shrunken by illness, and the skin unhealthily mottled. The woman beside him, not yet middle-aged, still elegant, though she has borne six children, seems already almost in mourning—her round grey hat and veil give her a widowed look. The senior partner, emerging from his private office to greet them with the grave deference appropriate to the client and the occasion, asks anxiously—

No. No, I can't do it. I do not know if Sir James was tall or short, or what kind of hat his wife wore; the crocuses may have been yellow; there may have been no pretty girls in Lincoln's Inn Fields that day. I do not know and cannot invent, for the Scholar is the servant not of Art but Truth. Forgive me, dear reader: my narrative must have its startingpoint nearly half a century later, when my own interest first became engaged in the affair.

CHAPTER 1

PROFESSOR TAMAR—MR SHEPHERD RANG AND SAID PLEASE COME TO LONDON AS SOON AS POSSIBLE. YOU CAN STAY AT HIS FLAT AND HE WILL GIVE YOU DINNER. HE SAYS IT HAS SOMETHING TO DO WITH A MURDER.

Awaiting me in my pigeon-hole at the porter's lodge of St George's College, the message perplexed me more than a little. If my former pupil Timothy Shepherd, now in practice as a barrister in Lincoln's Inn, wished to offer me hospitality, I was more than willing to oblige him: by the sixth week of the Trinity term my academic responsibilities were weighing heavy on my shoulders, and the prospect of a day or two away from Oxford was delightful. I could not account, however, for the pressing nature of the invitation; and as for this question of murder—

My step quickened by curiosity, I crossed the quadrangle and mounted the staircase to my rooms. Dialling the telephone number of Timothy's Chambers, I was answered in the tone of glum hostility which is characteristic of the temporary typist. She admitted with some reluctance that Timothy was available.

'Hilary,' said my former pupil, 'how good of you to ring back. How soon can you come to London?'

'Timothy,' I said, 'what is all this about murder?'

'Ah yes,' said Timothy, sounding pleased with himself. 'I thought that might interest you. Do you happen to recall, by any chance, the Remington-Fiske application?'

'Was that the one with the Greek boy, who had such a deplorable effect on Julia?'

'That's right. Do you remember it?'

I did, I did indeed.

It had been about three months earlier, a Thursday in late February. I had been persuaded by an obligation of friendship to attend a seminar in the London School of Economics. By a quarter past five I could endure no more: I slipped out into Lincoln's Inn Fields and sought refuge in 62 New Square.

Not pausing to announce myself in the Clerks' Room—Henry, the Senior Clerk, does not altogether approve of me—I ascended the bare stone staircase to the second floor, occupied by the more junior members of Chambers and commonly known as the Nursery. Timothy's room was empty. Knocking, however, on the door opposite, I was invited to come in.

Desmond Ragwort and Michael Cantrip, the usual occupants of the room, were seated facing each other at their respective desks, in attitudes which suggested a rather decorative allegory of Virtue reproving Wantonness. From the pinkness which qualified the chaste pallor of Ragwort's marble cheek and the unsanctified sparkle in the witch-black eyes of Cantrip I gathered that Cantrip had done something of which Ragwort disapproved—it was not so rare a circumstance as to arouse my curiosity.

Timothy, some three or four years senior to the other two, stood by the fireplace, supporting his long and angular frame by resting his elbow on the mantelpiece: he seemed to disdain the comfort of the large leather armchair facing the window, which from my position in the doorway appeared unoccupied. I was gratified by the warmth of his greeting.

'My dear Hilary, what a pleasant surprise. What brings you to Lincoln's Inn?'

'I am a refugee from a gathering of sociologists,' I said. 'I thought that your company would raise my spirits.'

'You mean,' said a voice from the depths of the armchair, 'that you thought we would take you for drinks in the Corkscrew.'

The voice had once been described to me by an impressionable county court judge, a guest on High Table in St George's, as resembling Hymettus honey slightly seasoned with lemon juice. Hearing it, I did not need the glimpse of blonde hair and retroussé nose afforded by a second glance at the armchair to know that it was occupied after all by the fourth member of the Nursery, Selena Jardine.

'Some such notion,' I said, 'had crossed my mind. What a fortunate coincidence that none of you is busy.'

'Not busy?' said Ragwort. 'My dear Hilary, you surely do not imagine that we have abandoned our labours at this early hour of the afternoon to engage in idle gossip? We are in conference.'

'That's right,' said Cantrip. 'We've all got to zoom along to old Loppylugs tomorrow to get him to do a trust bust.' Cantrip was educated—I use the expression in its broadest possible sense—at the University of Cambridge, and I do not always find it easy to understand him. From my acquaintance with him, however, I was now sufficiently familiar with the Cambridge idiom to gather that the members of the Nursery were all instructed in connection with an application under the Variation of Trusts Act to be made on the following day before Mr Justice Lorimer.

'With a view to saving our clients a large sum in capital transfer tax,' said Selena, 'we are varying the trusts in reversion on the interest of a lady in her late eighties, and not, alas, in the best of health. The saving depends on this being done in her lifetime, and we're rather anxious that there shouldn't be any defect in our evidence which might oblige us to ask for an adjournment. So we're going through it now to make sure it's in order.'

They decided, after some debate, that the evidence was not of a confidential nature, and that I might remain to hear it; they promised that after this we would adjourn to the Corkscrew. When I had settled myself in the least uncomfortable of the chairs provided for lay clients and solicitors, Selena began to read her client's affidavit.

I, Jocasta Fiske-Purefoy of Fiske House, Belgrave Place, London S.W.1, Widow, make oath and say as follows:
1. I am the Plaintiff in these proceedings and save where the contrary expressly appears the facts herein stated are within my own knowledge.
2. The purpose of this application is to seek the approval of this

11

Honourable Court of an Arrangement varying the trusts of the Will dated 20th March 1934 of Sir James Remington-Fiske Baronet (hereinafter called 'the Testator') who died on the 16th day of April 1934 and Probate of whose said Will was granted out of the Principal Probate Registry on the 30th day of May 1934.

3. A family tree showing the persons at present in existence who are or may become beneficially interested under the said Will is now produced and shown to me marked 'J. F.-P. 1.' The relevant certificates of birth, marriage and death are now produced and shown to me tied together in a bundle marked 'J. F.-P. 2.'

For the assistance of my readers, I have arranged for a copy of exhibit J. F.-P. 1 to be reproduced at the beginning of this volume. It will be observed, however, that the precise dates of birth, marriage and death of the baronet's descendants have been left incomplete—a circumstance which caused Selena some vexation: she did not, she said, expect much of her instructing solicitors, but she had imagined that even a dozy firm like Tancred's would have known how to prepare a family tree.

'We have the certificates,' said Ragwort. 'If I go through them while you're reading your affidavit and make a note of the dates, we can hand it to the judge at the hearing.'

'With apologies,' said Selena, still displeased, 'for it's not being properly sworn. Yes, thank you, Ragwort, that would be most kind.'

4. As appears from the said family tree the Testator was survived by his widow Lady Frances Remington-Fiske, who is still living, and by six children. His three sons, however, have all since died un-married and without issue, the younger two having been killed in action in the Second World War and the eldest having died some years later.

5. I am the eldest of the Testator's three daughters, being now 65 years of age, and have been married once, namely to the late Leonard Charles Purefoy. There was one child of my said marriage, namely my late daughter Petronella. Petronella was married once, namely to Rupert

*Galloway, and my granddaughter, Camilla Fiske-Galloway, is the
only child of the said marriage.*
*6. The second of the Testator's daughters was my late sister Lalage,
who was married once, namely to the late Arthur Robinson. My niece
Deirdre Robinson is the only child of the said marriage.*

'There are persons of great eminence,' I remarked, 'whose
surname is Robinson. But I somehow suspect a certain
coming down in the world.'

'You suspect rightly,' said Selena. 'After spending her first
youth—and indeed most of her second youth—in dutiful
spinsterhood, Lalage sniffed the permissive air of the Sixties
and ran off with a garage mechanic. I gather that the family
weren't too pleased.'

*7. My daughter Petronella and my sister Lalage both died in a tragic
accident when travelling in a motor-car driven by my sister's said
husband, who also suffered fatal injuries.*
*8. At the time of the tragedy Camilla was five years old and Deirdre
was one year old. It was decided that both children should come to live at
Fiske House, where I myself had resided with my mother since the death
of my husband. They both still reside with my mother and myself at that
address. Camilla is now 21 years of age and is in her second year at the
University of Cambridge, where she is reading Law. Deirdre is now 17
years of age and accordingly still a minor and is in her last term at
school.*
*9. My sister Dorothea is the youngest of the Testator's daughters,
being now 52 years of age, and has been married twice. Her first
marriage, namely to George Edward Fairfax, ended in divorce. She
now resides with her second husband, namely Constantine Demetriou,
who is of Greek nationality, at the Villa Miranda near the village of
Casiope in the island of Corfu. There are two children only of her first
marriage, namely Lucian and Lucinda Fairfax, who are twins and are
now 23 years of age. There is one child only of her second marriage,
namely Leonidas Demetriou, who is now 16 years of age and accordingly still a minor. All three children normally reside with my sister in the
said island of Corfu, though the twins engage extensively in travel and*

13

Leonidas is a pupil at Godmansworth College, an English boarding-school.
10. The Testator by his said Will—

'I say,' said Cantrip, 'shouldn't she say that someone's just waved a copy of the Will at her marked J. F.-P. thingummy?'

From the scandalized response of his colleagues I gathered that this was a very shocking suggestion. The Probate copy of the Will—that was to say, the photographic copy made in the Probate Registry and bound up in the document confirming the title of the executors to administer the estate—the Probate copy was considered to form part of an order of the Court and to need no verification. The Probate would be among the papers already left with the Judge's Clerk and would prove itself: to suppose otherwise was a grave solecism.

'It's all very well you talking about solipsisms,' said Cantrip. 'If I was poor old Loppylugs I'd rather have a few solipsisms than be made to plough through the Probate thingy. I bet it's one of the old-fashioned kind, all in hand-writing with no punctuation or paragraphs and running to umpteen pages.'

'No one is suggesting,' said Selena, 'that Mr Justice Lorimer should actually read the Probate. The solicitors, I devoutly hope, will have provided him with a nice typed copy, just like the ones we have ourselves. But that's for convenience, you see, not as part of the evidence.'

I endeavoured to look less perplexed than Cantrip by the fineness of this distinction.

—devised his residuary real estate (which principally consisted of certain agricultural land in the County of Wiltshire) to his trustees in strict settlement upon trust for his widow Lady Frances Remington-Fiske during her life with remainder to his eldest son James for life with remainder in tail to the eldest son of James to attain 21 with remainder in tail to the second and every other son of James to attain that age successively according to seniority with remainder in tail to the

eldest daughter of James to attain that age or previously marry with remainder in tail—

'Selena,' I said, 'is there any end to all this?'

'My summary,' said Selena, 'is almost ruthlessly concise. If set out in full, these provisions would run to eight pages.'

'I expect it's all this stuff about tails that's getting you down,' said Cantrip kindly. 'If a chap's got a tail, you see, what it means is that everything's got to be passed on to his eldest son, and then to his eldest son's eldest son, and so on until the Last Trump. So the chap with the tail can't get his paws on the loot and it might all be a bit sickening for him, but he can do a thing called barring the entail.'

Though a member of the Faculty of Laws in the University of Oxford, I am the first to admit that I am an historian rather than a lawyer. The concept of the entailed estate, however, was well developed by the end of the thirteenth century, and I may claim without immodesty to be familiar with it. I did not tell Cantrip this, for I knew he would not have believed me.

'It is the dearest hope of the English landowner,' said Selena, 'to father an unbroken line of male offspring, all large and red-faced and fond of hunting. But when making his Will he has to contemplate the possibility of an elder son dying, leaving only daughters, and to decide whether, in that regrettable event, his property should pass into the incompetent hands of a daughter or to some person of the preferred sex in a junior branch of the family. Sir James may be said to have preferred seniority to sex—that is to say, daughters of an elder son come in before sons of a younger son. I suppose,' she added with a sigh, 'that that's really rather progressive.'

She continued inexorably to recite the remainders over in favour of each in turn of the Testator's three sons and three daughters and their respective issue; but I cannot take so austere a view of the duties of the historian as to demand the attention of my readers for what failed to hold my own. I gathered, however, that the interests of the beneficiaries under the baronet's Will were conditional on surviving his widow, and that the interests of his daughters were subject to protective trusts—they would be forfeited on bankruptcy or alienation: in these circumstances, it was impracticable for the Will to be varied without the assistance of the Court.

My attention was revived by a mention of the value of the settled funds: a fortune of five and a quarter million pounds somehow excites interest.

11. The property now subject to the trusts of the Testator's Will consists of the agricultural land described in Part I of the valuation now produced and shown to me marked 'J.F.-P. 3' and the investments (representing the proceeds of sale of certain farms formerly comprised in the estate) specified in Part II of the said valuation. It will be seen that the present value of the said land is approximately £4,500,000 without vacant possession and that the value of the said investments on the day prior to the swearing of this affidavit was £753,000.

'That sounds,' I said, 'like a very comfortable little nest-egg—who in the end is actually going to get it?'

'If you had been paying attention,' said Selena, 'you would know that Camilla was going to get it, as the only descendant of the eldest daughter, provided she survives her great-grandmother. If she dies before Lady Remington-Fiske but leaves children, then her children will get it. If she dies without children, then Deirdre Robinson gets it, as the only child of the second daughter. If she also dies before the widow, then Lucian gets it, and so on. If all the Testator's descendants predecease his widow there's an ultimate remainder to the estate of his eldest son; but the eldest son, as it happens, left all he had to Camilla, so there's no problem about that.'

'And which of you,' I asked, 'is representing whom?'

'My client is Jocasta, but I'm going to be led at the hearing by Basil Ptarmigan. Technically, you see, though all this is really for the benefit of Camilla, it's Jocasta who's making the application. I thought the sums involved were large enough to justify her having leading Counsel.'

'And I,' said Timothy, 'appear for the trustees—Mr Tancred of our instructing solicitors and Camilla's father, Rupert Galloway. My responsibility on their behalf is to consider the Arrangement from the point of view of any unborn or unascertained beneficiaries who may become interested in the settled fund. Ragwort is in a rather similar position—he appears for Dorothea Demetriou, who has been appointed guardian for the purpose of these proceedings of the two minor beneficiaries.'

'Mrs Demetriou,' said Ragwort, 'has made it clear that she herself does not wish to receive anything from the settled fund. It accordingly seemed quite proper and convenient for her to act as guardian *ad litem* for her niece and her younger son and for me to represent her in that and her personal capacity.'

'I've got Camilla,' said Cantrip, 'but I couldn't swing it that I ought to see her in conference. Absolutely sickening, having a fantastically attractive bird on one's brief and not managing to meet her.'

'If you haven't met her,' I said, 'how do you know she's fantastically attractive?'

'If a bird's all set to come into five million quid,' said Cantrip, 'you don't need to meet her to know she's fantastically attractive.'

12. *I am advised that the settled fund will be exempt from capital transfer tax on the death of my mother but that if no action is taken before that time the tax prospectively payable on the termination of my own life interest at any time thereafter will be not less than three million pounds and may be substantially more. The purpose of the proposed Arrangement is to avoid this liability.*

13. *A draft of the proposed Arrangement is now produced and shown to me marked 'J.F.-P. 5.' It provides for my reversionary life interest to be extinguished in exchange for a capital sum of £200,000 to be paid to me on my mother's death. It also provides for the reversionary life interest of my sister Dorothea, which would be unlikely ever to fall into possession, to be extinguished without payment.*

14. *The Arrangement further provides for two funds of £20,000 each to*

17

be set aside on my mother's death and held upon the trusts therein mentioned for the benefit of the minor and unborn issue of Lalage and Dorothea respectively: in all practical probability, one such fund will be payable to my niece Deirdre Robinson absolutely and the other to my nephew Leonidas Demetriou absolutely.

'I don't quite see,' I said, 'why they should get anything. If they don't inherit, the Arrangement will have cost them nothing: if they do, they have the benefit of the tax saving.'

'Absolutely right,' said Cantrip, much pleased by this remark. 'Just what I said—"Don't give the little perishers a bean" was what I said. But Timothy and Ragwort went all obstructive about it.'

'On behalf of the unborn and minor beneficiaries,' said Timothy, 'we felt obliged to ask for some modest payment in respect of our negotiating position.'

'What they meant was,' said Cantrip, 'that if the little varmints were of age they could stymie the whole thing by just saying no. So if Camilla didn't want this thumping tax bill she'd probably have to slip them a few thousand quid to get them to cooperate. That's what they call a negotiating position.'

'We thought it right,' said Ragwort, looking up from his sheaf of certificates, 'to do no less for our young clients than they might, if of age, have reasonably done for themselves. Endeavouring to steer a moderate course between the avaricious and the quixotic, we suggested that a sum of forty thousand pounds, to be equally divided, would represent an acceptable douceur.'

I inquired whether Dorothea's adult children did not also want a douceur.

'No,' said Selena, 'they're being all *noblesse oblige*—delighted to help Camilla save tax and wouldn't dream of taking a penny for it. Their father, George Fairfax, is a successful merchant banker—I dare say they can afford to be high-minded. So we've simply put them on Cantrip's brief along with Camilla. Now, Hilary, if you'll stay quiet and not interrupt while we read the evidence about the protective trusts, explaining that there's no danger of Jocasta or Dorothea going bankrupt or anything, we'll all be able to adjourn to the Corkscrew.'

15. *My solicitor has carefully explained to me the nature of the acts and events whereby I might incur a forfeiture of my protected life interest. I have conscientiously considered whether I have ever done so and am satisfied that I have not. I am not extravagant, and live without difficulty within my present income, which derives from a settlement made on the occasion of my marriage. My mother intends to leave to me by her Will the house where we now reside and the sum payable to me under the Arrangement will be sufficient to enable me to discharge those household expenses which are at present borne by her. I respectfully submit that the protective trusts no longer serve any useful purpose.*

16. *I further respectfully submit that the Arrangement is for the benefit of all minor, unborn and unascertained persons who may become interested in the settled fund and ask that the same may be approved on their behalf.*

Sworn before me, a Commissioner for Oaths—

'And so forth,' said Selena. 'Would you like to read Dorothea's affidavit, Ragwort, as she's your client?'

'I haven't quite finished going through the birth certificates,' said Ragwort. 'Would you be kind enough to read it for me?'

Dorothea's evidence regarding her protected life interest closely resembled that given by her sister—naturally so, since Selena and Ragwort had used the same precedent. Her solicitor had explained to her with similar care the ways in which she might have forfeited her interest; she had considered with similar conscientiousness whether she might have done so; she was similarly unextravagant and able to live within her income. The house where she lived in Corfu was owned jointly by herself and her husband and she also owned a flat in Hampstead, used by her children and herself on visits to London. She earned a salary as artistic designer for a small ceramics factory near Casiope, of which she was part owner, and enjoyed a generous income—very generous, it sounded, in the circumstances—from the settlement made by her first husband on the occasion of their divorce. She respectfully submitted, and so forth.

'Ragwort,' said Selena, 'you look anxious. Is something the matter?'

'Do you happen,' said Ragwort, 'to know what the date is?'

'The twenty-sixth of February.'

'That's what I thought,' said Ragwort in tones of gloom. 'Deirdre's birthday was on the twenty-third.'

'Oh well,' said Cantrip, 'I don't suppose she expected us to send her a present.'

'Her eighteenth birthday,' said Ragwort. 'She's of age.'

Without perfectly understanding why, I perceived that the prospects of adjourning to the Corkscrew had receded. Ragwort, I would have supposed, could as competently represent a girl of eighteen as one of seventeen. But no, it was out of the question—it was the duty of her Counsel, now that she was of age, to make clear to her the nature of the Arrangement and her right to give or withhold consent; she might instruct him, after receiving such advice, to negotiate other terms than those agreed by Ragwort: Ragwort, if still representing her, would be severely embarrassed.

'It's no use,' said Timothy. 'They'll have to instruct separate Counsel for her. We'd better ring the solicitors and tell them. It's a pity, of course, given the urgency of the application—I don't suppose they'll manage to find anyone in time for it to be heard tomorrow.'

'Nonsense,' said Selena, 'we'll tell them to instruct Julia. I'll just ring through to 63 and make sure she's still there.'

Selena's expression, when she joined us an hour later in the Corkscrew, was that of a woman who thinks the past hour well spent. She took her place at the candlelit oak table and allowed Timothy to pour her a glass of claret.

It had turned out, she thought, rather satisfactorily. Julia was content to accept instructions, Tancred's to give them; the appropriate telephone calls had been successfully made;

and the girl Deirdre was now in a taxi on her way to Lincoln's Inn, where Julia waited to advise her.

'It will be good for Julia,' said Selena, 'to be involved in an ordinary, down-to-earth Chancery matter. With a pure Revenue practice, she's sometimes in danger of becoming a little out of touch with real life.'

Knowing that Julia's strategy for dealing with real life, on those rare occasions when she came across it, was to keep very quiet and hope it would go away, I feared that the grim practicalities of an application under the Variation of Trusts Act might prove too much for her; but the financial rewards, I supposed, would justify the risk.

'I did mention to Tancred's,' said Selena, 'that they were asking Miss Larwood to take the case at very short notice and that her Clerk would expect this to be reflected in the brief fee. Then I rang her Clerk, and told him what he was expecting. So I think that the fee should be not ungenerous.'

Timothy purchased another bottle of claret, and the conversation turned, as it so often does among the Chancery Bar, to the imperfections of their administrative and clerical arrangements. The tyranny of their Clerk Henry and the incompetence of the temporary typist were recalled in lingering detail and with copious illustrative anecdote. The time was passing pleasantly in this manner, and a third bottle had just been opened for us, when there stumbled through the doorway of the Corkscrew the figure of a woman: her dark hair was dishevelled, her clothing in some disorder; she gazed about her with anxious bewilderment, as if not knowing where she was, or where she ought to be. This being Julia's habitual demeanour, we suspected nothing amiss.

Traversing successfully—that is to say, without knocking anything over or tripping on anyone's briefcase—the distance from the doorway to our table, she sank wearily into one of the oak armchairs. I perceived at once that something was troubling her: her manner, when she greeted us, was more than usually distrait, and even her compliments to Ragwort lacked their accustomed fervour. She lit a Gauloise, drank a deep draught of claret, and looked apologetically at her friends.

'I don't quite see that it's my fault,' said Julia, 'but I don't think you're going to be pleased.'

'Of course it's not your fault,' said Selena kindly. 'What exactly is the difficulty? Didn't your client arrive?'

'No—no, it's not that. The solicitors delivered her in good order about half an hour ago, and left me to explain the Arrangement to her.'

'Can't she understand what it's about?'

'Oh, I think she has a reasonable grasp of the essential features.' Julia drank more claret, and drew deeply on her Gauloise. 'I was, of course, at pains to explain to her that she was not obliged to agree to it and could say no if she liked.'

'Of course,' said Selena. 'That was very proper of you, Julia.'

Julia looked doubtful.

'Dear me,' said Timothy, 'you don't mean she *does* say no?'

'She can't say no,' said Cantrip indignantly.

'Oh yes she can,' said Ragwort.

'I wouldn't say,' said Julia, draining her glass and gazing thoughtfully into its depths, 'that my client says no, exactly.' She brightened, as at some happy inspiration. 'It would be better to say, I think, that she instructs me to ask for an amendment to the Arrangement. A very small amendment, really—there would hardly be any re-drafting required. I do like this claret, I'm feeling much better now—may I have some more?'

'Of course,' said Selena. 'Would you like to tell us the precise nature of this small amendment?'

'The Arrangement as at present drafted provides, if my memory serves me, for a sum of twenty thousand pounds to be paid to my client on the termination of the existing life interest?' They nodded. 'The amendment we have in mind,' said Julia, 'is the substitution of a figure of one hundred thousand pounds.'

There was a shocked silence.

'A hundred thousand quid?' said Cantrip eventually, with apparent difficulty in finding his voice. 'If you think my client's going to fork out an extra eighty thousand quid, you must be even further round the twist than I've always thought. Come off it, Larwood old thing.' The professional exchanges of Chancery Counsel are not always characterized by such robust informality; but Julia and Cantrip were once on those terms conventionally called more intimate than friendship, and this perhaps accounts for it.

'My dear Cantrip,' said Julia, 'it's no use your saying "come off it". If your client wants our consent to the Arrangement, it will cost her a hundred thousand pounds. I should add that the figure is not negotiable. No doubt you will wish to take instructions—I gather Camilla's in London this evening, so there should be no difficulty.'

'Well, I'm going to advise her to tell your client to get lost. It's blackmail.'

'I'm sorry you feel like that about it, Cantrip, Isn't "arm's length negotiation" more the phrase you're looking for?'

'No, it jolly well isn't. "Blackmail" is the phrase I'm looking for.'

'Ah well—we have been friends too long, I hope, to quarrel over a question of semantics. You must advise your client as you think best, of course. I understand, however, that the prospective liability to capital transfer tax, if nothing is done in the lifetime of the widow, is not less than three million pounds. You will surely not allow a temporary sense of pique to expose your client to so severe an encroachment on her inheritance?'

'Look here, Larwood, do be reasonable – you can't seriously expect me to tell Tancred's to drag Camilla out of bed in the middle of the night—'

'It's only half past seven,' said Selena mildly.

'—well, drag her away from dinner in the middle of the evening, and tell her she's got to cough up another eighty thousand quid—'

'I'm afraid,' said Timothy, 'that it will be another hundred and sixty thousand. I'm sorry to add to your troubles, Cantrip, but if Deirdre's going to get a hundred thousand, I don't see how Ragwort and I can agree to less for the minor and unborn issue of Dorothea. The judge would think it very odd, you must see that.'

'Sweet suffering swordfish,' said Cantrip, clutching his forehead in an interesting dramatic gesture, 'there ought to be a law against it. All right—tell Camilla that she's got to cough up an extra hundred and sixty thousand if she wants this thing to go through and she's got until ten-thirty tomorrow morning to decide about it.'

'The urgency,' said Julia, 'is of not of my client's making. If Camilla needs more time to reach a decision, no doubt the application can be adjourned. I don't know, of course, how soon we could have another date for the hearing—I hear that the list is rather crowded . . . and the widow, I gather, is in her late eighties, and not, alas, in the best of health . . . Still, Cantrip, it's entirely for you to advise your client.'

'Time was,' said Ragwort, 'when a young woman just of age would not have thought it proper to obstruct the arrangements made by her elders for the preservation of the family fortune. Or, if indifferent to propriety, would not have thought it expedient. Has your client considered, Julia, how her present conduct may affect her expectations?'

'My client seems to think,' said Julia, 'that she can expect little from the generosity of her relations. In reaching this conclusion, she is perhaps influenced by the fact that the occasion of her eighteenth birthday passed entirely un-noticed by the rest of the family.' Julia, a sentimental woman, looked reproachfully at Cantrip, as if holding him personally responsible for this neglect.

'Oh dear,' said Selena. 'You mean they forgot it altogether? Not just its legal significance?'

'Altogether. There was not so much as a postcard. It was in striking contrast, I gather, to the celebration of Camilla's coming of age four years ago. So my client feels that she should take advantage of the present opportunity to secure her financial independence, and it seems to her that a sum of a hundred thousand pounds is the minimum required. She realizes that she won't have it until her grandmother dies, and that in the meantime the atmosphere in the home may be a little strained, but the prospect does not seem to trouble her unduly.'

'I see,' said Selena, rising from her chair. 'I'd better ring

Tancred's, I suppose, and see if they can arrange for us all to have further instructions from our clients before half past ten tomorrow. After that, perhaps we can all go and eat something. Aren't you joining us, Julia?' For Julia had begun that process of gathering things together which signifies her intention to depart.

'I'm afraid I can't. Deirdre's waiting for me in the bar at Guido's—I said I'd take her to dinner there.' She again looked reproachfully at Cantrip. 'Someone ought to do something to celebrate the poor girl's birthday.'

CHAPTER 2

On the following morning, having accepted the hospitality of the spare bed in Timothy's flat, I woke to find him making a hurried breakfast. At nine o'clock, if the efforts of their solicitors could achieve it, the parties to the Remington-Fiske application were to be gathered together in 62 New Square to receive advice and give instructions on Julia's minor amendment. In order to discuss certain preliminary matters with the other Counsel concerned, Timothy proposed to be there at half past eight.

There had been aroused in me a measure of curiosity about the family: I thought it would be of some interest to observe them at first hand, and I supposed there could be no objection to my presence.

'My dear Hilary,' said my former pupil, 'there is every objection. The relationship between Counsel and client is one of absolute confidentiality. We could hardly expect our clients to speak frankly to us of their most intimate personal affairs'—in Lincoln's Inn this means their financial affairs—'before an audience of gossip-mongering academics.'

When Timothy decides to be pompous, it is no use arguing with him. 'Very well,' I said. 'If that is your view, then naturally I respect it. I shall stay here and have a leisurely breakfast.'

'You can come to the hearing, if you like,' said Timothy,

generously offering me the same freedom to sit in the public benches as is enjoyed by every citizen, and every visitor to our shores, with an hour or two to wile away in the Law Courts. 'I think we're in Court 25.'

My mind was occupied, as I finished breakfast, with musing on the English law of entails, moulded through the centuries by the conflicting ambitions of the landowner and his heirs—his for a dynasty, theirs for cash. I was familiar, naturally, with the mediæval procedures for barring the entail by way of fine or recovery. It occurred to me, however, that I was wholly unfamiliar with the modern form of disentailing assurance, and had no idea what signs it might give of its ancestry. Impatient, as is the way of the Scholar, to remedy immediately such a *lacuna* in my knowledge, I realized with vexation that the libraries of the neighbourhood would not yet be open; but was pleased to remember, after a few moments, that a full set of the *Encyclopædia of Forms and Precedents* was to be found a mere five minutes' walk away, in the waiting-room at 62 New Square. I could consult it at once without disturbing anyone; and none of my friends, I hoped, would grudge me so modest a favour.

The heavy oak door leading to the Clerks' Room and the waiting-room was already open, as is usual in the daytime; but neither was occupied. I settled down in the waiting-room, in the little niche between bookcase and window, not troubling to provide myself with a chair; the Scholar, in pursuit of knowledge, is indifferent to physical comfort, and I was content to sit on the floor.

A few minutes later, happening to glance out of the window, I perceived the approach of a little group of people. They were led—I mean only that he seemed to know the way—by a man, as I judged, in his middle fifties. He wore the pin-striped subfusc which is the uniform of the professional man going about his business, and the signs of one who has prospered in his profession—a fullness of flesh and ripeness of complexion, claret-dark under thick white hair, not often seen in those obliged to frugality.

Tall as he was, an inch or two over six foot, he had no great advantage in height over either of the two women beside him, and a very slight inclination of the head was enough to show an attentive deference to the one walking on his right. She looked, I thought, accustomed to deference: iron-haired and angular of feature, she bore herself with that inflexibly upright carriage which can only be produced by a sound training in deportment and an absolute conviction of superiority. My attention was chiefly engaged, however, by the striking good looks of the girl on the man's left. Tall, as I have mentioned, with a dark fur jacket swinging loosely from her shoulders, she walked with her head thrown back a little, as if to drink in the air of the clear February morning, and seemed consciously to restrain the athletic vigour of her stride to avoid out-pacing her companions. Straight black hair, straight black eyebrows, the brightness of her eyes and the brilliance of her smile emphasized by a slight suntan—yes, she was splendid to look at. There was none the less, and despite the difference in ages, a sufficient family resemblance between the two women to make one think that the elder must once have been very handsome; and that the younger might some day be rather formidable.

I had thought at first that there were only three of them; but then I saw that there was another girl, small, almost dwarfish by comparison with the others. She was a pudgy, mouse-coloured, suet-faced little creature, pitifully plain by contrast with the dark girl—but I fear I flatter her, for her plainness was absolute, not comparative. She trailed along behind the others, head down, shoulders thrust forward, as though to advertise and reproach the effort she had to keep pace with them. By adopting this posture, and by stuffing her hands firmly into her pockets, she had begun to turn a rather elegant coat into something which could hardly be offered to a discriminating jumble sale.

They reached the flight of steps leading to the main door of 62 New Square. Obeying, it seemed, some instruction from the man, the plain girl remained at the foot. The others, ascending, were briefly hidden from my view; but a few moments later the door of the waiting-room opened, and they were within a few yards of me. Sitting, as I have said, on the floor between the window and the bookcase, I was

27

perhaps in a rather inconspicuous position—at any rate, none of them appeared to notice me; and I, absorbed in my researches, did nothing to draw my presence to their attention.

'There seems as yet to be no one in the Clerks' Room,' said the man in a tone of apology, as he ushered in his companions. 'It is rather an early hour by the standards of Lincoln's Inn, I'm afraid. If you would be kind enough to wait here for me, while I conduct Miss Robinson to Miss Larwood's Chambers—'

'In view of what occurred yesterday,' said the older woman, in a voice like the crack of a glacier, 'one can hardly regard with enthusiasm any further interview between Deirdre and this Larwood person. But I suppose it's unavoidable.'

'I can only say again,' said the man, sounding harassed, 'how sorry I am, Mrs Fiske-Purefoy—'

'And I can only say, Mr Tancred, that when one sends one's niece to an interview with one's family solicitor one does not expect her to return in the small hours of the morning in an advanced state of intoxication and demanding a hundred thousand pounds. At least, one would not have done in my day—no doubt I am very old-fashioned.'

'I can only say again, Mrs Fiske-Purefoy, how much I regret—'

'Nonsense, Mr Tancred,' said the girl, interrupting with vigorous firmness. She had a pleasant voice, though with echoes of the hockey-field. 'There's nothing for you to be in the least sorry about. I quite understand and it's not your fault at all. And it was very kind of Miss Larwood, of course, to take Deirdre out to dinner.' She sighed. 'Pity it wasn't some nice young man, but there you are—just her luck, poor old Dreary.'

'Camilla, my dear,' said the solicitor gratefully, 'you're most kind. I was sure I could count on you to understand the position. Now, may I leave you to take care of your grand-mother, while I see to Miss Robinson—I know Lincoln's Inn holds no terrors for you.' A little fulsome, I thought, from an established solicitor to a second-year law student—but she was, after all, an heiress. 'And then, I think, I had better look in at my own office again, to inquire if there is any news of your father or of Mrs Demetriou.'

'Yes, of course, Mr Tancred, I'll take care of everything. If anyone arrives in the Clerks' Room I'll explain who we are and why we're here.'

The solicitor made good his escape, and the two women sat down on the sofa of imitation leather at the far end of the room.

'Grans darling,' said the girl, 'I know you're cross, but don't take it out on poor old Tanks. He's a bit of a duffer, but he's doing his best, honestly.'

'Millie dear, Ronald Tancred's best is costing you a hundred and sixty thousand pounds. Would his worst be more or less expensive?'

'But Grans, I couldn't have left poor old Dreary without a bean, could I? I'd have had to do something for her when the time came. After all—' she sighed again. 'Well, one can't see her making a marvellous marriage or having a fantastic career, can one? So I don't lose anything by having it in the Court Order—it's probably quite sensible, actually. I don't mind that in the least—all I mind about is getting this wretched application over and done with.' Her voice was sharpened by a nervousness which surprised me, given the formal nature of the proceedings; but I remembered that some three million pounds were at stake.

Glancing again through the window, I saw that Tancred had fallen in with another tall man, wearing a camelhair overcoat, approaching from the direction of Lincoln's Inn Fields. After a brief exchange, the solicitor pointed towards 62 New Square, and the other proceeded obediently in the direction indicated. His bearing and mode of dress were those of a man who believed himself good-looking: I was too far away to know if the belief was justified.

'Daddy, you're here, how marvellous,' cried Camilla, springing up as he entered the waiting-room.

'Of course I'm here, Millie darling. I'm one of your trustees, you know. Besides, you didn't think I'd leave my little girl to go through this all by herself, did you?' One

29

might have supposed, from the sentimental quaver in his voice, that his daughter was on trial for her life.

'Rupert dear, what a relief to see you,' said the older woman. 'I haven't known where to turn—Tancred's useless, quite useless.'

'Mama-in-law, wonderful to see you. And looking magnificent as always.' Though the matrimonial link between Rupert Galloway and Jocasta Fiske-Purefoy had been severed by the death of Petronella some seventeen years before, they were still, it appeared, on terms of mutual affection. 'Now then, what's all the fuss about? I've had all sorts of messages from Tancred, and then I met the man himself on the way here, but I still don't know what's happening. He said you'd explain it, Millie. So what's it all about? I gather Deirdre's been making a nuisance of herself somehow, the little beast—I'm sorry, Mama-in-law, I know she's your niece and a sort of cousin of Millie's and I shouldn't say it, but she can be the absolute limit.'

'I should be the last to deny,' said Jocasta Fiske-Purefoy, 'that Deirdre has always been a most difficult child. So different from Millie, in spite of having the same upbringing. One is obliged, I fear, to speak of heredity.' Whether it was some remembered characteristic of her deceased sister Lalage which imposed on her this distasteful obligation, or of Lalage's equally deceased husband, it was impossible to tell.

'There's absolutely no crisis,' said her granddaughter firmly, 'and nothing to get cross with poor old Dreary about. If you'll just let me explain—'

Looking once more from the window, I had for a moment a sense of *déjà vu*, for again the substantial figure of Tancred was leading a little group of people towards 62 New Square, and as before two of them were tall, the third by comparison diminutive. On this occasion, however, the smallest of the group did not by any means trail unregarded behind the rest, but seemed on the contrary to be the centre of affection and interest. She had little obvious claim to be the focus of admiration: a bundle of mist-coloured tweed and jersey, her hair a wispy cloud of blonde and grey—middle-aged, there could be no gainsaying it; but her step was as quick and light as a young girl's, and she still had very pretty legs. The solicitor, half turning from time to time to look benignly down at her, had none of his former harried look: she had restored him, it seemed, to that confidence in his own superior judgement which is so necessary to the professional adviser. Between the two other members of the little party, who walked protectively on either side of her, there was as perfect a similarity as is possible between a muscular young man and a voluptuously built young woman; their copper-coloured hair and creamy white complexions would have enchanted a pre-Raphaelite artist; their look of robust health and exuberant spirits would have been his despair.

This then was Dorothea Demetriou, the youngest daughter of Sir James Remington-Fiske: difficult as it was to believe that she and Jocasta were sisters—it hardly seemed possible in nature that the bundle and the battle-axe should be offspring of the same union—I could have no doubt of her identity. The copper-haired twins, by the same token, must be Lucinda and Lucian Fairfax, the children of her first marriage. Their entry into the waiting-room was the occasion for much embracing and enthusiastic welcome.

'We're not terribly late, are we?' said Dorothea, a little breathless, her words tumbling over one another. 'We've been rushing about all over the place, trying to find some clothes to look respectable in. We had to break all sorts of speed limits coming down from Hampstead—well, Lucian did, Cindy and I just kept our eyes shut and prayed.'

'You're not a bit late, darling,' said Camilla. 'It's simply sweet of you all to bother.'

'Oh Millie, we couldn't let them make you pay all that horrible tax, of course we couldn't. But isn't it lucky we're in London? We meant to stay in Corfu until next month, because Costas can't leave until then, but we decided to come over early and have an export drive. I make Greek pots, you know, Mr Tancred—plates and bowls and ashtrays and things, just like the ones the archæologists dig up, but not so cracked. They're rather nice—you must come up to Hampstead and see them.'

'That would be delightful,' said the solicitor gallantly.

'So we've come to London to tell Harrods and people how nice they are and get lots of orders. The only thing is, I don't know if Leon can get here. I rang his headmaster and said it was frightfully important—family fortunes hanging in the balance and everything—and he said he'd send Leon up to London if he possibly could, but he was out on some sort of binge—Leon, I mean, not the headmaster—and the head-master didn't know when he'd be back. But Mr Tancred says it doesn't matter, because of him being under age—Leon, I mean, not you, Mr Tancred.'

'Quite so, Mrs Demetriou,' said the solicitor with rotund benevolence. 'Since Leonidas is only seventeen, his consent is legally valueless.'

'But if it doesn't matter what Leon says, why's it different with Deirdre? She's not twenty-one for ages.'

'Dolly darling, people come of age at eighteen now,' said Camilla. 'They changed the age of majority in 1969.'

'But Deirdre isn't eighteen—she was seventeen on her last birthday, wasn't she?'

'Her eighteenth birthday,' said the solicitor, 'occurred three days ago.'

'Oh no, it can't have done,' said Dorothea with tragic dismay. 'We haven't had a party, or given her a present or anything. Jo, it wasn't really, was it? You'd have reminded me.'

'My dear Dolly,' said her sister, 'had I remembered it myself, I should certainly have reminded you. But I do have other things to think about, you know, especially with Mother so unwell. I'm afraid that Deirdre's birthday, which is perhaps not one of the most significant events of the decade, escaped my recollection. I really think she's old enough not to make a fuss about it.'

'I ought to have remembered,' said Camilla. 'But I have had a frightfully heavy term—I've been simply snowed under with lectures and tutorials. I do feel rotten about it, though—poor old Dreary, no wonder she's feeling a bit bloody-minded.'

The members of the family now gathered in the waiting-room all seemed to be on terms of mutual affection: Deirdre being absent, harmony prevailed. The only exception that I could detect to this was a certain . . . absence of sympathy, perhaps no more than that, between Rupert Galloway and the Fairfax twins.

They had not met, apparently, for several years: it was in Corfu, I gathered, that the twins were generally reunited with their cousins—Camilla and Deirdre spent most of their holidays there; but Rupert did not accompany his daughter on these visits. Lucian and Lucinda, when he last saw them, would have been little more than schoolchildren: with the uneasy joviality natural to such an encounter, he remarked on how they had grown and inquired what they were doing these days.

'Lucian writes, I paint,' said Lucinda. 'That's our story anyway—and we usually stick to it.'

'We don't want Father to think we're layabouts, you see,' said Lucian. 'We're quite keen on him approving of us.' Remembering that George Fairfax was a successful merchant banker, I supposed that his approval might have a more than sentimental value to his offspring.

'Quite right, my boy, so you should be. Fine man, your father. I run across him from time to time, you know. Yes, he's a shrewd chap, is old George, I've got a lot of time for him.'

'I'm sure he'd be very pleased to hear that,' said Lucian. 'We know how much he respects your abilities as a businessman, don't we, Cindy?'

'Nice of you to say so,' said Rupert, apparently perceiving no ambiguity. 'But I'm not in the same league as George, of course. Just a modest flair for investment, that's all I can claim to have, and not always the money to back it up, unfortunately. Well, we must try to keep in touch a bit more—always glad to see you both, you know, any time you're in London.'

'We were in London in the autumn,' said Lucinda. 'We thought of coming to see you. But we weren't sure if you'd be pleased.'

'I'd have been delighted, my dear. You should have rung me.'

'We thought you might be tied up with all sorts of high-powered financiers, and so on,' said Lucian. 'We don't really move much in that sort of circle, you know. We thought if we turned up on your doorstep wearing the wrong clothes and talking in the wrong accents you might be frightfully embarrassed.'

A particular tone is used by young men apparently ingenuous to make observations apparently innocent in a manner apparently respectful with the intention of being extremely impertinent: one can hardly hope, in academic life, to be unfamiliar with it. I did not know quite what Lucian meant by these remarks; but I was very sure that it was not what he seemed to mean. From his sister came the sound of laughter imperfectly repressed. I thought that the Fairfax twins did not at all like Rupert Galloway.

It must eventually have occurred to someone in the Nursery that there would be nobody in the Clerks' Room, at this early hour, to take any notice of the clients' arrival or to show them where they ought to go. Selena arrived, her apologies silken, and with the assistance of Tancred arranged their distribution among their respective Counsel: Camilla and the Fairfax twins, the consenting adults, to be advised by Cantrip; Dorothea, as guardian *ad litem* of her younger son, by Ragwort; Rupert Galloway and Tancred himself, the trustees of the Will, by Timothy. Selena's own client was Jocasta Fiske-Purefoy; but Selena was to be led by Basil Ptarmigan QC, and plainly considered the soothing of formidable dowagers to be a task for leading Counsel. These arrangements made, she remained alone in the waiting-room.

'Hilary,' said Selena, 'why are you hiding behind the bookcase? I can see your reflection in the window-pane.'

'My dear Selena,' I said, rising, 'I had no intention of concealment. I wished to refresh my memory of the modern form of disentailing deed, and thought you would not object if I consulted your *Encyclopædia*.'

'It just shows,' said Selena, 'how one may be misled by appearances. One might so easily have thought, if one didn't know better, that you were deliberately eavesdropping on our clients.'

'There were people here, certainly,' I said, 'and I suppose they were your clients. Anyone who imagined, however, that their trifling exchanges could have distracted me from my researches would understand little of the mind of the Scholar.'

A telephone call to Julia informed her that the coast was clear—that is to say, that she could now bring Deirdre round to 62 New Square without risk of any embarrassing encounter with the other members of the family. When she arrived, however, she was without her client.

'She doesn't seem,' said Julia, 'to be feeling terribly well. I don't know why—we only had two bottles of champagne last night. I think your client must have been upsetting her, Selena. Still, I gave her an Alka-Seltzer and told her to sit quietly until she felt better. She doesn't have to be in Court for the hearing, does she?'

'No, of course not,' said Selena. 'None of them do, as long as we have their instructions. But they all seem to be regarding it as the trial of the century, so they might be rather put out if we said they needn't be there. By the way, Julia, you do realize, don't you, that Camilla's father—'

But I did not learn what it was that Julia should realize about Rupert Galloway, for at this moment a further visitor arrived in the waiting-room, inquiring anxiously if he had come to the right place and whether he was in time. It was the Greek boy.

There are Greek boys and Greek boys. There are many Greek boys, no doubt, who are fat and have spots; whose profiles are in no way reminiscent of fifth-century Athens; whose hair has not the blue-blackness of a cluster of ripe grapes; Greek boys, in short, who leave the observer baffled by Homer's reference to 'that most charming age when the beard first begins to grow'. Leonidas Demetriou was one of the others.

'Oh,' said Julia, looking at the Greek boy.

'Oh dear,' said Selena, looking at Julia.

'Oh,' said Julia again, 'you must be Leonidas.' She pronounced the name with the accent on the penultimate syllable, and the 'd' as a voiced fricative, like the last phoneme in soothe.

'Oh,' said the boy, with an enchanting smile, 'how delightful to find someone who speaks Greek.'

Julia's knowledge of the modern Greek language is confined, as I happened to know, to a few such essential phrases as 'good morning', 'good afternoon', 'where does the bus leave from?' and 'what beautiful eyes you have', supplemented, when this last proves inadequate for its purpose, by various passages learnt by heart from the work of the poet Cavafy; but she uttered no disclaimer.

Upon the other members of the family, when they again gathered in the waiting-room, she bestowed the vaguest of benevolent smiles, and went on gazing at Leonidas with the expression of a six-year-old contemplating a large slice of chocolate cake. During our progress to the Law Courts she continued to make him the sole object of her attention, pointing out to him, as if personally provided by herself for his entertainment, the lawns and historic alleyways of New Square, and burbling inaccurate fragments of the history of Lincoln's Inn. She let fall from time to time a word or two of Greek, as if it were with difficulty, and only out of courtesy to the rest of us, that she refrained from lapsing entirely into that language. When we arrived at the doors of Court 25, she prevailed on him to assist her in the adjustment of her wig and gown and the restoration to proper symmetry of her collar and white bands. It was all, as Ragwort said afterwards, perfectly disgraceful.

The application itself went smoothly enough, though Camilla, a few feet away from me in the public benches, sat through it looking as pale and tense as if the proceedings were of a criminal nature and she the accused: I reminded myself again how large a proportion of her inheritance was in issue. Rupert Galloway, sitting beside her, seemed to share her nervousness. I saw now that he was less good-looking than, at a distance, I had supposed he might be: a drooping blonde moustache failed to conceal the petulance of his mouth, and the slight wateriness of his pale eyes contradicted the authority of an almost Romanesque profile.

'As your Lordship will see,' said Basil Ptarmigan, 'we have thought it right to provide in the Arrangement some douceur for the unborn and minor issue of Lalage Robinson and of Mrs Demetriou. It is a hundred thousand pounds in each case.'

'That seems very generous, Mr Ptarmigan,' said Mr Justice Lorimer with approval, 'most generous.'

Julia turned her head to smile at Leonidas, as if it had been for his sake, rather than Deirdre's, that she had negotiated so liberal a provision.

I had found it a morning not without interest; so that when, some three months later, I stood in my room at St George's with the telephone in my hand and was asked by Timothy if I remembered the Remington-Fiske application, I was able to answer that indeed I did.

'But who,' I said, 'has been murdered?'

'I'm not at all sure that anyone has,' said Timothy. 'But the poor girl's certainly dead, and Julia thinks it's murder. If you get the next train to London, you can be in the Corkscrew by six-thirty or so, can't you? We'll tell you about it then and take you out to dinner.'

He rang off without telling me which poor girl was dead.

CHAPTER 3

The urgency of Timothy's invitation might have justified a taxi; but I was content, on a gentle May evening, to travel by Underground from Paddington to Charing Cross and from there walk at leisure to my destination, observing the streams of office-workers bound eagerly homewards from Kingsway and High Holborn. It was that season of the year when London is at her most hopeful and adventurous: her citizens go lightly clad, without raincoats or umbrellas; they plant geraniums on the window-sills of grey commercial buildings; they buy strawberries from men at street corners; they talk optimistically of British chances at Wimbledon.

Only the deepening blue of the sky suggested the approach of evening, and the sun still shone brightly on High Holborn. Little of it, however, was allowed to penetrate the interior of the Corkscrew, whose habitués are more at ease in a conspiratorial dimness. Timothy was waiting for me at one of the round oak tables, a bottle of Niersteiner already open.

'Timothy,' I said, 'will you please now abandon these childish devices to excite my curiosity, and tell me, simply and straightforwardly, which poor girl is dead and why Julia thinks it's murder?'

'Have you really heard nothing about it? I thought you'd have seen it in the newspapers—it was quite widely reported.'

'Recently?' I asked, puzzled, for I thought that a mention in the press of the Remington-Fiske family would have attracted my attention.

'About two months ago. On the day, to be precise, of the Oxford and Cambridge Boat Race.'

My ignorance was explained: I had spent the Easter vacation in the United States of America, dependent for English news on the *New York Times*. I had formed the impression that April had been a quiet month in England.

Timothy took from his briefcase a thin cardboard folder, from which he drew a newspaper cutting.

'This is the report of the inquest which was in the *Scuttle*. The reports in the other newspapers are much the same, but this is the fullest.' He pushed the cutting towards me across the polished oak table, and I leant forward to study it by the flickering candlelight. It was illustrated by a photograph of Camilla Galloway.

HEIRESS'S COUSIN IN DEATH FALL
AT CHAMPAGNE 'PICNIC'

A champagne and caviar lunch at the Mortlake home of Rupert Galloway, company director father of property heiress Camilla Fiske-Galloway, ended in tragedy when the heiress's eighteen-year-old cousin Deirdre Robinson fell to her death from the rooftop patio, a South London Coroner was told today.

Miss Robinson was alone on the patio and no one saw her fall. The other guests, watching the race from the windows of the room below, were unaware of the tragedy until alerted by screams from passers-by.

Raven-haired Miss Galloway, twenty-two, heiress to the multi-million estates in Wiltshire of the Remington-Fiske family, told the Coroner that her cousin had no reason to be depressed and had seemed to be enjoying herself. 'She was looking forward to watching the race,' said Miss Galloway. 'I suppose she must have leant over to get a better view and lost her balance. It's a terrible thing to have happened.' Mrs Dorothea Demetriou, an aunt of the dead girl, who was with her on the roof only a few minutes before she fell, confirmed that she seemed in good spirits.

Mrs Elizabeth Brown, thirty-two, a housewife, who was among the crowds gathered on the towpath, became the first person to be aware of the tragedy. 'I didn't see her fall,' Mrs Brown told the Coroner. 'I was watching the race. The boats were just going under Barnes Bridge and still quite close together, so it was rather an exciting moment. I heard a sort of thudding sound behind me, and looked round and saw her lying there on the pavement in front of the flats. I could see at once she was dead. I began screaming and a policeman came.'

The Coroner said there was nothing to suggest that Miss Robinson had taken her life deliberately. It would have been natural for her to lean over the balcony for a better view of the race and the evidence all pointed to her having accidentally overbalanced. Her balance might have been affected by the wine she had drunk at lunch: it was not excessive, but perhaps more than she was used to.

The jury returned a verdict of misadventure.

'I see,' I said. 'Poor Deirdre.'

'And Julia thinks it's murder,' said Timothy. 'She's really very worried. She seems to feel, you see—there are Cantrip and Ragwort. I'd better get another bottle.'

Resigned to the obligations consequent on three years' seniority, Timothy rose and moved towards the bar. Cantrip and Ragwort joined me in the circle of candlelight: I admired, as always when I see them together, the pleasing contrast between Cantrip's black hair and black eyes and the demure autumnal colouring of Ragwort.

'Hello, Hilary,' said Cantrip, 'we thought we'd find you here. Offer free grub and free booze, we said, and we'd have you here in two shakes of a mortarboard.'

'What Cantrip means is,' said Ragwort, 'that we were confident that an appeal from Timothy for your assistance would not go unheeded.'

'I don't yet know,' I said, 'why my assistance should be required. All I have heard so far is that Deirdre Robinson fell from a roof on the afternoon of the Boat Race, and Julia thinks it's murder.'

'Precisely so,' said Ragwort. 'And is greatly troubled by it.'

'Flapping like a moonstruck moorhen,' said Cantrip, 'and going on about Sir Thomas More and making everyone's life a misery.'

That Julia in a state of agitation would resemble such a bird as Cantrip had mentioned I could readily believe; the relevance of Sir Thomas More I would, I suppose, in due course discover; but why, some two months after the event, there should suddenly be this anxiety as to the cause of Deirdre's death—

'Because of the letter,' said Cantrip. 'Hasn't Timothy told you?'

There are days on which Julia does not open letters. She is overcome, as I understand it, by a sort of superstitious dread, in which she is persuaded that letters bode her no good: they will be from the Gas Board, and demand money; or from the Inland Revenue, and demand accounts; or some much valued friend, and demand an answer. If a letter arrives on such a day as this, she does not open it but puts it carefully away, to be dealt with when she feels stronger. After that, I had always supposed, it is never seen again.

'That, certainly,' said Timothy, returning with the wine, 'is the normal course of events. You will remember, however, that there are also periods of reform, during which we are promised a new, improved and more organized Julia. They generally don't last long enough to matter much. But they always begin, of course, with a tidying of papers: that's how she came across this.' He again opened his briefcase.

The letter was amateurishly typed, though on paper of excellent quality; the postmark on the envelope which had contained it was four days earlier than the date of the Boat Race.

> Fiske House,
> Belgrave Place,
> Tuesday.

Dear Miss Larwood,

   I have found out something interesting and I want you to tell me what to do about it. Can you meet me at seven on Saturday at that place we had dinner at? Ring me at home if you can't make it, but don't leave any messages with anyone.

> Yours sincerely,
> Deirdre Robinson

Not the most graceful of letters, from a young woman asking a favour of a comparative stranger; but that might perhaps be shyness. I was not surprised by the letter's effect on Julia. In the circumstances it had something of the quality of a deathbed request, and Julia would feel a sense of guilt that she had not complied with it—though, had she done so, she would have waited in vain for Deirdre, who by seven o'clock on the Saturday of the Boat Race had already the best of all excuses for failing to keep her engagements. She had wanted to tell Julia of something she had discovered; some childish and trivial secret, very probably, of no interest to anyone; but she had died without telling it. I could understand that Julia would feel troubled.

The letter lay mute and unhelpful in the candlelight, like the embodiment of some small, resentful ghost.

'I suppose,' I said, 'that you could take it to the police.'

'Yes,' said Timothy, frowning slightly at his wineglass. 'Yes, we did consider that. But it's not really evidence of anything, is it? If the police did nothing, Julia would remain uneasy. On the other hand, if they did reopen the case, several perfectly innocent people might be quite unnecessarily upset.'

'So she got this idea,' said Cantrip, 'that we ought to do it ourselves. Rootle about and look for clues, you know, but being all tactful and unobtrusive, so as not to upset anyone. Well, what I said was, if you get half the Chancery Bar crawling along the towpath with magnifying glasses looking for bloodstains, it might be a lot of things, but unobtrusive isn't one of them. Apart from which, I said, I couldn't see it was any of our business—after all, if the bird's family aren't fussed about her getting pushed off the roof, why should Julia worry about it?'

'That proved,' said Ragwort, 'to be an ill-advised remark.'

'Too right,' said Cantrip. 'It was when I said that that she got all miffed and started talking about Sir Thomas More and the traditions of the English Bar. This Thomas More chap was something in history—you ought to have heard of him, Hilary.' His tone implied, however, that he did not suppose I had. 'Julia thinks he's hot stuff, and she reckons that if someone had bumped off one of his clients he'd have done something about it. She went on about him for ages.'

'Sir Thomas More, saint and martyr,' said Ragwort, 'as of course you know, Hilary, was the only member of Lincoln's Inn ever to be canonized: a very proper object of admiration for Julia, and indeed all of us. Were it possible, however, to dwell excessively upon so improving a topic, one might be tempted to say that Julia had done so.'

'You bet one might,' said Cantrip. 'Anyway, if he was allowed to waste time playing detectives instead of getting on with his paperwork, he can't have had a Clerk like Henry. The thing is, you see, we're all frantically busy at the moment, and we just can't spare the time. So what we thought we'd better do,' said Cantrip happily, 'was get you to do it, Hilary. It's just your sort of thing—digging up odds and ends of gossip and finding out things that aren't your business.'

I remarked with some coldness that my own time was not

so entirely undisposed of as my companions appeared to believe, and I doubted whether my academic responsibilities would allow me to undertake the task they envisaged for me. If they wished merely to prevent Julia from talking about Sir Thomas More, I supposed some simple but humane form of gag would sufficiently serve the purpose.

'What Cantrip means is,' said Ragwort, 'that your flair for research and your training in the methods of Scholarship seemed to us to make you uniquely qualified to conduct the investigation. That *is* what you meant, isn't it, Cantrip?'

'Oh rather,' said Cantrip.

'And we ventured to hope,' continued Ragwort, 'that by this stage of the summer term the burden of your academic duties might be less onerous than at other times of the year.'

'I'm afraid,' said Timothy, 'that Julia will be quite upset if you won't do it. She has great faith in your detective powers, you know, since that trouble she had in Venice. She often says that if it weren't for you she might still be languishing in a dungeon under the Doge's Palace.'

In this, as it happens, she spoke no more than the truth. When she had been suspected by the Venetian police of responsibility for a crime of passion, it had been my own investigation which had established her innocence and secured her freedom: I have written elsewhere of these events.* A recognition of my achievement was not, however, so widespread in Lincoln's Inn that I could be unmoved by it. Besides, for all her failings, I am fond of poor Julia, and would not wish to think of her distressed. Upon the understanding that I might look towards New Square for such assistance as their professional engagements would allow, I consented to give my mind to the question of Deirdre's death.

Cantrip was obliged to leave us. He attends on Friday evenings at the offices of the *Daily Scuttle*, where it is his function to peruse the items intended for the Saturday issue of that journal and to damn to deletion those likely, in his professional opinion, to expose its proprietors to civil or criminal proceedings. Some of my readers may think that his

* *Thus Was Adonis Murdered*

educational disadvantages—for which, I have always said, he is rather to be pitied than blamed—would render him unsuited to such a task; but the *Scuttle* is fortunately one of those periodicals which eschew, so far as possible, all words of more than two syllables, so that very little of it is incomprehensible to him.

'Cantrip,' I said, 'while you're there, could you see if you can discover from your Fleet Street colleagues any further details of the evidence given at the inquest?'

'I'll have a bash,' said Cantrip. 'With lots of subtlety and discretion, of course. Toodle-pip all of you—I'll see you later in Guido's.'

His departure from the Corkscrew coincided with the arrival there of Julia and Selena, both looking rather at their best. Selena wore a round-necked dress of sky-blue cotton, most becoming to herself and to the season: I remembered, seeing her, that the Courts had risen for Whitsun, and a member of the Bar could be seen in bright colours without inviting the inference of a declining practice. Julia also wore something in holiday style, of a design sufficiently *dégagé* to suffer little from the loss of a button or two.

It occurred to me that Julia herself was the only one of us who had had any personal acquaintance with the dead girl. Deirdre Robinson had seemed to me, from the little I had seen of her, to be peculiarly lacking in any attractive qualities; but I supposed that Julia, on the evening they had spent together, might have perceived in her client some hidden charm or talent.

'No,' said Julia sadly. 'No, not really. She was, as you say, very plain, and rather dull, and she didn't seem to like anyone very much. But I still think it matters if someone pushed her off the roof.' Julia spoke as if expecting contradiction. 'One's protection from acts of violence doesn't depend, in a civilized society, on being talented or attractive or making people like one. It depends on the law. That, as I understand it, is the distinguishing characteristic of civilization: to protect those one likes or loves is no more than the merest barbarian might do.'

'No doubt,' said Timothy. 'But why should the whole

44

burden of defending civilization and the rule of law fall on the members of New Square?'

'I would suggest,' said Julia, absent-mindedly flicking her cigarette ash into her wineglass, 'that those of us who have made the law our study and our profession have a more than ordinary responsibility to uphold the principles upon which it rests. It is a responsibility acknowledged in the traditions of the English Bar and the rules which govern our conduct. One can't refuse to act for someone, for example, because one dislikes or disapproves of them.'

'No,' said Timothy. 'One can't pick and choose one's clients.'

'Because otherwise there would be people who could find no one to represent them, and would be prevented from defending or enforcing their rights: the law would be applied for the benefit of some and not of others, and this would be inconsistent with the principles on which it is based. If the law is personal and partial in its application; if it defends only strength and restrains only weakness; if it varies and veers and wavers to meet the demands of power or the expediency of the moment—then it no longer has the quality of law: our civilization is built on sand, and we slide back before we realize it into that state of Nature in which, as we are told, the life of man is solitary, poor, nasty, brutish and short.'

'Yes, indeed,' said Selena. 'These are very proper sentiments, Julia, and do you credit. Do you feel better now?'

Julia, however, continued for some time after this to discourse on the high principles and noble traditions for which Sir Thomas More had gone to the scaffold and Erskine May had resigned high office. I blame for this sort of thing the authors of the *Guide to Professional Conduct* which is handed out wholesale to all those called to membership of the English Bar: they have seen fit to include in it a number of sensational and romantic tales about barristers behaving well and acting on principle and so forth; and have too little considered, in my opinion, what effect these may have on impressionable persons such as Julia, who misunderstand things and take it all seriously.

'My dear Julia,' I said at last, 'do not distress yourself

further about these matters. I have consented to undertake the inquiry, and there is no need for you to worry any more about civilization or the rule of law or what Sir Thomas More would have done. Sir Thomas will understand that you have done your best, and when civilization crumbles it will not be your fault at all. It is only fair to tell you, however, that I shall engage in the investigation without sharing your belief that it is a case of murder.'

She gave me a look of polite but distrustful inquiry, as if suspecting me of a wish to evade my task or excuse in advance a lack of zeal in its performance.

'Don't you see,' I said, 'that it's the wrong girl who's dead?'

Murder is unusual. The irritations, disappointments, envies and desires of everyday life are generally resolved in some manner less extreme. When it occurs, then, or is thought to have occurred, there must be looked for to account for it some unusual feature in the surrounding circumstances—some unusual wrong to be avenged, some unusual passion to be assuaged, some unusual advantage to be obtained.

A personal fortune of five million pounds is unusual. To gain possession of it, it is conceivable that someone might behave in a manner quite contrary to custom and convention. At a gathering, therefore, of the descendants of Sir James Remington-Fiske a murder would be not wholly unaccountable.

But one would expect it to be the heiress who was murdered.

'Camilla, however, lives and flourishes, and the supposed victim of your imagined crime is the insignificant poor relation. The rich, my dear Julia, commit many wrongs against the poor; but they seldom murder them, and hardly ever for gain.'

Julia sat silent in the candlelight, perceiving the force of my argument but unpersuaded by it.

'Morever,' I continued, 'it cannot be said that Deirdre's death is mysterious or unexplained. There has been an inquest and evidence has been given and the Coroner is satisfied that it was an accident. The probability surely is that he is right?'

'Oh, but he can't be.' It was Selena who answered, surprising me by her firmness. 'However Deirdre came to fall from the roof at Rupert's flat, it can't have happened in the way the Coroner thought. Julia and I have been there, you see, and we know it can't. I think we had better tell you—if Timothy and Ragwort don't mind hearing it again—the story of the Grateful Client.'

CHAPTER 4

The story of the Grateful Client had its beginning in November of the previous year, when Selena received instructions from Tancred's to appear in a possession action in the Wandsworth County Court. The lay client was Rupert Galloway, whose landlords were seeking to forfeit the lease of his penthouse for an alleged breach of the covenant not to use it for any profession or business. Rupert admitted that the penthouse had become the registered office of Galloway Opportunities Limited, a company of which he was the managing director, and that the company's affairs were conducted from that address; but he denied, and wished Selena to deny on his behalf, that this amounted to a breach of the covenant.

'What opportunities,' I asked, 'does this company provide?'

'You could say,' said Selena, 'that it gives those wishing to invest in commodity futures the opportunity to take advantage of Rupert's expertise—that's how Rupert puts it. Or you might say that it gives Rupert the opportunity to speculate with other people's money. It's a question of how you look at it.'

She had thought the case difficult but not hopeless. There were, she proposed to argue, two distinguishing features which characterized the carrying on of a business—the attendance of customers and the employment of staff; if these were absent, there would be no breach of covenant. She assumed, and Rupert confirmed, that his clients did not come in person to the penthouse to buy and sell cocoa futures. As to employing staff—she had asked Rupert specifically whether he employed anyone to assist him with the company's affairs, and he had firmly assured her that he did not: his daughter sometimes helped out by typing a few letters for him, and one of his girlfriends did the same thing; but that, he said, was all.

When, therefore, it was revealed in evidence on the first day of the hearing that a young lady, identified by the diligence of the landlords' inquiry agent as being on the books of a leading secretarial agency, had visited the penthouse from 10 o'clock in the morning until 1 o'clock in the afternoon on three days a week for a period of months, Selena was rather cross.

'Cross,' said Julia, 'is not quite the word. You expressed the desire, on your return to Lincoln's Inn, to boil your client in oil and feed him very slowly to man-eating piranha fish.'

Reproached for his duplicity, her client had claimed that the young lady from the secretarial agency was in fact the girlfriend whom he had mentioned, and had sought to imply, by various winks and leers, that the purpose of her visits was more amorous than secretarial. It seemed to Selena, however, that their regularity was uncharacteristic of a romantic association.

'On the basis of our own experience,' said Ragwort, 'I should have thought it even more uncharacteristic of an agency typist.'

Selena had spent an evening intended for better things in revising her closing speech to accommodate in her definition of non-business use the employment of a part-time secretary. She had felt, on concluding her labours, quite pleased with the result, and when she delivered the speech on the following day had thought that the judge listened not unfavourably. On the day fixed for judgement, however, she had found herself engaged in the High Court, which naturally took precedence over the Wandsworth County Court. Julia, having no unalterable commitments on that day, was prevailed on to take her place.

Finding Wandsworth County Court was an enterprise, according to Julia's account of it, of more or less equivalent difficulty to tracing the source of the Blue Nile; but she had surmounted the rigours of the journey, and arrived, albeit flushed and breathless, in time to take the judgement—which was, of course, in Rupert's favour.

'I wouldn't have thought,' said Timothy, 'that there was any "of course" about it—it sounds like a very near thing.'

'When Selena tells us,' said Julia, 'that she was quite pleased with her closing speech, we may safely conclude that it was the finest piece of advocacy ever heard in south-west London—our success was not in doubt. All that remained for me to do was to bow and ask for costs, and be taken to lunch by the lay client.'

'This last,' said Ragwort, 'was not among your professional duties.'

'Not in the narrow sense—but these little gestures of gratitude on the part of the lay client do not occur so commonly that one ought to discourage them. It was unfair, of course, that Selena should have done all the work and I should have the lunch; but it seemed better that Rupert should buy lunch for me than that he should not buy it for anyone. And it is fair to say that it was a very good lunch at a rather attractive little French restaurant in Putney.'

While giving him credit, however, for the excellence of the meal, she had thought him unduly complacent about his success, which he seemed to attribute rather to the merits of his case than to the brilliance of his Counsel. He confessed to having felt some anxiety when his solicitors entrusted the case to a young lady, but he had to admit, he said, that Miss Jardine had done it very nicely—

Julia, recounting this, choked on her Niersteiner.

—very nicely, he said, though of course it was a very simple and straightforward case, and the landlords had had no chance of winning: when one looked properly at the evidence, as Miss Jardine herself had pointed out to the judge, they really had no case at all. Still, she had done it very nicely. Recalling the care of Selena's preparation and Rupert's own unhelpfulness towards success, Julia had thought it right to make clear to him that but for his good fortune in being represented by one of the most persuasive advocates in Lincoln's Inn he would even then have been seeking accommodation on the Thames Embankment; and had added that that, in Julia's opinion, would have been a just reward for his ingratitude.

'It was kind of you to say that,' said Selena, turning her glass thoughtfully between her fingers. 'I shouldn't like you to think that I don't appreciate it. Although as things turned out—'

Startled by the vehemence of her indignation, Rupert had remarked that she seemed to be a great admirer of Selena's; to which Julia answered that indeed she was, for to know Selena and not to admire her was a thing impossible.

'Julia,' said Ragwort, 'have you no sense at all?' A foolish question, since he knows she has not.

'Julia was not to know,' said Selena, 'that Rupert is a rather—unsophisticated sort of person.'

The lunch had thereafter proceeded amiably. At its conclusion Rupert had invited Julia to bring Selena to a little party he was holding at the end of the following week; it would be the sort of thing, he said, that he thought they might find amusing. She had attached, at the time, no particular significance to these words or the manner in which they were said.

'I believe we have reached a part of the narrative,' said Timothy, 'which may not be suitable hearing for the Revenue silks whom I see gathered at the next table. Shall we adjourn to Guido's?'

No more was said, as we walked along Kingsway in the warm May evening, of the affair of the Grateful Client. Not until we were comfortably installed in Guido's and all necessary choices had been made between asparagus and tagliatelli, grilled sole and scampi Nizzarda, Valpolicella and Frascati, did Selena resume her narrative.

'Thinking,' said Selena, 'that if Rupert wished further to express his gratitude in the form of food and drink it would be unkind of us to discourage him, we made our way on the appointed evening to his penthouse in Mortlake. It is on the fifth floor of a rather elegant block of flats close to Barnes Bridge, with a view across the river to Duke's Meadows. The door was opened by a red-haired girl, quite substantially built, wearing a black dress and black stockings and a little white pinafore.'

'In brief,' I said, 'an old-fashioned parlourmaid.'

'Your "in brief" is appropriate, your "old-fashioned" less so. When I say she was wearing stockings rather than tights, I do not speak from surmise. I am able to add, again without surmise, that they were secured by a black lace suspender belt. You may conclude that the dress was very brief indeed.'

'Quite disgraceful,' said Ragwort.

'We hung up our coats and she led us into the drawing-room. It was a nice spacious drawing-room, the result, I imagine, of knocking two rooms into one, with a balcony and French windows on the side looking on to the river. The furnishing was of the sort designed to be recognized as opulent—Wilton carpets and leather sofas and so forth.'

'If I may say so,' said Julia, 'it was not the quality of the furniture which most immediately engaged one's attention. It was the presence in the room of a number of people with no clothes on.'

'Yes,' said Selena a little reproachfully. 'Yes, Julia, I was coming to that. Ah good, here's the asparagus.'

'You should have left forthwith,' said Ragwort, 'pausing, if at all, only to utter a brief denunciation.'

'It was possible,' said Julia, 'that Rupert meant well and did not intend us to be disconcerted. In which case, we would not have wished to appear so.'

'And even more possible,' said Selena, 'that he did not mean well at all and intended us to be very disconcerted. In which case still less would we have wished to appear so. Moreover, we had travelled half way across London in an inconvenient direction to enjoy his hospitality, and I at least did not intend to leave until I had my money's worth. We accepted the champagne offered us by the parlourmaid person, and sat down on one of the sofas to consider our position. Julia was afraid that we might be committing some kind of solecism by not taking our clothes off; but I thought we could regard the occasion as one at which dress was optional. So we kept them on.'

'Looking round at our fellow guests,' said Julia, 'one could not help feeling that they would have done well to do likewise. I refer in particular to those of the male sex. With the exception of our host—who was, I am relieved to say, more formally clad in a pair of black leather bathing trunks—with that exception they were all entirely naked; and they were, alas, well past the age at which a man may carelessly disrobe and be confident of being an object of desire and admiration.' Julia sighed. 'To be naked with elegance, even for the most slender and graceful young man, is a severe test of deportment. The scene before us, therefore, despite a well-advised dimness of lighting, was one neither pleasing to the eye nor conducive towards desire.'

'On the other hand,' said Selena, 'the champagne was excellent.'

Mindful of his duty as host to ensure their entertainment, Rupert had completed their introduction to the quasi-parlourmaid: her name, it appeared, was Rowena, and she was the girl about whom, as Rupert put it, Selena had been so severe with him—that is to say, the girl from the typing agency whose visits had obliged Selena to revise her closing speech. Perhaps prejudiced on this account, Selena had not much cared for her; but she had seemed to Julia to be a pleasant, good-natured sort of girl—a conclusion drawn from the circumstance that she constantly filled their glasses. She also offered them some fudge, which she described as being 'something rather special'.

'I thought she meant,' said Julia, 'that it was homemade.'

'No doubt it was,' said Selena. 'It also had—how shall I put it?—a decidedly North American flavour. I did suggest, Julia, that it would be better not to eat too much of it.'

'As always, I would have done wisely to act on your advice; but it was rather delicious fudge, and I was quite hungry. You will be interested to hear, Hilary, that it had a most remarkable effect—even on Selena after a very modest quantity. She cast off all conventional restraints and devoted herself without shame to the pleasure of the moment.'

I asked for particulars of this uncharacteristic conduct.

'She took from her handbag a paperback edition of *Pride and Prejudice* and sat on the sofa reading it, declining all offers of conversation. I have never known you, Selena, so indifferent to the demands of social obligation. I, on the other hand, talked a good deal, though not as I recall with great lucidity: I was trying, for some reason which now escapes me, to explain to Rowena the effect of Section 478 of the Taxes Act; but I kept forgetting half way through my sentences how they were meant to end, so I fear that I may have given her an imperfect understanding of these provisions. I also found that the fudge had made me thirsty, and in consequence of this I drank more freely of the champagne than I might otherwise have done.'

'I don't think,' I said, 'that fudge and champagne mix well together, Julia.'

'No,' said Julia sadly, 'no, they don't. A realization of this came suddenly upon me, obliging me to make my way in some haste to the bathroom. The bathroom, however, proved unsatisfactory. It was in many respects an admirable bathroom—marble walls, gold taps, and a bath the size of a paddling pool. It did not, however, afford the privacy which was my objective. The bath, you see, was full of people—I can't say exactly how many, since they were rather tangled up together.'

'How,' I asked, 'did you resolve your difficulty?'

'I said I was terribly sorry and withdrew, not knowing what to do next. But fortunately I found Rowena just outside the bathroom door: she told me that there was another one en suite with Rupert's bedroom, and offered to conduct me there. I accepted with alacrity, and in due course emerged feeling much better. Rowena had waited for me in the bedroom, intending—or so I supposed—to escort me back to the centre of the social whirl. She showed no inclination, however, to leave the bedroom: she said there were some very interesting things in Rupert's wardrobe and that if I liked she would show them to me. I could hardly say that I wasn't interested, could I?'

To say so, I perceived, would have seemed to Julia a breach of the rules of polite conduct which had been impressed on her during her schooldays. I inquired the nature of the interesting objects.

'Sundry items of leatherwear, various whips and things, one or two pairs of handcuffs—I found it difficult to know what comment was appropriate: such phrases as "Oh, how nice" didn't seem entirely suitable. What Rowena, for some reason, expected chiefly to interest me were various items of clothing, apparently intended for some kind of dressing-up game. There was a nurse's uniform, I remember, and also a navy blue gymslip. Rowena giggled a good deal about the gymslip, and said that it was the costume that Rupert liked her best in. It featured, evidently, in some kind of fantasy in which he undertook the role of schoolmaster. She seemed very anxious that I should try it on. The idea, to be candid, did not greatly appeal to me—I did not think it at all a becoming garment. She grew so insistent, however, that I could not politely refuse.'

Ragwort, at this point, covered his eyes with his hand in a gesture of elegant despair.

'I had accordingly put on the gymslip, and was trying to persuade Rowena that it really did not at all suit me, when the disturbance occurred. But Selena is in a better position than I am to tell you about that.'

Selena, having concluded her dealings with her sole meunière, accepted the invitation to resume the narrative.

'The party had increased in informality, with the encouragement, I suppose, of the fudge, not to speak of various other substances being smoked or sniffed by our fellow guests. Scenes similar to that noticed by Julia in the bathroom were now occurring in various parts of the drawing-room, and Rupert had begun leaping about with a flashlight camera taking photographs of everyone. He frequently interrupted his artistic activities, however, to urge me to take my clothes off and enjoy myself—this made it very difficult for me to concentrate on *Pride and Prejudice*. Isn't it curious how intolerant some people are of other people's pleasures? Was I pestering Rupert to put his clothes on and read Jane Austen? No, I wasn't. Was he prepared to show me a corresponding indulgence? Not a bit of it. On the contrary, he became quite peevish and aggrieved—"If you and your girlfriend," he said "are just going to sit there and not do anything, I think it's a pretty poor show."'

'He was evidently under some misapprehension,' I remarked, 'as to the nature of your friendship.'

'Evidently—as I say, he's a rather unsophisticated sort of person. But even if we had been on such terms as he supposed, it would still have been frightful cheek to expect us to make a public demonstration of it. I began to feel, in spite of the champagne, that it was time we were leaving. I was still waiting, however, for Julia to return from the bathroom, when, as she says, there was a disturbance—people banging loudly on the front door and shouting for admittance. Their precise words being "Open up there, this is the police."'

Selena paused, and thoughtfully sipped her Frascati.

CHAPTER 5

The words 'Open up there, this is the police' tend to have a dampening effect on almost any social gathering. The initial response to them of Rupert's guests had been a panic-stricken immobility, which held them frozen for several seconds in the attitudes in which the moment found them; then, disengaging with amazing rapidity from their various mutual entwinements, they had scrambled headlong for the doorway giving access to the roof, leaving their host to deal as he thought best with the unwelcome intrusion.

'Rupert,' said Selena, 'failed notably to behave like a respectable householder whose home is his castle and who does not suppose himself to be living in a police state. The proper course of action for such a person, when the police demand entry, is to ask politely by what authority they do so and to take steps, before opening the door, to verify their

55

answer. This sensible precaution has the further advantage of enabling the householder, should he happen to be dressed only in a pair of black leather bathing trunks, to change into some more orthodox costume before confronting the forces of law and order. Rupert, however, did not seem to think of this—the last of his guests had hardly disappeared from the drawing-room before he was opening his front door, with apologies for the delay, to admit his more recent visitors: two heavily bearded but quite personable young men, one tall, the other taller, wearing the distinctive uniform of the Metropolitan Police.'

Making vague reference to 'information received', they had proceeded to search the drawing-room. Rupert, green-gilled and glassy-eyed with apprehension, had offered no protest; Selena, not being present in a professional capacity, felt that it would be officious to volunteer any on his behalf. She ventured to suggest, when they took possession of the flashlight camera, that they would wish to give Rupert a receipt for it, and something was rather grudgingly scribbled on a page of one of their notebooks; otherwise her role was that of disinterested spectator. It was not until they gave signs of proposing to search the other rooms in the flat that she began to feel serious disquiet.

'I thought, you see, that if they went into the bathroom they would find Julia there, still perhaps feeling not quite well, and it might be upsetting for her.'

'As it happens,' said Julia, 'I was no longer in the bathroom, but on the balcony of Rupert's bedroom—Rowena had thought it the best place to go when the disturbance started. Something rather curious happened while we were out there—there was a snow shower. Not an ordinary snow shower, you understand, falling alike on the just and unjust, but one confined to the balcony and falling exclusively on Rowena and myself. At least, so it seemed at the time; on closer investigation, we found that what was falling on us was not snow at all, but a quantity of little twists and packets of paper. It appeared that those on the roof, thinking it inadvisable to remain in possession of whatever they had been sniffing and smoking and putting in the fudge, were attempting to dispose of the evidence; but they evidently didn't realize that the balcony extended some distance further than the roof, so obstructing the free passage of their dejectamenta to the safe anonymity of the public highway. Selena, of course, didn't know about this at the time.'

'No,' said Selena. 'No, I didn't. I thought, as I have said, that if the police searched the flat they would find you in the bathroom, perhaps feeling not quite well, and I felt anxious. If I had known that they would find you on the balcony, unconvincingly disguised as a schoolgirl and surrounded by little packets of illegal substances, I would not have felt less so.'

She had accordingly thought it right to inquire casually whether their visitors happened to have a search warrant or anything of that kind. The taller one, who seemed to be the spokesman, admitted that they had not; but they supposed, he said, that if Mr Galloway had nothing to hide he wouldn't mind them taking a look round to see that everything was above-board. Ignoring anguished looks and attempted disclaimers from Rupert—who fortunately, however, seemed by this time incapable of coherent speech—she answered firmly that Mr Galloway would mind very much indeed.

'The taller one shrugged his shoulders and said that if that was our attitude they'd better go back to the station for further orders, and he hoped we wouldn't blame them if it looked suspicious in their report. I assured him that we wouldn't and they took their departure. Together, of course, with Rupert's flashlight camera.'

I heard in Selena's voice a note of irony, and the upward curve of the corners of her mouth was a fraction more pronounced than usual. I began to think that things were not what they seemed.

'While Rupert went up to the roof, to tell his guests that the forces of law and order had now retreated and they might safely return to the comfort of the drawing-room, I telephoned Mortlake police station. I told them that we had received a visit from a PC Golightly, that being the signature on the receipt for the camera, and a colleague of his whose name I did not know. They informed me that there was no one among their officers of that name, and that none of their force had been sent that evening to the address I mentioned.'

'It just shows,' said Ragwort, 'how careful one should always be to behave like a respectable householder. Even if one isn't.'

'Especially if one isn't,' said Julia.

'Thinking,' continued Selena, 'that Rupert would be interested in this information, I followed him on to the roof. He became, on hearing my news, extremely indignant. Uttering various intemperate threats, he went to the parapet and looked over, in the hope of catching some glimpse of the impostors making their departure. I too, from curiosity rather than indignation, tried to look over the parapet. But it was too high for me to see anything nearer than the far bank of the river. So you do see, Hilary,' said Selena, leaning back and finishing her Frascati, in the manner of one who brings a well-rounded narrative to a logical and satisfactory conclusion, 'you do see, don't you, that it can't have been an accident?'

My curiosity about the spurious policemen had distracted my mind a little from the chief purpose of the narrative. Not allowing myself to be provoked into any precipitate inquiry as to its relevance, I refilled all our glasses with sufficient deliberation to permit myself time for thought.

'I suppose,' I said eventually, 'that you are—let me see, about five foot four, Selena?' She nodded. 'The parapet then, if you could not see over it, must be of a similar height. And Deirdre—Deirdre, I seem to remember, was rather a small girl. Two or three inches shorter than you, I fancy?'

'At least that,' said Selena.

'And your suggestion is, I suppose, that a young woman who chooses to watch the Boat Race from a balcony some two inches higher than herself—'

'Must be singularly indifferent,' said Julia, 'to the outcome of the contest.'

'While the notion of her leaning over it becomes, I agree, distinctly improbable. Are you quite sure, Selena, about the height of the parapet? It seems odd that it should be so high as to obstruct the view of the river.'

'Quite sure,' said Selena. 'I thought at the time what a pity it was. It does, however, prevent the roof terrace from being overlooked from the other blocks of flats in the neighbourhood: it seems that the designer preferred privacy to prospect. And it would be more sheltered, I suppose, if one were sitting out there with a breeze blowing.'

I asked Selena if it would be possible for her to draw for me a plan of Rupert's flat. The product of her labours with ballpoint and table napkin, being possibly also of some interest to my readers, is reproduced below.

I was still studying it when Cantrip arrived, showing no signs of weariness from his labours in Fleet Street. The waiters of Guido's gathered round him with affectionate solicitude: it is their desire to encourage all their clients to a comfortable and prosperous plumpness, and Cantrip is an enduring challenge to them. The slenderness of Ragwort may be attributed to restraint; but Cantrip's look of artistic semi-starvation survives any quantity of pasta or profiteroles.

'They've kept you very late,' said Timothy. 'Has the gossip columnist been sailing more than usually close to the wind?'

'No,' said Cantrip. 'No, it's not that—I've been chatting up this bird. Hang on a minute while I order some food, and I'll tell you all about it.'

'No doubt,' said Ragwort, with weary distaste. 'You generally do.'

'All right then, I won't,' said Cantrip. 'What I thought

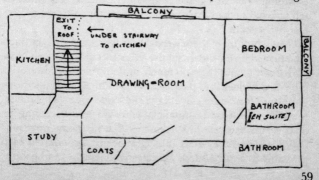

59

was, if you were still trying to find out about Deirdre, you might all be quite interested. But if you're not, I won't bother.' Turning a shoulder towards Ragwort in a manner indicative of pique, he addressed himself to the nearest and most attentive waiter. 'I'll have a steak, please. You needn't cook it much, I'm practically dying of hunger.'

'Why?' said Selena. 'Who was this girl, Cantrip?'

'Oh, no one special.' Cantrip was elaborately casual. 'Just a bird on the staff of the *Scuttle*. She covered the inquest on Deirdre. And I'll have some mushrooms with it and lots of fried potatoes and some salad.'

'Cantrip, don't tease,' said Julia. 'Tell us what she said.'

'Shan't, so there,' said Cantrip with dignity. 'Not until Ragwort takes back his malicious innuendo.'

'A malicious innuendo? On my part? My dear Cantrip,' said Ragwort, 'what can you mean?'

'You know jolly well what I mean. What you innuended was that I kept boring you sick with unsavoury stories about my success with birds, and I want a retraction and an apology. That means you've got to say it's not true and you're sorry you said it.'

'My dear Cantrip,' said Ragwort, 'of course it's not true that you bore me with unsavoury stories of your success with women. I find them quite entertaining. And if I've said anything which could be construed as implying otherwise, then I am very sorry.'

Mollified by this graceful apology, Cantrip consented to tell us what he had learnt of the circumstances surrounding Deirdre's death.

'The whole lot of them were there—you know, all the ones who turned up for the trust bust. It's a sort of family tradition for Rupert to give them all lunch on Boat Race day. Looks as if he mostly does it to please Camilla—the word is it's quite important for him to stay on the right side of her. He fancies himself as some kind of financial whiz kid, but everything he does seems to come unstuck—mention his name near our City Desk and they start talking about bargepoles. So he's probably in a rather dodgy position moneywise, and people think he's counting on Camilla to do the grateful daughter bit when she comes in for the loot.'

'There were no other guests,' I asked, 'apart from members of the family?'

'Old Tancred was there—you remember, our instructing solicitor. Not in a professional capacity—as an old family friend. Well, that's what he told the Coroner. I expect he just slid under the door when he heard there was free booze going—you know what solicitors are like.'

The attentive waiter now placed before Cantrip an enormous steak, surrounded by mushrooms and fried potatoes, murmuring as he did so a few coaxing words in Italian, as if fearing that without encouragement his customer would eat no more than a mouthful: Cantrip applied himself to dispelling these anxieties.

'I imagine,' said Selena, thoughtfully sipping her brandy, 'that Mr Tancred is another person whom Rupert might be anxious to keep on good terms with. Tancred's may be a rather dozy sort of firm, but they're very respectable. If I were engaged in dubious business ventures, I believe I might find it quite convenient to be able to say they were acting for me.'

'I'm surprised,' said Timothy, 'if Rupert's activities are as dubious as you seem to think, that Tancred does go on acting for him.'

'I suppose,' said Selena, 'that if he refused to act for Rupert he'd risk losing the Remington-Fiske business altogether. He would be more inclined, I dare say, to give the benefit of the doubt to Camilla's father than to many other clients.'

The presence of the solicitor at Rupert's luncheon party could easily be attributed, it seemed to me, to no sordid motive on either side, but to a sociable desire on Rupert's part to dilute the preponderance of femininity. Even with Tancred there, the men would have been outnumbered by five to four.

'No,' said Cantrip, looking up briefly from his steak, 'it was an even number. Sorry, I forgot—Dorothea brought her husband. Her second husband, I mean, the Greek one. Constantine whatsisname. He's a professor of something at

Athens University, and this bird on the *Scuttle* says he writes poetry.'

I happened at this moment to be raising my coffee cup to my lips: I returned it carefully to its saucer, not trusting my hand, at such a moment, to retain its steadiness. 'Cantrip,' I said, 'you don't mean that Dorothea's husband is Constantine Demetriou the poet?'

'I don't know,' said Cantrip. 'That's his name, and this bird says he writes poetry. Is it something to get steamed up about?'

The mention in connection with the case of a name so distinguished, so deservedly honoured throughout the civilized world no less for political fortitude than for literary achievement, was, as my readers may easily imagine, a complete astonishment to me. I had known, of course, that Demetriou had spent the years of his exile in England—indeed, I had several colleagues who were friends of his from that time: I had even been vaguely aware, perhaps, that he had an English wife; but the notion of his being Dorothea's husband had not crossed my mind for a moment. His full name had been mentioned, I dare say, in her affidavit; but it is a common one in Greece, and there had been no roll of drums or blare of trumpets to mark the greatness of the man referred to.

'Really, Cantrip,' I said, 'I should have supposed that even in Cambridge—'

Yet even those who did not share Cantrip's educational disadvantages were but dimly aware, it seemed, of Demetriou's eminence: Julia had seen his name in an *Anthology of Modern Greek Verse*, purchased to improve her acquaintance with that language; Ragwort, well-informed from his earliest years on the affairs of the world, remembered that the poet's outspokenness had obliged him to leave Greece precipitately during the regime of the Colonels; Selena had heard him spoken of with admiration by my young colleague Sebastian Verity, the customary companion of her idler moments—I would have expected no less of so ardent Hellenist; Timothy shook his head apologetically.

O tempora, O mores.

62

'Very well,' I said at last, perceiving how useless were further reproaches, 'on the day of Deirdre's death, ten people had gathered in Rupert's flat to take lunch together and afterwards to watch the Boat Race. They happened to include one of the greatest European poets of the twentieth century, of whom none of you, apparently, has ever heard. Very well. Were you able, my dear Cantrip, to gather from your interesting friend any further details of what occurred?'

'They all had lunch on the roof,' said Cantrip, his powers of communication still a little restricted by steak and mushrooms. 'Then they sort of drifted down to the drawing-room to watch the start of the race on television. Deirdre was the last one left up there. But Dorothea went up to get some glasses or something, and stayed and chatted for a bit. Then she came back to the drawing-room, and a bit after that there was all this hullabaloo beside the towpath. They didn't know at first it was anything to do with Deirdre—they thought it was just people getting stirred up about the race. But it wasn't. That's all there is to it, really.'

'The question appears to be, then,' I said, 'whether any of the party could have returned to the roof unobserved in the interval between Dorothea's descent to the drawing-room and Deirdre's more precipitate departure. Is there anything to indicate how long that might have been?'

'The Fairfax twins were on the drawing-room balcony, and they say Dorothea came back just after they'd got their first sight of the boats. And the witnesses on the towpath are pretty definite about Deirdre having fallen just as the boats were going under Barnes Bridge. So it depends how far you can see down river from Rupert's drawing-room balcony.'

'I'm not sure,' said Selena, gazing thoughtfully into her brandy glass. 'It was fairly dark when Julia and I were there. There's a bend in the river, isn't there, at Chiswick Steps? I don't think one could see further than that. Does anyone know how long it would take for the boats to cover the distance between Chiswick Steps and Barnes Bridge?' She looked hopefully at Cantrip, who can generally be counted on to be well-informed on matters of a sporting nature.

'The record's 3 minutes 43 seconds for that stretch,' said

63

Cantrip. 'That was your lot in 1953—cheating, I expect. This year's time must have been a bit longer—say 4 minutes, at the outside.' He devoured his last fried potato as ravenously as he had the first and looked sadly at his plate.

'It isn't very long,' I said.

'We are led to believe,' said Julia, 'that it is a sufficient time to enable us to make all necessary preparation in the event of a nuclear attack. It must surely be ample, therefore, for a straightforward little murder?'

I perceived that Julia was not readily to be dissuaded from her opinion. I myself, though I did not share it, felt a certain uneasiness: the question of the height of the parapet . . . it seemed an absurdly obvious point for the police to have overlooked.

'They didn't,' said Cantrip. He sat back in his chair with his hands clasped behind his head and his elbows pointing upwards, like sharp strenuous wings.

I raised an eyebrow.

'The highly-trained staff of the *Scuttle*,' said Cantrip, 'i.e. this bird, did a spot of tireless in-depth investigation i.e. bought a pint for one of the local fuzz. What the fuzz think is she chucked herself off on purpose. They worked out it couldn't be an accident, because of the wall being too high, so she must have meant to do it. But they didn't see any joy in saying that at the inquest—needless distress and all that to the rest of the family, and no good to Deirdre.'

'A reasonable view,' said Selena.

'This bird thinks there's more to it than that. The way she sees it, it's all due to money and influence. Money and influence being what the Remington-Fiske crowd have got bucketfuls of—you know, probably all went to school with the Home Secretary's grandmother. So someone tipped the wink they weren't to be embarrassed by anyone suggesting Deirdre did it on purpose. Well, that's what this bird thinks. She was at the L.S.E.,' he added, as if in explanation.

'An opinion,' I said, 'may be held by a graduate of the London School of Economics and none the less be true.'

'Anyway,' continued Cantrip, not looking convinced, 'the fuzz didn't say anything at the inquest about the wall round the roof being too high to fall off. And the Coroner didn't ask. And all the family said how bright and breezy Deirdre had been that afternoon, which this bird says is what you'd expect them to say. So the verdict was misadventure and everything was tickety-boo. But what the fuzz really think is that Deirdre did it on purpose.'

Physically, no doubt, it was entirely possible: a girl five foot two in height does not lean over a parapet of five foot four; but if resolved to throw herself over, she may easily scramble on to it. As to her reasons—well, she did not seem to have been of a notably light-hearted disposition: comparing her own position with Camilla's, it would not be surprising if she were discontented; and the young take desperate remedies for discontent. The police, with great experience in such matters, believed that she had done so: could we not with good conscience accept that they were right?

'No,' said Julia, 'no, I don't think we can. The police don't know about the letter. Whatever suicidal inclinations she might have had at any other time, we know she didn't intend to die on the Saturday of the Boat Race; she intended to come and have dinner here at Guido's and tell me about some discovery she'd made. Something she thought was interesting.'

'No doubt when she wrote to you that was her intention. Suicide, however, is a matter of impulse: a degree of despair may be reached, my dear Julia, at which the prospect of having dinner with you in the evening is an insufficient inducement to survive the afternoon.'

It was in vain, however, that I sought to reason with her. Julia has moments of unforeseeable stubbornness: encouraged by more than her fair share of Frascati, she now showed a disposition to begin talking about Sir Thomas More again.

I inquired, with resignation, what arrangements could be made for me to meet further with the descendants of Sir James Remington-Fiske.

CHAPTER 6

Victoria—ah, Victoria, starting-point of all true journeys, all southward voyages of pleasure or exploration, all escapes, all elopements, all flights from financial and emotional creditors. At the thought of her infinite possibilities what pulse could fail to beat faster?

'My dear Hilary,' said Ragwort, 'we are only going into Sussex.'

'You fail,' I answered, 'to discourage me. It is a charming county for a visit.'

Under the grimy sunlight which filters through her vaults of corrugated glass there prevails an atmosphere of almost Continental exuberance—the bars and station cafés strive gallantly for a Parisian look, and it is possible, even on a Sunday morning, to purchase not only a newspaper but also a coffee and croissant: waiting for a train to take us to Godmansworth, Ragwort and I availed ourselves of this circumstance.

Godmansworth College, possibly known to my readers as a public school of sound if unflamboyant reputation, had the privilege at that time of including among its pupils Leonidas Demetriou and among its teaching staff, as junior Classics master, a boyhood friend of Ragwort's—a young man by the name of Peter Hayward. A telephone call on the previous day had conveyed to Ragwort's friend my own passionate desire to visit the celebrated pleasure gardens, laid out in the eighteenth century by William Kent, which were not, however, open to the general public at any time convenient to me. The young schoolmaster had issued with a good grace the invitation which, had he wished to, he could scarcely have withheld. Ragwort had further mentioned, splendidly en passant, his brief professional acquaintance with Leonidas; the possibility, as Ragwort supposed it to be, that the boy might be going up to Oxford in the following year; the thought that it might be pleasant for him, in that event, if he already had one or two friends there; and that if Peter cared, therefore, to invite him to join us for lunch . . .

'I didn't speak,' said Ragwort, as our train clattered happily through the green countryside, 'of your influence with the Admissions Board. I thought it would be wrong, since so far as I know you don't have any. If Peter, however, should somehow have gained the impression that you do, it would be unkind to disabuse him.'

'He surely cannot imagine,' I said, a little shocked, 'that the prospects of Leonidas securing admission to Oxford could be affected by any personal partiality which might be entertained by a senior member of the University?'

'He may,' said Ragwort, 'have some such notion . . . no doubt it is quite misconceived.'

'My dear Ragwort,' I said with some severity, 'certainly it is. Admission nowadays is based entirely on merit. The boy is the son of one of the greatest poets of our time: at Oxford, whatever may happen elsewhere, I hope that will always be accounted sufficient merit to secure entry, without resort to influence or patronage.'

The village of Godmansworth, a cluster of redbrick houses enfolded in the gentle Sussex hills, lay becalmed in the drowsiness of a warm summer Sunday. The cobbled High Street, deserted by all save a sleeping tabby cat, became after fifty yards or so no more than a country road: in the fields on our left browsed a few indolent cattle; on our right lay woodlands, unruffled by any breath of wind; all was rustic tranquillity. There was nothing to prepare us for any scene of violence or alarm.

We turned, about a mile from the village, down an avenue of chestnut trees, at the far end of which could be seen the façade of the great eighteenth-century mansion which is now Godmansworth College. There was no sound to be heard but the distant humming of bees, the warble of a wood pigeon, and, as we drew nearer, the high clear voices of boys singing in the chapel. The avenue divided; and we followed a path which led us round the western wing of the house, away from the sound of the singing. The terrace on the west looks out across the former deer park: we paused there to admire the distant prospect of the lake, an agreeable vista charmingly interrupted by a coppice of oak trees.

A figure emerged suddenly from the coppice, running with the swiftness of panic, yet with such graceful lightness that I could scarcely believe it was any girl of flesh and blood who fled so desperately through the long grass, her fair hair streaming wildly, her thin white dress savagely dishevelled, but rather that the dryad inhabitant of the oak trees was in flight from some gross and violent intrusion. The youth who a moment later appeared in enraged pursuit was well suited to the role of satyr: a heavy, hairy, hulking sort of boy, with a look, even at a distance, of loutish brutality. The fugitive seemed at first to be gaining ground; but stumbled; was overtaken and seized; and cowered pitifully from the instantly threatened blow.

It had not, I confess, occurred to me—so rapidly and unexpectedly had these events taken place—that any practical assistance ought to be offered to the victim. Ragwort, however, murmuring 'Quite disgraceful' in the severest tone, had begun to remove his light-weight sports jacket.

'My dear Ragwort,' I said, 'do you really think . . . ?'

But it would take more than any such mild remonstrance to deter Ragwort from what he conceived to be his duty. He threw down the jacket, and set off at great speed towards the scene of action. Pausing to retrieve the garment so impetuously discarded, I followed him at a more leisurely pace.

The dryad was not enduring her wrongs in silence. I could not distinguish the words in which she reproached or pleaded with her assailant; but they were uttered with an astonishing fluency, and in a rhythm curiously familiar to me, which for several seconds I sought in vain to identify. Continuing to struggle, she again managed to break free and once more, though with her head still turned to continue her tirade, began to run away from the coppice in the direction of the house.

Ragwort, as my readers may recall, was at the same time running away from the house in the direction of the coppice, at a speed which admitted of neither check nor swerve.

Collision in such circumstances was scarcely to be avoided: I was close beside them before either recovered breath.

'Oh dear,' said Leonidas Demetriou, removing his blonde wig, 'I'm terribly sorry. It's Mr Ragwort, isn't it?'

'My dear Ragwort,' I said, assisting my young friend to his feet, 'you might reasonably imagine, I suppose, that a dryad would address her ravisher in Greek; but surely you could not expect her to achieve *ex tempore* the actual metre of classical tragedy?'

'Poor Tomkinson is quite upset,' said Leonidas, demurely pouring sherry in Peter Hayward's oak-panelled study, 'at being suspected of an attempted ravishment. He's very respectable, and wants to go into the Stock Exchange. I've told him, of course, that after today's incident it will be quite impossible—unless we can all be persuaded to keep it very dark.'

Leonidas had changed from the floating white chiton which he had worn to rehearse the title role in Euripides' *Helena* into more conventional garments. There remained about him, even so, something curiously equivocal—that slight wariness, that imperceptibly more alert apprehension, that attentiveness even in repose to the evidence of the senses, which is found in those who in some alien environment never cease to watch for danger or advantage: in migrants between countries or classes; in those conscious of some unorthodox erotic preference; in spies; and in cats always, however domesticated.

'I do hope he didn't believe you,' said Peter Hayward. Fair-haired, fresh-complexioned, with the square-cut features which seem incapable of guile, the master looked more boyish than the boy.

'Of course he didn't,' said Leonidas. 'Even Tomkinson has more sense than that.' But he smiled as he said this a rather Byzantine smile, full of malice and intrigue.

We talked for a while of Euripides. The open-air performance of the *Helena* which was shortly to mark the ending of the Godmansworth summer term was under Peter Hayward's direction: having sometimes been prevailed upon by the undergraduates of St George's to undertake a similar responsibility, I was well able to sympathize with the difficulties of his task. I happened, moreover, to be at that time rather particularly well-informed about the play itself. A few days before my young colleague Sebastian Verity had sought my advice as to how he might persuade Selena to enter into some more formal—that is to say, matrimonial—arrangement; knowing well how attached she is to the darling douceurs of the single life, I had thought it kind to divert him from so unfruitful a topic. I invited him to tell me about an article he had lately published in one of the learned journals, and which I had heard much praised, concerning the transmission of the texts of Euripides, with particular reference to the *Helena*. The diversion proved so successful, and he addressed me at such length on the discrepancies between the L Codex and the P Codex, that I almost repented of having raised the subject. I now had the pleasure, however, of displaying more learning than I was truly possessed of.

I was recalled with some reluctance to the purpose of our visit. It would be prudent, said Ragwort, if I were to gratify at once my desire to see the gardens: Leonidas, perhaps, would be kind enough to act as my guide, while Ragwort himself assisted his friend in the final preparations for lunch. He gave me a glance intended to remind me that I should make the most of the opportunity to question Leonidas. Peter Hayward gave his pupil a rather similar look, intended no doubt to remind him that he should not waste the opportunity to impress favourably a fellow of St George's.

The boy did very well. Familiar, or contriving to appear so, with the history of the distinguished family who had formerly lived at Godmansworth, he diligently pointed out to me how it was reflected in the design and architecture of the place. Traces remained of the manor house built by the first to be eminent, the businesslike adventurer knighted by the first Elizabeth; his grandson, by two judicious marriages, sufficiently improved his fortune to buy a peerage from James II and rebuild the house in the style of the English Renaissance, with that grand simplicity which disdains all ornament but its own harmonious proportions; a more re-mote descendant, rising to an earldom under one of the Georges, had commissioned William Kent to design the gardens—a created Arcadia, in which duchesses and states-men might play at nymphs and shepherds.

Over winding paths silent with moss the chestnut trees spread a network of translucent green. Wherever the eye might have wearied of shade there was a shaft of sunlight; wherever it might have surfeited of green it found the dark glow of a copper beech, the purple of a rhododendron, or a wild pink hyacinth among the grass. At the highest point was a little rotunda, with grey stone columns of the Ionic order: the paths all led towards it, but with a teasing circuity; catching a glimpse of it through the trees and thinking to walk in that direction, one somehow lost sight of it; and at last came upon it again as if unexpectedly, with a sense of discovering by chance some hidden and mysterious place.

I sat down on the shallow steps of the rotunda to admire the view laid out with such careful carelessness for that purpose. With perhaps an equally studied abandon, the boy lay full length on the grass nearby, the sunlight through the leaves dappling him with shadows. I reminded him (though I thought he already remembered) of our previous brief meeting, and expressed my regret at its tragic sequel.

'Deirdre? Yes, poor Deirdre.' His tone did not imply any depth of personal grief.

'Forgive me,' I said, 'if the subject is too painful to speak of. You were, I dare say, on very close terms with your cousin?'

He gave me a slightly satirical look, knowing that his manner had not suggested that. 'She and Millie used to spend a lot of time with us when we were living in England. And after we went back to Corfu, they generally stayed with us for the holidays. So I suppose we'd seen a good deal of each other. But I'm afraid I didn't like her much—you will think, perhaps, Professor Tamar, that I ought not to say so?'

He smiled again his malicious Byzantine smile, as if mocking the convention which he imputed to me. His eyes

71

were not dark, as his colouring led one to expect, but a bright clear shade of blue—the colour of lapis lazuli.

'My dear boy,' I answered, 'I am an historian—my profession largely consists of speaking ill of the dead.'

'You see,' he went on, as if feeling after all some need to justify himself, 'there was nothing she seemed to like. She didn't like sailing or dancing or having lunch in the taverna or anything else the rest of us did. But if we didn't take her with us, she complained of being left out. And if we did, she just kept saying how miserable she was until we had to take her home again.'

'Irritating,' I said. 'One should think it fortunate, no doubt, that your cousin's death is not a deep personal loss—at least to you. I fear it must have been so to your aunt and grandmother—they brought her up, I believe?'

'My grandmother is very old, Professor Tamar, and used to people dying. And Aunt Jocasta has been controlling her feelings for so long, I'm not sure she has any left to control. They brought up Deirdre, after all, because they could hardly avoid it: her parents died in a car accident, you know, and her father had no relatives. But of course they never cared about her in the way they do about Millie.'

For Jocasta, no doubt, it was a natural preference: to favour a daughter's child above a sister's is a customary inclination. I remembered, moreover, that her daughter had died in the same accident as Deirdre's parents—if she blamed them for it, her feelings towards their child could hardly be unequivocal. But the girl's grandmother, it seemed, without these motives, had also regarded Camilla as entitled to be preferred—as though she were marked by priority of inheritance to be the favourite of affection as well as fortune.

'You think, then, that there was no one,' I said, 'who was much affected by your cousin's death?'

'My mother was rather upset, I think. She was quite fond of Deirdre—at least, she tried to be. Poor Mama—she believes that if one loves people they become lovable: nothing disillusions her.' The malice of his smile was qualified by an indulgent tenderness. 'And she was upset, of course, about the way it happened. She was the last person Deirdre talked to, and she had to give evidence about it at the inquest. It was all rather horrid for her.'

A lizard lying motionless in the warm sunlight was startled by some over-sudden movement of my hand, and disappeared with the swiftness of mercury through a crack in the weather-marbled stone. I wondered how far I might venture to pursue my questions without seeming more than idly curious.

'No doubt it is always disagreeable,' I said, 'to be required to give evidence in court. One may be asked questions one would prefer not to answer, for some reason quite unconnected with the case in hand. I speak generally, of course—I do not imagine there was anything which your mother would not have wished to tell the Coroner.'

'As you say,' said the boy, as if the thought amused him, 'there's always something. She wouldn't have wanted, for example, to tell him about the row between Rupert and my father.'

As one might have expected, it had been about politics.

In the cause of family harmony, Dorothea had sometimes in previous years coaxed one or more of her children to attend Rupert's Boat Race luncheon party and present an appearance of amiability; but this, I gathered, was the first occasion that her husband Constantine had been among the guests. The poet, in recent years, had been very little in England, and the two men had seldom met; not often enough, certainly, to be friends; not often enough, it was rashly assumed, to be enemies.

Hostilities opened almost at once. The poet made some reference, as they sat down to lunch on the roof terrace, to the years he had spent in England when his native country was under the rule of the Colonels. Rupert took the opportunity to say that he personally had a lot of time for the Colonels, who had at least done something to get the Greeks to pull themselves together a bit. The poet responded with thoughtful civility, as if to a rather abstract proposition put forward in some impersonal political dialogue. Rupert said that he personally would rather see the Colonels back in power than a pack of so-called intellectuals who whined about free speech and probably took their orders from Moscow. And so forth: despite various attempts by those about them to change the subject to one less acrimonious, the two men continued thus throughout lunch.

From time to time during the meal there were exchanged between Leonidas and Camilla the apologetic glances and grimaces commonly employed by the young to deplore their parents' conduct and their own inability to control it. The other guests, on the pretext of wishing to observe on television the scenes preliminary to the start of the Boat Race, escaped one by one to the comparative tranquillity of the drawing-room; but Leonidas and his cousin continued to hover anxiously on the outskirts of the battlefield, watching for some opportunity to separate the combatants. Deirdre also, indifferent to the dispute and its outcome, chose to remain on the roof terrace.

Hopes of a cease-fire were raised when Rupert, at his daughter's persuasion, went downstairs to make coffee for his guests; but the poet insisted on following his host—it would be discourteous of him to do otherwise, he said with apparent sincerity, when they were in the middle of such an interesting conversation.

'Parents,' said Leonidas, with a sign of remembered weariness, 'can be very difficult.'

'They have suffered,' I said, 'a traumatic experience—you must make allowances.'

Obedient to an appeal from Camilla that he should go after them and make sure they didn't come to blows, Leonidas also went downstairs. In the kitchen, where Rupert was making coffee, battle had again been joined: Rupert was telling Constantine that he personally believed in old-fashioned democracy, and thought that anyone who didn't should be put up against a wall and shot. It seemed to Leonidas, watching them, that his father's Olympian serenity was driving Rupert into a kind of frenzy, as though the need to make the other man lose his temper had become with him an overmastering passion: his hands shook as he filled the coffee percolator, and there was sweat on his forehead.

The thought occurred to Leonidas after a few minutes that his own presence was not improving matters. He accordingly retreated to the drawing-room, and sat down with his Aunt Jocasta in front of the television set to watch the start of the Boat Race. Camilla, when she joined them, looked reproachfully at him; but he indicated, with an apologetic shrug of the shoulders, that he had done his best in the role of peacemaker and proposed to do no more.

The Fairfax twins had already installed themselves on the drawing-room balcony with a bottle of Rupert's champagne: they would not have felt that Boat Race Day was Boat Race Day (said their half-brother tolerantly) if they had not jumped up and down waving blue handkerchiefs and shouting 'Come on, Oxford' for at least ten minutes before the boats came into view. From time to time they called out to those round the television set to inquire who was leading and at what stage in the course. Leonidas joined them when the boats were approaching Chiswick. As he passed the kitchen he heard Rupert, more enraged than ever, asking whether Constantine was calling him a fascist.

His recollection was very clear of the moment at which the boats first came into view from the balcony, since it was also the moment at which Rupert was heard shouting that he wasn't going to be called a fascist by a greasy little Greek gigolo.

'And that, of course,' said Leonidas, 'was altogether too much.'

The poet had come out of the kitchen looking, as his son described it, all grand and patriarchal, and said they must leave at once: he evidently took it for granted that his stepchildren, as well as his wife and son, would accompany him in his departure. He stood in majestic silence while Lucinda went to call her mother to come down quickly from the terrace. When Dorothea, bewildered, appeared in the drawing-room, he told her only that Rupert's opinion of him was such that he could no longer accept his hospitality.

'And we would have left,' said Leonidas. 'But Lucian was still on the balcony—poor Lucian, he was really quite keen on seeing the Boat Race—and he noticed something odd going on on the towpath. And it was because of Deirdre, of course.' He sighed: he had told me of these events in the light and ironic tone appropriate to an account of social discomfiture recollected in tranquillity, and seemed almost to have forgotten that the quarrel between his father and their host had not been the chief catastrophe of the afternoon. 'Poor Deirdre. But you will understand, Professor Tamar, that my mother would not have wished to tell the Coroner what Rupert said to my father.'

The boy looked very graceful and at ease, lying on the grass beside the little temple, and I thought how well the surroundings became him: if the designer of the garden had had the power to choose not only the shrubs, flowers, trees, temples and statuary but also some living inhabitant for his Arcadia, it would have been, I could not doubt, a boy who looked like Leonidas—with the same delicately carved profile, the same grape-black hair, the same olive-tinted smoothness of complexion. There was something about him, all the same, which reminded me that there is a darker side of Arcadia: the gods who have their birthplace in that remote and mountainous region are not the good-natured and reasonable deities who have their home on Olympus, and their purposes are not always benign.

'I quite understand,' I said, 'that your mother would not have cared for so an offensive a remark to be repeated in the newspapers. It seems surprisingly fortunate that nothing was asked which obliged her to mention it. I should have supposed—but I am very ignorant of such matters—that the Coroner would have inquired rather closely about the time immediately preceding your cousin's death: to establish, for example, exactly how long she had been alone on the roof terrace.'

'He mostly wanted to know what sort of mood she was in—whether she seemed at all depressed, and so on. We were able to tell him, as it happened, that she had been in unusually good spirits.' There was again an ironical note in his voice, which I could not quite account for. 'My mother noticed at lunch how pleased she seemed to be, and asked her if she had something special to be excited about.'

'And had she?'

'Yes, so she said. It was still a secret, she said, but when we knew about it it would be a great surprise for us. My mother of course assumed she was talking of some love-affair. But it wasn't really quite like that. She had the sort of look she used to have when she'd found something out that she knew you didn't want her to know—it was rather a habit of hers. You could tell, if you knew her, that she meant the surprise to be an unpleasant one for us—something that would make her the centre of attention, and make us all wish we'd been nicer to her.'

'It sounds,' I said, 'like a rather disagreeable form of high spirits. But at least you can be satisfied that her death was accidental.'

He had been lying on his side, looking towards me. He now made a quarter turn and lay on his back, his hands clasped behind his head. I could not tell, therefore, with what expression he said, 'Oh no, Professor Tamar, it wasn't an accident.' His tone, however, was one of detachment; of slight irony; and a certainty that sounded like knowledge.

The honey-scented air was almost unnaturally still. Leaves, flowers and shadows were as motionless as stone, and the birds were no longer singing. It is in such conditions, I have heard it said, that cattle and goats and certain other animals may behave wildly and unpredictably, as if in terror of some unseen presence.

'I understood,' I said, 'that the verdict was accident.'

'It couldn't have been an accident,' said the boy. 'The wall around the terrace is too high to fall from by accident.'

'But you say that your cousin behaved as if she were in good spirits?'

'I say that she behaved, Professor Tamar, as if she expected to be the centre of attention and make us all wish we'd have been nicer to her. Yes. How else could she have done that except by killing herself?' He turned towards me again, looking at me with his curious lapis lazuli eyes; and what he said seemed for a moment quite reasonable and persuasive.

77

I thought it idle to question him further: if he knew more of his cousin's death than he had already told me, I could not doubt that the knowledge was very dark indeed. And yet it occurred to me—the young have such curious consciences— that it might be no more than remorse for some slight or unkindness to her which persuaded him to believe, with that certainty which sounded like knowledge, that she had committed suicide. Since the habit dies hard of discouraging the young from thoughts considered morbid—

'My dear boy,' I said, 'that is altogether too fanciful, you know. People do not commit suicide in such a mood as you have described—I do not believe for a moment that your cousin killed herself.'

This afterwards proved to have been a most dangerous remark.

CHAPTER 7

'Did you happen to notice,' inquired Selena, 'if he had a cloven foot? Or do your suspicions rest entirely on his being olive-skinned and having blue eyes? No doubt it is a most sinister combination, almost conclusive of his guilt; but there are unimaginative persons—such as sit on juries, you know—who might regard it as a quite natural consequence of his having a Greek father and an English mother.'

In the coffee-house at the top of Chancery Lane which is, on weekday mornings, the customary meeting place of the junior members of 62 New Square, Ragwort and I had given our account of our expedition into Sussex. Selena was disposed, as my readers will have gathered, to regard with scepticism the uneasiness I had felt during my conversation with Leonidas Demetriou.

'Did you,' she continued, turning to Cantrip, 'have a similar sort of time in Cambridge? Was the Black Mass being said in your College chapel? Were there witches weaving spells in the Senior Common Room? Were there warlocks waltzing in the quad?'

It had been arranged that Cantrip would make a weekend visit to his alma mater, where he would attempt to contrive some meeting with Camilla. I had not supposed that much would come of it; but had not wished—for the boy meant well—to wound his feelings by saying so.

'No,' said Cantrip, with regret. 'No, nothing like that. I had quite a jolly time, all the same. I went along to my College and dug out my ex-tutor—decent old geezer by the name of Grocklehurst. Taught me all I know about Equity and Succession.'

I knew Professor Grocklehurst a little personally, and well by reputation. Though not entirely sound, in my view, on the development of the action of *assumpsit*, he was a scholar of no small ability—I had often wondered by what youthful error or evil stroke of fortune he had found himself exiled to Cambridge.

'So I hauled him off to the nearest hostelry,' continued Cantrip, 'and poured booze down him until he was feeling pretty genial, and then I told him about my hopeless passion for Camilla.'

'My dear Cantrip,' said Julia with some alarm, 'I do hope the attachment is fictitious?'

'Oh, absolutely, but I had to think of some reason for wanting to see her again, didn't I? Anyway, it was all dead easy, because it turned out old Grockles was teaching Camilla Equity and Succession as well. And he was having a breakfast party on Sunday morning, so he said he'd invite her along and I could try my luck. He didn't fancy my chances much—he reckoned there'd been a lot of chaps trying to chat her up since she came to Cambridge, and none of them had got anywhere. I said they were probably all callow undergraduates and it would be a bit different if the chap doing the chatting up was a smooth and sophisticated man of the world.'

'I dare say it would,' said Ragwort. 'But what exactly is the relevance of that to—? Oh, I see—my dear Cantrip, do forgive me for being so obtuse.'

I asked if the heiress had accepted Professor Grocklehurst's invitation.

'Oh, like a shot—chuffed as chocolate about it. Grockles's breakfast parties are rather a big deal socialwise—I mean, getting asked to them means you're part of a sort of intellectual élite.'

'Cantrip,' I said, 'were you, when at Cambridge, a frequent guest at these gatherings?'

'Oh, rather,' said Cantrip.

My heart bled for Grocklehurst.

'And is Camilla,' I asked 'a member of this élite?'

'Well, not really. Bright but not brilliant, you know—that's what Grockles thinks, anyway. But she wants to come to the Bar, and she's frightfully keen and hardworking—always asking for extra reading lists and spent the last summer Vac working in a lawyer's office to get experience. You wouldn't catch me doing that sort of thing if I was due to get my paws on five million quid—but there's no accounting for tastes. She's one of those all round birds, though—plays tennis for her College and might get her blue for swimming.'

'A paragon,' said Selena, 'of the Victorian virtues. *Mens sana in corpore sano* and no sex life. I wonder if she takes cold baths.'

'We may be about to learn,' said Ragwort, 'that under the influence of Cantrip's sophisticated charm her coldness melted like the snow in summer. I assume, Cantrip, that at this breakfast party you maintained the appearance of amorous pursuit?'

'Well, I had to, hadn't I? Mind you, I don't say I mightn't have chatted her up a bit even if I hadn't had to—she was looking quite fanciable. Anyway, I shovelled scrambled eggs down her in a worldly and sophisticated sort of way and it all went like a breeze. There was some fairly stiff competition from a chap from Trinity—fancied himself on account of being a baronet or something—but he never had a chance, because what she wanted to hear about was the inside story of life at the Bar. So in the end I took her off to lunch, leaving the Trinity chap standing at the post.'

'That,' I said, 'was no doubt most gratifying. Did you manage to persuade her to talk about Deirdre at all?'

'Of course I did, or I wouldn't be telling you about it,

would I? I gave her a couple of martinis to soften her up, and then I said what rotten luck it was about Deirdre falling off the roof—you know, the manly sympathy bit. And she said pretty much the same as your Greek kid—you know, about Deirdre being a bit of pain and not much loss to anyone. Well, she didn't put it like that—but the general picture was that Deirdre falling off the roof hadn't exactly left an aching void in her life and she thought it'd be hypocritical to say it had. The way she saw it was that Deirdre'd always been miffed about not being the one who was going to get the loot, and the only way she could get her own back was by being fairly bloody-minded all the time—always whining and telling tales and so on. Well, that's the way Camilla saw it. But then she went all stiff upper lip and said that Latin thing about mortuaries.'

'The phrase you have in mind,' said Ragwort, 'is *"de mortuis nil nisi bonum"*—that of the dead one should say only what is good.'

'That's the one,' said Cantrip, impressed by his friend's erudition. 'She didn't actually seem to be able to think of anything good to say about Deirdre, but she obviously thought it was a bit off to go on saying what a ghastly brat she'd been. So I kept on with the manly sympathy bit, but laying off the personal tragedy angle and putting more emphasis on the frightful shock aspect—you know, grimness of having to cope with the fuzz and the newspaper chaps and the Coroner and all that. And she went all stiff upper lip again, and said yes, it had been pretty grim, but specially grim for Aunt Dolly—that's Dorothea.'

'Presumably,' I said, 'because Dorothea was the last person to talk to Deirdre before she died.'

'Well, partly that. But mostly because of her husband— that's the poet chap. The poet chap thought it was all his fault.'

Someone judged this a suitable moment to remind Cantrip of our empty cups and that it was his turn to buy coffee. I waited with some impatience to learn why Constantine Demetriou considered himself responsible for Deirdre's death.

'Because of having this bust-up with Rupert. They were going on at each other all through lunch, the same as the Greek kid told you they were, and everyone else getting jolly fed up with them. But Camilla reckoned it was all the poet chap's fault. The poet chap's some kind of lefty, and Rupert can't stand lefties at any price. So the poet chap shouldn't have stirred things by talking about politics. That's the way Camilla sees it.'

Leonidas blamed Camilla's father, she blamed his—it was a pleasing instance of filial piety.

'So everyone else was trying to take no notice and concentrate on the Boat Race. But just as it got to the exciting bit and the boats came in sight from the balcony the poet chap suddenly went all huffy about something Rupert said, and said he was leaving at once and where was Dolly. So Cindy— that's the ginger-haired bird—had to go and call Dolly down from the roof and Dolly came down and left Deirdre on her own there. So when Deirdre started leaning over to see the boats going under Barnes Bridge there wasn't anyone there to hold on to her ankles. And that's why the poet chap reckoned it was all his fault, because if he hadn't lost his temper and insisted on leaving, Dolly would still have been up there to act as ankle-gripper.'

I reflected with admiration on the tormented subleties of the artistic conscience. I was surprised, however, that the boy Leonidas had given me no hint of his father's feelings.

'Shouldn't think he knew about them,' said Cantrip. 'I don't mean the poet chap did the conscience-stricken bit there and then. But next day, when Camilla went round to Hampstead, she found Dolly all weepy and upset, and that's when Dolly told her that the poet chap thought it was all his fault and she couldn't persuade him it wasn't and she didn't know what to do. So I don't suppose he'd done the conscience-stricken bit to anyone except Dolly.' Cantrip, who had contrived to combine his narrative with the consumption of a doughnut, now licked his fingers and looked regretfully at his empty plate. 'Well, that's as far as I got, really. I thought Camilla would think it a bit funny if I asked her exactly where everyone was standing and whether anyone happened to slope off to the loo—it's not the sort of thing birds expect to be asked about when they're being chatted up over lunch.'

Cantrip had done well, and I thought it right to say so. If he had failed, as it afterwards proved he had, to ask Camilla the one question which might even then have given me an inkling of the truth, he is hardly to be blamed: I freely confess that I myself might not have thought to ask it.

'Were arrangements made,' inquired Ragwort, 'for a further meeting?'

'I said if she gave me a buzz next time she was in London I'd feed her the odd chip or two, and she seemed quite chuffed at the prospect. But it won't be for two or three months—she's going straight out to Corfu to stay with Dolly as soon as term's over. She's got a boat of her own out there, so she's reckoning to spend most of her time sailing. That's when she's not swotting up on Equity and Succession and all that.'

A digression ensued: Selena was reminded that in some three weeks' time she herself would be sailing in the same waters. She spoke a trifle defensively of the enterprise, for the courts would still be sitting: but Henry, it seemed, had so arranged her professional obligations over the past year as to disrupt at short notice her plans for Christmas, Easter and the present short Whitsun vacation, and she had at last rebelled. She had told Henry, kindly but firmly, that during the second fortnight in June the wheels of justice must roll on as best they could without her assistance: she would be sailing a small boat round the Ionian Islands in the company of her friend Sebastian Verity, out of reach of any form of long-distance communication which might demand her return to Lincoln's Inn.

While Selena spoke joyfully of the prospect of sailing on the wide, blue, Henryless Ionian, I reflected on what we had learnt from Leonidas and Camilla. Could murder still be thought of as even a remote possibility? The timing was very fine: the dispute between Constantine Demetriou and Rupert Galloway had reached its climax at the moment when the boats came into view from the balcony; assuming that this was when they passed Chiswick Steps, we had calculated that four minutes would have been available before the moment at which Deirdre was known to have fallen; but this was now reduced by the time taken for the poet to announce his departure, for Lucinda to be sent to call her mother, and for Dorothea herself to come downstairs from the roof. Both accounts, moreover, had given the impression that all the members of the family were present in the drawing-room—or at least on the balcony or in the adjoining kitchen—when Dorothea returned to it. The only person whose presence there had not been expressly mentioned was—

'Ah, Mr Tancred,' said Selena, anticipating my words, though in a tone more cordial than any I had thought to employ. Turning my head, I saw approaching our table the substantial figure of the Remington-Fiske family solicitor. He returned Selena's greeting with equal warmth.

'Ah, Miss Jardine—this is an unexpected pleasure. May I join you? Unless,' he added, observing how many members of 62 New Square were gathered round our table, 'I am intruding on a Chambers meeting?'

'Nothing like that,' said Selena. 'A purely informal gathering. Do join us—you know Professor Tamar, don't you?'

'Ah yes, I do, of course—how are you, Professor Tamar?' said the solicitor, disguising with a rather excessive enthusiasm for our present meeting his inability to recall our last. I thought it kind, when he had settled himself beside Selena, to remind him that it had been on the occasion of the proceedings under the Variation of Trusts Act, when I had chanced to be visiting Chambers.

'Ah yes, of course.' The syllabies rolled mellow and rounded from his tongue. 'How long ago it seems—extraordinary to think it was only in February.'

'I was sorry to read,' I said, 'of the tragic sequel.'

'The death of poor Miss Robinson? Ah yes, a very sad business. A dreadful ordeal for Miss Galloway, of course—indeed, for the whole family.'

'I believe,' I said, 'that you yourself were present when the accident occurred? It seems fortunate—if anything can be so described in such a connection—that the family should have been able to turn to you immediately for your advice and support.'

'I did what I could, naturally. I can hardly claim, however, that such events are within my normal professional experience.' His enthusiasm for me seemed to be cooling.

'Of course not. None the less, one cannot doubt that your presence at such a time would have been of the greatest assistance. In dealing with the police, for example—a lay person without the benefit of professional advice might say all manner of things to the police which prudent reflection would have left unsaid.'

'There was no question of that, Professor Tamar. None of the family had any reason to be anything but entirely candid with the police.'

'Oh,' I said rather quickly, for his tone suggested a desire to treat the subject as closed, 'I did not intend to suggest that they had. But the fact that you yourself were a witness—'

'Do let us talk,' said Selena 'of something more cheerful.'

My readers will be surprised, perhaps, at this intervention in my questioning of a witness so providentially met with and so material to the subject-matter of my investigation—an investigation, as my readers will recall, undertaken at the particular request of the members of 62 New Square, who might thus have been expected to support me in my inquiries. But no such matter: they had observed my questioning of Tancred with every sign of increasing apprehension; and Selena, as I have said, now chose to change the subject.

Success at the Bar, my readers should further recall, is seldom achieved by offending solicitors.

The conversation consisted thereafter of innocuous legal gossip. It was not until Tancred's departure—an appointment at his offices in Lincoln's Inn Fields prevented him from lingering—that the subject of my inquiry was touched on again.

'By the way, Miss Larwood,' he said as he rose to leave us, 'talking of the Remington-Fiske application, I don't suppose—I believe I did mention to your Clerk some weeks ago that the probate seemed to have gone astray somehow—I don't suppose you happened to come across it at all?'

Julia at this showed signs of agitation. She turned the colour of a tomato with something on its conscience, and answered with quivering over-emphasis: 'No, I haven't, Mr Tancred. I don't have the probate. I never had the probate. There was never any reason for me to have the probate. So there's no possibility of my now coming across the probate.'

'I really think,' said Selena, 'that that must be right, Mr Tancred. You wouldn't have put it with Julia's papers, would you? You'd have lodged it in Court. And when the hearing was over, the Judge's Clerk would have handed it back to you.'

'Yes,' said the solicitor doubtfully. 'Yes, that would be the usual thing, certainly. But I remembered that Miss Larwood had been kind enough to accept instructions at very short notice, and might not have had a complete set of papers. In which case, it occurred to me, the Judge might have handed her the probate for her assistance in the course of the hearing.'

'He didn't,' said Julia. 'I should certainly have remembered so signal a favour. It must have been lost in your office, Mr Tancred—someone took it out, I expect, to check the investment powers or something of that nature, and forgot to put it back again.'

'That's really most unlikely, you know, Miss Larwood. We wouldn't keep an original probate with our ordinary working papers, you see. We would have a copy of the Will on our current file—the final draft, probably, or a copy taken from it—and that's what we would use for ordinary reference purposes. We would keep the original probate safely in a strongbox, and only take it out when absolutely necessary.' He spoke benignly and a little complacently; for he perceived, I suppose, that Julia would not have thought of such a system, but would have been careful to keep any original document in a place where it could easily be referred to, and spilt coffee over, and mixed up with other papers having nothing to do with it.

'I know what must have happened,' said Selena with

triumph, as if hitting on an explanation which when once thought of was manifestly true. 'If the probate was with the papers when you left them with the Judge, Mr Tancred, and you haven't seen it since, the Judge must have it. He was looking at the affidavits, I dare say, and he put the probate on one side and misplaced it—used it to mark his place in a Law Report, I expect, and then forgot about it. I think your best course, Mr Tancred, would be to have a tactful word with his Clerk.'

'Well, you may be right, Miss Jardine—I'll do as you suggest, certainly. But if Miss Larwood would be so kind as to have another look for it . . .' With a tolerant smile at Julia to show he meant no unkindness, the solicitor took his leave of us.

'It's an extraordinary thing,' said Julia, 'how every solicitor who loses a piece of paper anywhere in the area of Greater London always claims that it's my fault. It seems to be an official policy of the Law Society.'

'The notion is certainly rather widespread,' said Ragwort, 'that if any document goes missing in a case in which you have been concerned it's probably somewhere on your desk.'

'And it usually is,' said Cantrip. 'Are you taking the line this one isn't?'

'Of course it isn't,' said Julia. 'Selena has just conclusively established that it can't be.'

'No,' said Selena absent-mindedly. 'No, of course it can't. But it might be a good idea, perhaps, to have just one more look for it among your papers.'

I asked what exactly it was that Julia should not have had but had none the less managed to lose. If, as I vaguely imagined, it was the original Will of the late Sir James Remington-Fiske, the matter seemed to be serious: I wondered if its loss might give rise to difficulty when the time came for Camilla to enter upon her inheritance.

'Good heavens, no,' said Selena. 'Nothing like that. The probate is the official grant of representation to the executors, with an office copy of the Will bound up inside it. The original Will is filed at the Probate Registry. So there'd never be any serious problem about finding out what it said, even if Tancred lost every single copy on his files.'

'You mean,' I said, 'that the loss of the probate is of no consequence?'

'None whatever,' said Julia, her spirits evidently rising. 'So even if I had lost it, which I haven't, it wouldn't matter in the least.'

'It could be rather a nuisance from the conveyancing point of view,' said Timothy. 'You see, Hilary, whenever any of the land is sold a memorandum is supposed to be endorsed on the probate to prevent the same land being sold twice over. So a future purchaser might be rather cross if it couldn't be produced.'

Julia looked discouraged again.

The notion drifted idly across my mind that it is not unheard of for a solicitor to embezzle funds of which he is trustee; and it seemed, from what Timothy had said, that a solicitor who had done so might find it convenient to lose the probate.

It was perhaps unwise to voice these thoughts aloud, for they were immediately received by my companions as asserted and established fact. It seemed to them the most natural and probable thing in the world that Mr Tancred should behave in such a manner as I had surmised. He was, after all, a solicitor: a member, that was to say, of a profession noted for its lack of financial scruple, owing its entire prosperity to delay in paying Counsel's fees, and whose invariable practice it was, when the affairs of a client had been mishandled, to put the blame for it on some poor, innocent, hardworking member of the Bar. Only Timothy expressed doubt, and that on merely practical grounds.

'It wouldn't be quite as easy as you seem to think,' he said. 'The tenant for life would have to be a party to the sale, remember, and the purchase money would be paid into a joint account in the names of both the trustees.'

'Hilary is about to remind us,' said Selena, 'that the tenant for life is an elderly lady, not, alas, in the best of health, who probably signs anything that her solicitor puts in front of her.'

'And that the co-trustee,' said Ragwort, 'is Rupert Galloway—a disreputable financier hoping to benefit from his daughter's generosity when her inheritance falls into possession. Hilary would suggest, no doubt, that the more flexible sort of conscience might see little harm in anticipating that generosity.'

'So the way you see it, Hilary,' said Cantrip blithely, 'is that Tancred and Rupert were in cahoots to trouser some of the trust fund? And Deirdre found out about it somehow, so Tancred did her in to stop her spilling the beans. Do you reckon Rupert was in on that as well?'

I was obliged to disclaim so adventurous a flight of reasoning. I had merely been speculating on the possible explanations for the loss of the probate: I had not suggested for a moment that the solicitor had any responsibility for Deirdre's death.

'Yes, you did,' said Cantrip. 'You were just going to anyway, when he came creeping up on us all suddenly like that. Jolly sinister, if you ask me—probably trying to slip arsenic in our coffee, to stop us exposing him.'

'Oh, I hardly think so, Cantrip,' I said, I fear a little acidly. 'He must surely be aware that he is in no danger of exposure from any of the members of 62 New Square. It was clear from your attitude, when I attempted to question him, that none of you would do anything to embarrass a solicitor, however homicidal, from whom your Chambers so regularly receive instructions.'

They were apologetic. It was true, they said, that they had been a little embarrassed at my persisting in a topic of conversation so plainly distasteful to Mr Tancred. If, however, he was a murderer, then I might rest assured that they would decline all further work from him, whatever the brief fee and however cross Henry might be about it: no Barristers' Clerk could expect his principals to receive instructions from hands steeped in the blood of innocent beneficiaries, and they would tell Henry so in no uncertain manner.

I advised them not to be premature in making such a sacrifice, for there was at present no reason to believe Mr Tancred guilty of any crime. He was the only one of the available suspects whose presence in the drawing-room at the material time had not been specifically remarked on by either of our witnesses; but it was possible that they had merely thought it of insufficient interest to be mentioned; conversely, if one of the others had left the drawing-room on some natural and trivial pretext, one would not expect their absence to have been expressly alluded to.

'You mean,' said Cantrip, 'if one of them nipped off to the loo, Camilla wouldn't have bothered telling me about it?'

'Precisely so,' I said. 'Nor Leonidas to tell me.'

'It would be an unconvincing pretext,' said Selena, 'for someone really meaning to go up to the roof terrace. The door leading to the bathroom and the one leading to the staircase are at opposite ends of the drawing-room. I think the excuse would have had to be that they wanted something from the room at the foot of the staircase—the one Rupert calls his study.'

Julia now asked me what arrangements I intended to make to interview Rupert Galloway.

'My dear Julia,' I said, 'to interview Rupert at this stage would be either premature or pointless. The only person I could usefully talk to would be Dorothea—her evidence is crucial, but she is in Corfu. Well, it is possible that something can be arranged. I have had it in mind to spend a little time in Corfu—I have friends there who have kindly said I am welcome at any time—but not until September.'

'You're not suggesting,' said Julia, 'that we do nothing until September?'

'There is nothing we can do,' I answered.

I perceived from her reproachful gaze that she felt her confidence in me to have been misplaced. She did not know exactly what Sir Thomas More would have done; but she plainly thought that he would have done it before September.

CHAPTER 8

To keep Julia confined permanently in her room at 63 New Square, however ample the arrangements for her comfort and well-being, would provoke some objection, I suppose, from one of the humanitarian societies: misguided in my view—Julia, if allowed to wander unrestrained about London, can only come to harm, and it is no kindness to permit her to do so. A truth sufficiently demonstrated by the events which occurred on my next visit.

It was the day, some three weeks later, on which Selena was to leave for the Ionian Islands. At midday, however, I found her still at her desk, looking rather pink and shiny-nosed, her fair hair rumpled and the sleeves of her white shirt pushed back to the elbow, as if she expected by merely physical effort to dispose of the pile of papers which surrounded her.

'It isn't really as bad as it looks,' she said, leaning back and drawing a deep breath. 'I've only two Opinions and a Statement of Claim to do, and Sebastian isn't collecting me until five o'clock. I ought to have finished them by then—in manuscript, that is. Having them typed depends on the temporary typist.' Her optimism seemed to fade a little. 'Still, if the worst comes to the worst, they can be typed next week, and Julia can sign them off for me.'

I inquired if Julia was any better than she had been when I last saw her—that is to say, whether she had recovered at all from her anxiety about Deirdre and the traditions of the English Bar and so forth.

'No,' said Selena, after a moment's reflection. 'No, I don't think one could say she was better. It would be more accurate to say—' she paused in apparent search for the *mot juste*—'that she's worse. Yes, considerably worse. It's all Cantrip's fault. His friend on the *Scuttle* reminded him that Rupert Galloway was one of the people involved in that unpleasant business at Rustington a few years ago. Do you remember anything about it?'

The Rustington affair had been one of the more colourful scandals of its day; but though at the time I had followed it with interest I did not now recall the details. A number of moderately celebrated persons—bankers, politicians, television panellists and so forth—had enjoyed the hospitality of a well-known businessman at his house on the Sussex coast; the festivities had been of an unconventional and boisterous nature; and a girl had died, apparently by drowning. Some rather unsavoury suggestions had been made as to the cause of death, though none, if my memory served me, of deliberate murder. I did not, however, remember any mention of Rupert in connection with the affair.

'I don't imagine,' said Selena, 'that he was distinguished enough to attract much notice in the newspapers, but he was certainly among the guests. Well, Cantrip told Julia, and Julia thinks it's significant—she won't believe that Rupert's presence on two occasions when young women have met with unnatural deaths is merely an unfortunate coincidence. And she feels that something should be done.'

I said that I was sorry to hear it: I had rather hoped that Julia would by this time have forgotten about the whole matter.

'By no means,' said Selena. 'So it's very fortunate, Hilary, that you're in London again: you can reassure her that you're still investigating and all the resources of scholarship will be devoted to discovering the truth. I think you should go straight round to 63 and tell her so—it will be a great comfort to her, and leave me free to get on with my paperwork.'

In 63 New Square, however, I was told by Julia's Clerk that she had as yet made no appearance there: in the afternoon, he added with touching confidence, I could be sure of finding her, since she had an important conference at half past two; but of her present whereabouts he had no idea.

Selena, when I returned with these tidings, was too much preoccupied to express any great curiosity. She was correcting the most recent product of the skills of the temporary typist—an Opinion on the title to certain freehold land comprised in the estate of an ancient and noble family—and the task seemed to be distressing her. She took particular exception, as I recall, to the description of the fifth Earl as the sun and air of the fourth.

'I could understand it,' she said in the tone of one trying hard to be reasonable, 'if I had been dictating. Muriel has been typing for us, after all, for only six months, and cannot be expected to be familiar with technical terms. But how does she manage to do it when she's simply copying from manuscript?'

It was, I explained, an instance of the phenomenon known to students of textual criticism as *dictation interne*: the copyist, mentally repeating the words of the original, copies them not as he sees them but as he imagines hearing them—it is a fruitful source of error.

'Most interesting,' said Selena. 'Some day, Hilary, you must tell me all about it. Some day, that is, when I don't have a plane to catch and three sets of papers to finish.'

I sought in vain to persuade her that she should pause from her labours for a light but nourishing lunch in the Corkscrew: she had brought sandwiches, and proposed to eat them at her desk. The other members of the Nursery being all engaged in court, I resigned myself to lunching alone.

On my way down the steps of 62 New Square, however, I encountered Ragwort, returning from the Law Courts in triumph: he had been applying, I gathered, for something called a Mareva injunction, and despite the perjured evidence and meretricious argument deployed against him, had succeeded in obtaining it. He was sufficiently elated to be prevailed on to join me in the Corkscrew.

I listened with attentive admiration to the full details of his victory; but towards the end of the meal I made some passing reference to Julia's absence from Chambers. Ragwort frowned.

'One would not wish,' he said, 'to speak critically of one's friends. It has to be admitted, however, that Julia is not wholly free of the sin of sloth. If she woke up this morning and found herself with no immediate engagements, it is quite possible that she simply went back to sleep again. And she is capable, in that case, of failing to wake up again in time for her conference at two-thirty, which I understand to be rather important. Shall we stroll along to Bloomsbury and make sure she's up and about?'

'By all means,' I said. 'It will be an opportunity to see Carlotta, which is always delightful.'

Julia occupies as her residence the top story of a dilapidated Victorian house near the British Museum, owned by the celebrated historical novelist Carlotta Benares—my readers will doubtless be familiar with her work, though a tendency to emphasize the more sentimental aspects of history has prevented her enjoying the critical esteem which would be the just reward for her painstaking research. I am always pleased to see her, for we have several enemies in common.

She greeted us in her customary splendour of black lace and topaz, and offered us madeira and macaroons. Ragwort is a favourite in her affections, for she regards him as being 'the right man for Julia': she does not know, I think, that he has rejected Julia's matrimonial proposals with as much firmness as those of a less honourable nature. Myself also she greeted with great goodwill, being eager to know my opinion of a colleague in the world of Scholarship who had written unfavourably, in a review of her most recent novel, of her understanding of military tactics in the reign of Richard III. The same man, as it happened, had once published an impertinent comment in one of the learned journals on a little article of my own concerning the statute De Donis: I was happy to assure Carlotta that he was a person of no intellectual consequence, and reported by a reliable source to change his underwear only once a year.

Of Julia, however, there was no sign. At about half past eight on the previous evening she had triumphantly announced that she had at last finished her Opinion on Part XV of the Taxes Act and intended to reward herself with dinner at Guido's: Carlotta had not seen her since and was beginning to be anxious.

Returning once more to 62 New Square, we found Selena in not wholly amicable discussion with the temporary typist,

94

who seemed to feel that she was being unduly critical of a newly typed Statement of Claim.

'You did say,' said the temporary typist, in a tone of accusation, 'that you wanted it in a hurry.'

'Yes,' said Selena. 'Yes, Muriel, it's quite true I said that. But I didn't actually mean that I wanted you to leave bits out.'

'It's only one paragraph, Miss Jardine. I don't suppose anyone'll notice.'

'I know it's only one paragraph, Muriel, but it does contain allegations which are essential to my client's case. I really can't just leave it out.'

'Well,' said the temporary typist, 'you could write it in in handwriting, couldn't you?'

'I suppose I shall have to,' said Selena with a small sigh, 'but it's going to look very messy. It hardly seems worth typing it at all if half of it is going to be in manuscript. It's quite a long paragraph—I don't understand how you came to miss it out.'

This was unreasonable, for the error was a natural one. I saw, looking over Selena's shoulder at her draft, that the missing paragraph had begun with the same half-dozen words as that which succeeded it: the typist, having copied them for the first time, would have looked back at the draft to see what followed; the same phrase, occurring again a few lines later, would have caught her eye; and she would have continued from that point, omitting what lay between.

'It is an instance,' I said, 'of the mistake known as haplography—a fruitful source of error in ancient and mediaeval manuscripts. I cannot doubt, Selena, that you are familiar with it: just such a blunder in the P Codex of the *Helena* is central to the argument in Sebastian's recent article on the texts of Euripides. You will remember, moreover, from your own studies of Roman Law that Professor Daube's brilliant reconstruction of the celebrated crux in *Celsus*—'

'Hilary,' said Selena, 'do you wish me to lie down on the floor and scream?' I recalled that she thought the day unseasonable for the discussion of textual criticism, and said no more on the subject.

The temporary typist having departed in dudgeon, we told Selena of our visit to Bloomsbury and of Julia's failure to return there. Selena looked puzzled and frowned a little.

'Perhaps she spent the night somewhere and has gone straight back to Chambers. I'll ring William and see if she's there.'

But Julia's Clerk was equally without news of his missing principal, and had begun to regard with some disquiet the approach of the hour appointed for her conference. Selena now looked perceptibly anxious.

'Did you say she was meaning to have dinner at Guido's? Let's see if they've any idea what's happened to her.'

An eavesdropper on Selena's conversation with Guido's would have gathered that on the previous evening she had lent her umbrella—a rather pretty and distinctive umbrella, with an ivory handle carved in the shape of a horse's head—to her friend Miss Larwood; that Miss Larwood, before departing for her morning's engagements in the High Court, had confessed to having left it somewhere—she thought in Guido's; and that Selena would like it back. She would be most grateful if they could look and see—there was silence while search was made.

'She didn't? . . . didn't leave anything at all? How strange—unprecedented. Was there anyone with her to remind her not to forget things? . . . Ah . . . Ah, I see . . . I wonder if it's anyone I know—did you happen to catch the name? . . . No, I don't think so . . . Well, she must have gone on somewhere else and left my umbrella there. You wouldn't know of course—oh really? . . . yes . . . thank you, that's most kind . . . yes, I'll try there.' Replacing the telephone receiver, she began to arrange her papers in separate bundles, each neatly tied up in pink tape.

'Selena,' said Ragwort severely, 'very little of that was true.'

'Losing one's umbrella,' said Selena, 'seems less eccentric, somehow, than losing Julia.'

'I gather,' I said, 'that she dined at Guido's last night. Are we to understand that there was someone with her?'

'She arrived alone, but when she was about half way

through her meal a red-haired signorina came in, who seemed to be a friend of hers—that is to say, Julia seemed pleased to see her and invited her to share her table. They drank much wine and were very happy. When they had finished their meal, the red-haired signorina asked the waiter to call a taxi for them—to go, it seems, to a place called Vashti's House. It's a sort of nightclub in Chelsea.'

'Vashti's?' said Ragwort with austere disapproval. 'Vashti's has a most unsavoury reputation. I have heard it spoken of as a place frequented by females of unnatural propensity, seeking companions in disgraceful conduct.'

'I have heard it spoken of,' said Selena, 'as an agreeable little establishment where single women may enjoy one another's company in relaxed and convivial surroundings. Still, we're clearly thinking of the same place.' She now rolled down her sleeves and put on the black linen jacket which would have completed the suitability of her costume for an appearance in Court. 'The discothèque in the basement will be closed, of course, in the daytime. I believe, however, that there is a wine bar on the ground floor under the same management. With reasonable expedition, we should be able to get there in time to present ourselves as customers for a late lunch.'

Remembering her aeroplane and her paperwork, I did not suppose that any trifling danger to Julia's merely moral welfare would persuade her to set forth so precipitately for Chelsea. I inquired what more there was to it.

'It seems,' said Selena, 'that the name of her red-haired friend was Rowena. That was the name, you remember, of the girl at Rupert's party—the one dressed as a parlourmaid. It sounds as if Julia's trying to investigate Rupert; and in view of the Rustington business and so forth, I'd really rather she didn't.'

To a place of such ambiguous repute as Vashti's my readers will wish no precise directions. Nor, indeed, am I in a position to give them: it is my custom, when being driven by Selena on any errand which she considers urgent, to keep my eyes firmly closed. When at last it seemed safe to open them, we were somewhere in that area of South-West London where the artistic overlaps the opulent, no doubt to their mutual advantage.

Having reflected during the journey on the best means of obtaining news of her missing friend, Selena had concluded that it was in the character of one who loved not wisely but too well that she was most likely to attract sympathetic assistance. She proposed, therefore, to enter the wine bar in that state of solitary dejection appropriate to one misused in an affair of the heart: Ragwort and I would appear to be strangers to her, but would endeavour to find a table in close proximity.

The interior decoration of Vashti's House has a certain Moorish quality: arched recesses in whitewashed walls, a floor of terracotta tiles, many curls and arabesques of black wrought-ironwork. Our orders for lunch were taken by a tall, dark girl, short-haired and aquiline-nosed, dressed in a costume reminiscent of the bull-ring—very tight black trousers, white shirt and scarlet cummerbund.

It being now almost two hours since our lunch in the Corkscrew, neither Ragwort nor I found any difficulty in disposing of our slices of quiche lorraine and their accompanying salads. Selena, on the other hand, sitting alone at the next table, toyed listlessly with the contents of her plate; considering the frugality of her lunch, the performance did her credit. She drank her glass of wine, however, with unaccustomed rapidity, and forthwith asked for another.

'Are you all right, love?' inquired the girl in black trousers, as she brought the second glass.

'Yes, I'm fine, thank you,' said Selena, in a tone of wretchedness bravely dissimulated. 'It's only . . .' She concluded with a wan smile and a sad little shrug of the shoulders.

'If you're fine,' said the dark girl, 'why are you sitting there not eating anything and looking like a wet Sunday in Highgate Cemetery?' Selena repeated the wan smile and the sad little shrug, throwing in for good measure an understated but moving gesture of the hands. Construing this as an invitation to act as confidante, the girl sat down, facing her earnestly across the wrought-iron table.

98

'I wouldn't like you to think,' said Selena, 'that I'm jealous or possessive or anything.'

'Of course not, love,' said the girl in black trousers. 'Just who is it you're not jealous and possessive about?'

Sipping her second glass of wine, Selena explained that she had a friend of whom she was very fond; who was, she believed, fond of her; but who sometimes behaved unpredictably and as if indifferent to her feelings. On the previous evening, although aware that Selena could not accompany her, she had announced an intention to visit Vashti's House; and she had not returned.

'So you'd like to know who she came with?'

'I'd like to know who she left with,' said Selena, with some asperity.

The dark girl, it seemed, had been serving in the bar of the discothèque on the previous evening, and might be able to assist; Selena described Julia.

'Strewth,' said the girl, 'you don't mean the woman who dropped things?'

'Yes,' said Selena. 'Yes, that sounds like Julia. What exactly did she drop last night?'

'Well, love, you might ask "What didn't she?"' said the dark girl, looking at Selena with what seemed to be a mixture of pity and amazed admiration.

'Oh dear.' Selena's anxiety, I thought, was only partly feigned. 'She does sometimes tend to get a trifle exuberant.'

'Has exuberant got an "x" in it?'

Selena admitted that it had.

'I think your friend's the woman who put it there.'

The particulars of Julia's exuberance were so deplorable, it seemed, as to require telling *sotto voce*, and Ragwort and I heard no more of the conversation. Save for occasional murmurs of apology and extenuation, Selena took little active part in it. Eventually she sighed, tendered payment for her lunch, and rose to leave.

'If you take my advice, love,' said the dark girl, handing her her change, 'you'll forget about her. All right, so she's got curves. So's a roller-coaster got curves—it doesn't mean you can have a steady relationship with it.'

'You know how it is,' said Selena, 'when you're fond of someone.' With a final wistful smile she took her departure, leaving the dark girl to shake her head in resigned acknowledgement of the power of passion over judgement.

'We weren't able to hear the whole of your conversation,' said Ragwort when we rejoined Selena in her motor-car. 'You'd better tell us the worst.'

'It appears,' said Selena, 'that Julia was thrown out. Her conduct fell short of the standards of decorum which Vashti's expects of its clients.'

'It can't have done,' said Ragwort. 'There aren't any.'

'There are and it did. The attitude of the management is that they want people to enjoy themselves but they have to draw the line somewhere. They drew it at Julia.' Selena inserted her vehicle into the stream of westbound traffic. 'No doubt she was simply trying to enter into the spirit of things and do what was expected of her. But she does seem to have overdone it rather.'

'Did you discover,' I asked, 'at what hour she was ejected? And in whose company?'

'At about two o'clock in the morning. And she was still with the parlourmaid person—the girl called Rowena. It seems that Rowena was staying in the flat of a friend of hers—a friend of the masculine gender—while he was away on holiday. They apparently intended to go back there and console themselves by drinking his whisky.'

'Selena,' said Ragwort, perceiving that we were now moving briskly westwards along the Embankment, 'where are we going?'

'Mortlake, of course,' said Selena.

Among the amenities of the opulent block of flats in which Rupert Galloway resided was an entryphone device; but our arrival at the main entrance coincided with that of another visitor, who obligingly held the door open without inquiring our business. The lift conveyed us with unnatural smoothness to the top floor of the building.

Neither the first ring at Rupert's doorbell nor the second

caused the door of his flat to be opened to us.

'There's no one there,' said Ragwort.

'No one who chooses to answer,' said Selena. 'Fortunately, however, it seems to have the same kind of lock as the main door to the Nursery.' She began to search for something in her handbag.

'What exactly,' said Ragwort, with a certain apprehensiveness, 'is the relevance of the door to the Nursery?'

'I know how to open it without a key. Cantrip very kindly showed me how, in case I accidentally locked myself out. Ah, here we are.' She took from her handbag a credit card widely publicized as ensuring entry to places from which the holder might without its aid be excluded.

'My dear Selena,' said Ragwort, 'are you proposing to commit a burglary?'

'Certainly not,' said Selena, dexterously inserting the plastic rectangle between the door and the doorpost. 'We don't intend, do we, when we have entered the flat, to steal or maliciously damage any property, or ravish any woman therein or cause grievous bodily harm to any person?'

'No,' said Ragwort, 'of course not.'

'In that case it isn't burglary. The book about criminal law that I read for Bar exams was quite clear on the point. Ah, that's it.' She regarded the open door with the satisfaction natural in one who successfully displays a little-used accomplishment.

Cautiously she led the way into the entrance-lobby, and from there, with even greater circumspection, into the drawing-room. The room was expensively furnished and of not unpleasing proportions, though curtains of woven hessian drawn across the full-length windows, shutting out the afternoon sunlight, gave it a slightly funereal look. Selena looked carefully about her, as if Julia might be hidden somewhere behind one of the vast leather sofas or the cocktail cabinet of chrome and tinted glass; but the room was plainly unoccupied.

'I think,' she said, after a pause, 'that we ought to try the bedroom.'

The door on our right led to a short corridor, off which there opened the door to the bedroom. Selena tapped on it and received no answer. After a moment's hesitation, she turned the knob and went in, closely followed by Ragwort. I heard her draw breath rather sharply.

'Oh lord,' said Ragwort.

On the bed lay Julia, dressed in a small quantity of black underwear and only partly covered by the sheet flung carelessly over her. She lay at an awkward angle, her head thrown back, her dark hair spread in tangled disorder across the pillow, one bare arm trailing limply over the edge of the bed. She looked pale and curiously peaceful.

CHAPTER 9

And was, I need hardly say—though I must confess to a childish hope, unbecoming perhaps to the Scholar, of having aroused in my readers some measure of interesting apprehension—no more than soundly asleep.

Gently awoken by Selena, she appeared pleased by our presence, though less surprised than the circumstances seemed to warrant: she apparently regarded it as natural that Selena should discover her whereabouts by some system of telepathy. It was, she said, lighting a Gauloise, very kind of us all to come and find her: it had not been her intention to put us to so much trouble.

'And what, pray,' said Ragwort sternly, 'did you expect us to be put to, when you disappeared in dubious company without a word to anyone and having as your destination the abode of a man of unsavoury proclivities connected with at least two violent deaths? We have all been much inconvenienced and extremely worried. Really, Julia, what were you thinking of?'

'I acted,' said Julia, 'for the best.' She paused to allow us to admire the excellence of her motives. 'I was sitting in Guido's, remembering how I'd taken Deirdre there and feeling rather troubled in my conscience. I couldn't help thinking—if you will forgive my saying so, Hilary—that our investigation had been less than energetic. So when Rowena came in, whom we knew to be on intimate terms with Rupert, it seemed little short of providential. You will agree, Ragwort, that to forgo so remarkable an opportunity would have savoured of the impious.'

'Hm,' said Ragwort.

'She greeted me like a long-lost friend, so there was no difficulty in engaging her in conversation, and since Rupert was our only mutual acquaintance it seemed natural to ask for news of him. She told me that she was at present living here in his flat, during his absence on holiday—he doesn't like leaving it unoccupied. You will be interested, perhaps, to know that he is spending his holiday in Corfu.'

'Not, surely,' said Selena, 'with the Demetriou family? Not after what passed between him and Constantine on Boat Race Day?'

'No, not exactly. He travelled out there with his mother-in-law, the formidable Jocasta, and she's staying with the rest of the family in the villa at Casiope. But Rupert is at some hotel or other. His object is to spend some time with his daughter—he complains that now she's at Cambridge he hardly sees her. Rowena is sceptical about his motives: she believes them financial rather than sentimental. Rupert, it seems, is in rather urgent need of money—his company needs an injection of capital, as he calls it, of the order of fifty thousand pounds before the middle of July. Failing this restorative treatment, there is likely to be unpleasantness from the Department of Trade—embarrassing questions, you know, and murmurs of fraud.'

'That,' said Selena, 'does not surprise me. But how does he expect Camilla to help? She won't have any capital until her grandmother dies.'

'The notion is that the trustees of the settlement should invest part of the trust fund in Galloway Opportunities. Rupert seems to believe that if Camilla and her grandmother both agreed to it, Tancred as his co-trustee would be obliged to cooperate.'

'Well,' said Selena, wrinkling her nose, 'he wouldn't have

to—Camilla's interest is contingent, after all, on surviving her grandmother. But if the life tenant and the probable remainderman both say that that's what they want, it might be embarrassing for him to refuse.'

'So Rupert thinks; and thinking so has set out for the Ionian Islands to persuade his daughter of the inestimable benefits of such an investment. That, at any rate, is the construction placed by Rowena on his actions. She told me all this within minutes of our meeting, and since it seemed that reticence was not her watchword, I felt the acquaintance was worth pursuing.'

'My dear Julia,' said Ragwort, 'are you quite sure that you were the one pursuing it?'

'It is true,' said Julia, looking rather pleased with herself, 'that Rowena showed a flattering willingness to remain in my company. She seemed to feel there was some sort of bond between us—in addition, that is, to the bond which must naturally exist between any two women who have shared the same balcony disguised respectively as a parlourmaid and a schoolgirl while the premises within were raided by the police. In the matter of erotic preference, you see, she regards herself as inclining rather towards her own sex than the other—in her dealings with men, she likes to see her role as that of courtesan. She is,' added Julia in an explanatory tone, 'a rather old-fashioned and romantic girl.'

'Oh quite,' said Ragwort. 'And she is under the impression that you share her preference?'

'There was, you may remember, a misunderstanding on Rupert's part—and also, in consequence, on Rowena's—as to the nature of the friendship between Selena and myself. It seemed sensible, in the circumstances, not to correct it—I do hope, Selena, that you don't mind?'

'I am resigned,' said Selena, 'to its being an impression widely held in South-West London.'

'We adjourned after dinner, at Rowena's suggestion, to a sort of nightclub she knows in Chelsea—a place, I need hardly say, with an exclusively female clientele. I rather enjoyed myself there. But I must have done the wrong thing somehow, because they asked us to leave.' Julia looked puzzled and a little hurt at the recollection. 'So we came back here and drank brandy and talked about men. Rowena is inclined to regard them as an overrated sex. My own view, as you know, is that their many failings should all be forgiven them for the sake of the incomparable pleasure which they are sometimes capable of giving. To say so, however, would have been inconsistent with the impression I was seeking to give to my own tastes—I was rather at a loss, therefore, for any persuasive argument in their defence.'

'Is Rupert,' asked Selena, 'exempt from her disapproval?'

'Oh, by no means—he was cited as the chief example of every defect to which the unfair sex is subject. I don't think Rowena really likes him much—she seems to be wearying of the schoolgirl's uniform routine. So I managed to learn a good deal to his discredit, though nothing, unfortunately, with any direct bearing on Deirdre's death: he hadn't talked to her about that, beyond telling her it had happened. I did try to look round the flat for clues, but I didn't find any.' Julia looked crestfallen.

'And how,' inquired Ragwort, 'did the evening conclude?'

'As to that,' said Julia, 'I have no very clear recollection— I had drunk a good deal of wine and a certain amount of brandy, and that may well account for it. In due course, no doubt, I must have gone to bed.'

'And the Rowena person,' said Ragwort, with inquisitorial sternness, 'must also have gone to bed. To, we are compelled to suppose, the same bed.'

'No doubt, my dear Ragwort, since there is only one. Considering, however, the lateness of the hour and the amount we had drunk, I cannot think it likely that anything of an improper nature occurred.'

'Hm,' said Ragwort. It was not an expression designed to convey unqualified belief.

'So the next thing you remember,' said Selena, 'is waking up and finding us here?'

'Oh no,' said Julia, a little surprised. 'Rowena woke me up at about ten o'clock, when she had to go to her agency, and gave me a cup of coffee. But I found, in spite of the coffee, that I was in that state of health in which one cannot usefully give

105

one's mind to the Taxes Acts. The sensible thing seemed to be to take one or two Alka-Seltzers and go to sleep again. But I knew, of course, that I mustn't sleep too long, because of my conference this afternoon. So that's when I rang and left my message for you.'

'What message?' asked Selena, puzzled.

'Saying where I was, and asking you to ring me at midday or so to make sure I was awake.'

'Julia,' said Selena, 'with whom did you leave this message?'

'With your temporary typist, of course. And she must have given it to you,' added Julia, with the first dawning of anxiety, 'or you wouldn't be here.'

'Something,' said Ragwort wearily, 'will have to be done about that girl.'

The cries, wails, protests and lamentations with which Julia received the news that it was now half past three and that she had irretrievably missed her conference, the clutchings of the forehead, the tearings of the hair, the knockings over of bedside tables, the rushings about wrapped only in a sheet—all these would be too pitiful to recount, and were so indeed to observe. I withdrew to the drawing-room.

The opportunity could not be disregarded to examine the scene of the supposed crime which I had undertaken to investigate. Going through the door at the far end of the drawing-room from that which led to the bedroom, I found myself at the foot of a wooden stairway. I ascended; but the door to the roof terrace was locked, and there was no key to be found in its immediate vicinity. Disappointed, I descended again. The door at the foot of the staircase opened without resistance into a room furnished as an office: a person trained in accountancy and having leisure to peruse the contents of the filing cabinets would perhaps have learned much of Rupert's business dealings; but to me the room disclosed no secrets.

I returned to the drawing-room. A glance through the archway on my left persuaded me that the kitchen area held nothing of interest to the investigator. I went out on to the balcony: below me, beyond the road and the now deserted towpath, the Thames wound peacefully under the Victorian ironwork of Barnes railway bridge, the afternoon sunlight dancing on its mud-coloured surface; on the other side of the river the willow trees at the edge of Duke's Meadows dipped low into the water. The prospect was a most agreeable one; and it occurred to me, after a little reflection, that it was also conclusive of my investigation.

I heard Selena's quick, light footsteps in the drawing-room behind me. Having reached, it seemed, the final stages of the complex process of making Julia ready for departure, she was inquiring whether Julia might have brought a coat with her: and whether she happened, if so, to know where she might have put it. From the direction of the bathroom came the answer, a little muffled, that there might well have been a coat, a sort of beige sort of raincoat, and it might very possibly be found in one of the cupboards in the entrance lobby. Rummaging sounds ensued.

'Selena,' I called, 'tell Julia to come out here and look at the view from the balcony—it will have a soothing effect on her. You and Ragwort will also find it of interest.'

'Julia's still dressing,' answered Selena, amid sounds of further rummaging. 'And Ragwort's tidying the bedroom, and I'm looking for Julia's raincoat. We don't have time to stand about looking at views.'

'I ask but a moment,' I said. 'And you will not regret it.'

At last they all three joined me on the balcony—Julia washed, dressed, brushed and combed, Ragwort modestly complacent at the tidiness of the bedroom and Selena a little dusty but triumphant in her search for the beige raincoat. I invited them to stand at the corner of the balcony from which they would have the best view downstream—that is to say, towards Chiswick—and asked them what they could see.

'The river?' said Julia, with a helpful and intelligent expression, as if anxious to know if this was the right answer.

'Part of the river,' said Selena. 'About as far as the top of Corney Reach.'

'Remarkably little of the river, really,' said Ragwort. 'In fact, the view downstream is rather poor—I can't imagine why you think it's interesting.'

'You will remember,' I said, 'that it was from here—'

A key turned in the lock of the front door.

Why this sound should have caused us to shrink back into the corners of the balcony as if to escape detection in some criminal act, I cannot now readily explain, for Selena had been satisfied that we were committing none. To have entered premises by manipulating the lock with a plastic credit card perhaps has some curious psychological effect, making one think that one's presence may be unwelcome.

There followed sounds of the putting down of luggage, and of voices. I recognized the tones of deferential gallantry in which I had previously heard Rupert address his mother-in-law. They had evidently returned together from Corfu; and Jocasta had broken her journey home to Belgrave Place in order to be provided with certain papers relating to Rupert's company. (Knowing and cynical glances were exchanged by my companions on the balcony.) We heard her decline offers of refreshment.

The papers, it appeared, were in the little room furnished as an office. We suffered a moment of anxiety while Rupert went in search of them, for Jocasta employed the time in drawing back the heavy hessian curtains; but she did not look out on to the balcony, and our presence remained undetected.

'Here we are, Mama-in-law,' said Rupert. 'Capital Statement and Profit and Loss Account for Galloway Opportunities Limited. All duly audited, of course. If there's anything that isn't clear, just give me a ring.'

'I'm sure there'll be no need. I'm only taking them because you insisted on it, Rupert—it's really quite unnecessary. Mother and I have complete confidence in your judgement.'

'I know you have, bless you,' said Rupert, with great warmth and sincerity. 'That's exactly why I don't want anyone to be able to say that I've talked you into something without explaining what's involved. What I want to make absolutely clear is that I'm not saying this is to your mother's advantage in purely financial terms. It might even mean a reduction in income—the whole thing's geared to capital growth. It's for Millie's sake I want to do it.'

108

'My dear Rupert, you surely know by now that Mother's only too delighted to help Millie in any way she can.'

'Well, I do know that, of course.' Rupert seemed now almost overcome by an intensity of emotion which it would have been unmanly to express. 'Your mother's been wonderful, simply wonderful—there's no other word for it. If it hadn't been for her generosity—well, I don't mind admitting it, there's no way I could have given Millie the sort of upbringing she was entitled to. I'm not a rich man, you know, Mama-in-law—not by comparison with the sort of fortune Millie's going to inherit. But I do have a little bit of a flair for investment, and when I became one of the trustees I hoped I'd be able to use it for Millie's benefit. Like any father, I suppose—wanting to feel I've done something for my little girl. But everything I suggest gets blocked by Tancred—all this rigmarole about the Trustee Investments Act and God knows what. I don't mind telling you, Mama-in-law, I've come pretty close to losing my temper sometimes.'

'Tancred's an imbecile, I've always said so. One would not, of course, like one's solicitor to be too clever to be respectable; but Tancred goes too far to the other extreme.'

'Well, he's certainly no fireball when it comes to investment. I sometimes think he'd like the whole fund still to be in Consols.'

'My dear Rupert, I do see how frustrating it must have been. But there's no difficulty, is there, now that Millie's of age? Tancred has to do what she and Mother ask him to.'

To this Rupert made no immediate answer, but instead renewed the offer of alcoholic refreshment—evidently as a polite preliminary to pouring a drink for himself. When he spoke again, his remarks had no apparent connection with the previous topic.

'Mama-in-law, may I have a word with you about Millie? I'm—well, I'm just a bit worried about her. To be absolutely candid, I wish she weren't quite so thick with Dolly's kids—I sometimes feel they count for more with her than I do. As if they were her family and I was just—well, some kind of distant relative.'

'Nonsense, Rupert. Millie's devoted to you. She's very close to the twins, naturally—they practically grew up together. And Dolly's house in Corfu is like a second home to her.'

'Don't I know it, don't I just know it?' Whatever doubts I had previously had of Rupert's sincerity, I now thought his bitterness entirely genuine. 'And what sort of home is it? The whole household revolving round that prize charlatan Dolly's got herself married to, like some kind of little plastic god. Lucian and Lucinda sitting round pretending to be writers and artists and not doing a damn thing except lie in the sun and drink retsina. Lucian dressing like a hippy and Lucinda dressing like a tart—not just dressing like one, either, from some other things I've heard.'

'Really, Rupert—'

'Well, I've heard remarks made when she goes into bars in Casiope that I wouldn't like anyone to make about Millie, that's all. What that girl needs is a good spanking, if you ask me. And Dolly, of course, is the last person in the world to have any idea of imposing discipline. I'm not blaming her—it's up to a father to impose discipline. Well, you can't see Demetriou doing anything to keep the twins in order, can you? Even if he really were their father and not just a stepfather. No, it's George Fairfax I blame. The twins are his children, after all—you'd think he'd take a bit of interest in the way they're brought up.'

'He was anxious, I think, not to embarrass Dolly by interfering with her life after her marriage to Constantine— he's very fond of her. Men do get fond of Dolly, you know.' She spoke without jealousy, but rather with a proprietorial pride in her sister's attractiveness.

'No, really, Mama-in-law, it's one thing being civilized about the divorce and so on, and another leaving his children to be brought up with no supervision and no discipline and running wild all over the place. And don't think I'm saying this behind George's back—I've said as much to his face. I don't see all that much of him—he's out of my league financially, and I'm the first to admit it—but when I do see him I speak my mind. I've even written to him. I happened

110

to hear last summer that Lucian had got mixed up with an even more unsavoury crew than usual, and I thought George ought to know about it. But he didn't even bother to reply.'

'I had no idea,' said Jocasta, 'that you felt so strongly.'

'I haven't seen much of the twins since they left school, and I thought the adult world might have knocked a bit of sense into them. But they're worse than ever. No standards, no manners, no respect for authority, no respect for anything. They lounge about making silly private jokes and giggling over nothing, not doing a hand's turn of work, and sponging on Millie whenever they get the chance. They make me sick, and that's a fact.' Rupert paused. 'Sorry, I suppose I shouldn't be talking like this—they are family, after all.'

'You did say,' said Jocasta, 'that you wanted to talk about Millie.'

'Yes,' said Rupert. 'Yes, that's right.' He still seemed to have difficulty in coming to whatever might be the point. There was a further clinking of ice and hissing of soda.

'I had thought,' said Jocasta, 'that you and Millie were getting along particularly well together during the past fortnight.'

Her words provoked a melancholy sigh. 'So did I, Mama-in-law, so did I. Thought she quite enjoyed having her old dad about to squire her to restaurants and the casino and that sort of thing. Yes, I'll admit it, I had the idea I'd got a pretty good relationship with my daughter. Until yesterday.' Another heavy sigh. 'Shows how wrong you can be.'

'My dear Rupert, you astonish me. I thought that yesterday was delightful.'

'Well, it didn't start too well from my point of view. The original idea, you remember, was for me to help Camilla sail the boat down to Gouvia and meet the rest of you in town for dinner. Then Dolly's kids decide at the last moment that they want to come along for the ride, so bang goes my idea of having Millie to myself for the day. Still, they were off as soon as we'd moored at Gouvia—scared they might have to help with tidying the boat up, I expect. That's when I remembered that Millie hadn't signed that letter yet—you know, the one to Tancred about changing the investments. So I suggested perhaps she might like to sign it right away and let me bring it back to London with me. And do you know what she said? She said she'd have to think about it. That hurt, Mama-in-law, it hurt.'

Further cynical glances were exchanged on the balcony.

'Really, Rupert, if that's all that's worrying you, I think you're making far too much of it. She naturally wouldn't want you to think her the sort of girl who signs things of that kind without thinking about them.'

'I'm her father, Mama-in-law—it's pretty wounding to find she doesn't trust me. Or doesn't trust my judgement.'

'My dear Rupert, I'm quite sure that's not at all what she meant.'

'Wasn't it? You haven't heard the whole story yet. I told her, of course, that she was entitled to think it over if she wanted to. Tried to make a joke of it—said I hoped she didn't think her old dad would try to pull a fast one on her. To which she said no, of course not, but fifty thousand pounds was a lot of money and she didn't want to do anything silly; she'd gathered that the business of the company was dealing in commodity futures, and she'd heard it could be a rather risky market. So I said I was very pleased to see her taking an interest in financial affairs and asked where she'd got her information. And do you know who she'd been talking to?'

'My dear Rupert, I have no idea.'

'That know-all little pansy Leonidas, if you please. Has an economics lesson once a week at his so-called public school, reads the *Financial Times* on Wednesdays and Saturdays and sets up as an expert on the Stock Market. The twins are bad enough, God knows, but at least they're good British stock. But when I find that slimy, slithering little half-caste Levantine trying to turn my own daughter against me—well, I'm sorry, Mama-in-law, but I could wring the little pip-squeak's neck for him.'

It was at this point that Julia sneezed. The pollen count was high, and the poor creature is susceptible to it.

'Rupert,' said Jocasta, 'what was that noise outside?'

Rupert stepped out on to the balcony. His mouth, when he perceived our presence, fell open under its drooping moustache; his watery blue gaze, as it passed from one to another of us, held much of surprise and little of delight. He seemed about to speak. With a smile of infinite complicity and infinite reassurance, Selena raised her forefinger to her lips and gently shook her head: it was a gesture, as I understood it, designed to suggest that our presence on Rupert's balcony was in some way connected with aspects of his private life of which he might prefer his mother-in-law to remain unaware. After a moment of perplexity and hesitation, Rupert understood it in a similar sense: he withdrew from the balcony.

'It's nothing, Mama-in-law—something on the towpath—my cleaning woman must have left the windows open.'

CHAPTER 10

'Properly regarded,' said Selena, as she settled in the driving-seat of her motor vehicle and prepared to drive us back to Lincoln's Inn, 'that all passed off rather well. I don't say that Rupert was entirely satisfied with our explanation for being on his balcony; but at least he accepted it without the rather searching cross-examination to which we might have been subjected by Jocasta, had she still been present when we offered it.'

'We were obliged,' said Ragwort, 'to tell a quite extraordinary number of lies.'

'My dear Ragwort,' said Selena, 'whatever can you mean? We said that Julia had been invited to Rupert's flat for a drink by his friend Rowena: that was true. We said that we had come to collect her and take her back to Lincoln's Inn: that was true. We said that we were in some haste and must leave at once: that was entirely true. How can you possibly suggest that we told any lies?'

She elected not to cross the river by the bridge at Chiswick but to remain on the south side of it until we reached Hammersmith—a distance which she covered with such rapidity as to move me to remark diffidently on the possible existence of a speed limit.

'In normal circumstances,' said Selena, 'I would be quite willing to oblige you by dawdling along at any speed you found comfortable—say five miles an hour or so. You will perhaps recall, however, that I am hoping to catch a plane to Athens this evening, with a view to sailing round the Ionian Islands. The crew—namely Sebastian—has been instructed to report promptly for duty at 17.00 local time—or, as you landsmen would say, five o'clock this afternoon. To arrive late might seriously impair the authority of the skipper—namely mine—for the duration of the voyage.'

I perceived in her manner the blithe insouciance of a woman who had cast aside the responsibilities of practice at the Chancery Bar: it was as if she already breathed the salt Ionian air and her hand rested not on the steering-wheel of her car but on the tiller of some graceful sailing craft, cutting swiftly through the blue water. Knowing that in such a mood there could be no reasoning with her, I adopted the policy previously mentioned of keeping my eyes closed.

'I'm very sorry,' said Julia. 'I'm afraid it's my fault. I'll explain to Sebastian, if we're late, that it's due to my embroiling you in a criminal investigation.'

I had not told them, I now realized, that our investigation was concluded, and that no crime had been committed. I thought it prudent to delay this disclosure until Selena had completed her negotiation of the streams of traffic moving rapidly round Hammersmith roundabout.

'We have been told,' I said, 'that Rupert's insult to Constantine Demetriou—that is to say, the Greek gigolo remark which resulted in Dolly being called down from the roof terrace—was uttered at the moment when the boats first came into view from the balcony. Between then and the moment at which Deirdre is known to have fallen we have supposed that a resolute person would have had time to ascend unobserved to the roof terrace and make a murderous attack on Deirdre.'

'The timing,' said Selena, 'seemed fine but not impossible.'

'Quite so, if we had been right in assuming that the boats would have come into view when they passed Chiswick Steps. But the fact is that it is quite impossible from Rupert's balcony to see anything like so far as that. The front of the building is at a slight angle to the river bank: the view upstream is admirable, but downstream, as Ragwort rightly remarked, it is very poor—one can see no further than three or four hundred yards below Barnes Bridge. That is about a quarter of the distance to Chiswick Steps—the Boat Race crews would take, I suppose, no more than a minute to cover it. Which leaves, you see, no time at all for any attack on Deirdre. No one could have gone up to the roof before she fell without meeting Dolly on the way down from it. Indeed—'

'You were,' said Ragwort, 'about to say?'

'I was about to say,' I said, 'that very little time can have passed between the moment at which Dolly left the roof terrace and Deirdre either fell or jumped from it. Almost no time at all.'

'You surely aren't suggesting,' said Ragwort, 'that Dolly herself—? Oh nonsense, Hilary, she's a simply delightful woman.'

'She is indeed,' I said, 'a most charming and attractive woman. The study of history, however, demonstrates that charming and attractive women are not incapable of murder. You do see, don't you, that if murder was committed she is the only person who had time to do it? On Boat Race Day, remember, and at so crucial a point in the contest, there would have been a considerable commotion on the towpath: it would have taken a minute or so for those watching from the balcony to become aware of anything amiss. If she had thrown her niece over the parapet and immediately descended to the drawing-room, I dare say they would all have believed that she was already downstairs when Deirdre fell.'

'Hilary,' said Selena, 'you aren't serious about this, are you?'

'No,' I said. 'No, as it happens, I am not. I agree that she couldn't have done it—she isn't tall enough.'

'And a study of history demonstrates, I suppose,' said

Ragwort, 'that women of short stature *are* incapable of murder?'

'The commonplace experience of lifting a suitcase into a luggage-rack demonstrates the muscular effort required to raise a heavy object above one's head. If Dolly had ever trained as a weight-lifter, it is conceivable that she might be able to lift a young woman of similar height and weight to herself over a barrier some two inches taller; otherwise not—I am satisfied that the possibility may be excluded.'

We continued eastwards in silence. It was not until we reached Trafalgar Square, where buses, pigeons and wandering tourists, all equally indifferent to impatient toots of the horn, reduced our speed to that of an unhurried pedestrian, that Selena spoke again.

'I'm glad,' she said, 'that there's no question of murder. It means we can stop being anxious about Camilla.'

Unaware that we had begun to be anxious about Camilla, I invited her to explain her meaning.

'Well, you've always said, Hilary, that you didn't think it was murder because the wrong girl was dead.'

'Yes,' I said. 'I have always taken the view that if a murder were to take place in the Remington-Fiske family it would be the heiress who was murdered.'

'And it's quite true, of course,' continued Selena, as she edged her way forward into the Strand, 'that if anyone else in the family had wanted to inherit the estate, they would have had to dispose of Camilla. But Deirdre was the next in line of inheritance, so she was the only one for whom that would have been enough. Anyone else would have had to get rid of both of them. And there's no particular reason, is there, why they should do so in order of seniority?'

The crew after all arrived before the captain. We found my young colleague Sebastian Verity sitting in Selena's room in 62 New Square, peacefully reading a copy of Homer's *Odyssey*—a graceful young man, grey-eyed and silken-haired, of agreeably poetic appearance. His name will perhaps be known to my readers—though the work has not reached so extensive an audience, even among the discerning, as its artistic and scholarly merits would deserve—for his verse translation of the *Idylls* of Theocritus, published some fifteen months prior to the events here related.

He rose and came forward to greet us with an eagerness astonishing in a young man who expected to spend the next two weeks being tossed about on the Mediterranean in a small, damp, dangerous sailing-craft. I reflected, however, that at the prospect of spending a fortnight in Selena's company in a cell in Wormwood Scrubs the eyes of my young colleague would have shone with an equally rapturous delight; such is the effect of passion on a tender and devoted heart. Despite the adverse consequences which such familiarity might have on shipboard discipline, Selena allowed herself to be embraced.

'The first question is,' he said, 'whether I should begin immediately to address you as "sir" or may continue to call you Selena until we are on board.'

'I shall be quite content,' said Selena, 'to be addressed as "skipper", provided that it is done in a suitably respectful manner.'

'Those of you,' said Sebastian, 'who have seen Selena only on dry land will probably think of her as a reasonable, good-natured, easy-going sort of woman, and may find it difficult to credit the transformation which takes place as soon as she sets foot on a sailing-boat. I think it's because of the books she reads. She spends the winter months, you know, reading books about sailing and seamanship—they all seem to recommend that the conduct of the ship's captain should be modelled as closely as possible on that of Captain Bligh of the *Bounty*.'

'Sebastian,' said Julia kindly, but with a certain sternness, 'we think that you exaggerate.'

'By no means,' said Sebastian, 'quite the contrary. I wouldn't venture to tell you, Julia, of the dangers and appalling living conditions which are the fate of anyone who puts to sea with Selena. If you were to imagine me clinging precariously to the rigging in the sort of howling gale which she describes as a nice, lively little breeze, or think of me scrubbing decks and pumping bilges from dawn to dusk under the merciless sun, pleading in vain for a small sip of retsina to cool my thirst—no, Julia, it's more than your gentle heart could bear. You would want to report the whole thing to the Court of Human Rights or someone.'

'There is,' said Selena, 'not a word of truth in this.'

'Sebastian,' said Ragwort, 'we believe every word you say. We ask ourselves only by what compulsion, knowing all this, you were persuaded to enlist for the voyage.'

'Seafaring,' said Sebastian, 'as of course you know, has from ancient times been a vital element in the Greek way of life, and has had a great influence on their thought and literature. I am anxious to achieve an insight into the sufferings and privations which would have been endured by the ordinary Greek seaman in the periods of which I profess the study. I dare say I'm overdoing it rather—one can hardly imagine that a freeborn Athenian of the fifth century, for example, however poor and economically exploited, would have submitted to quite such despotic treatment as I must look forward to. Still, I am doing my best.'

'When we go aboard,' said Selena, 'I shall be revenged for this.'

'Your explanation,' said Ragwort, 'reflects great credit on you. But it occurs to us, from our recollection of certain passages in classical literature, that rough words and harsh discipline were not the worst that an Athenian sailor—a young and personable Athenian sailor—might have had to face at the hands of his officers: advantage, we fear, would sometimes have been taken of his subordinate status to make him the instrument of sensual gratification. Have you considered, Sebastian, that you may be placing yourself in a similar danger?

'Hilary will confirm,' said Sebastian, 'that in the cause of Scholarship no sacrifice is too great.'

Having wished our friends a happy and prosperous voyage and waved them farewell from the great gateway between New Square and Lincoln's Inn Fields, Julia and Ragwort

118

and I turned by common consent in the direction of the Corkscrew. The weather, which had been charming, became suddenly grey and blustery, with a suggestion of rain: we quickened our step, and Julia put on the raincoat which she was carrying.

'My dear Julia,' said Ragwort, as we walked through Great Turnstile, 'I do not wish to appear critical, but would you care to tell us how in the world you came to purchase that raincoat? It's at least two sizes too small for you.'

'It *is* rather tight across the shoulders,' said Julia. 'Indeed, quite uncomfortably so. I rather wish you hadn't mentioned it, Ragwort—I've never noticed before.'

'It might be better,' said Ragwort, 'if you didn't have so much in the pockets.'

'I don't have anything in the pockets,' said Julia. 'I emptied them yesterday in the cause of neatness and order. Oh.' Seeking to demonstrate the emptiness of her pockets, she had produced from one a cellophane-wrapped box, containing, according to its label, a bottle of expensive scent, and from the other a thick brown envelope. 'I don't remember why I've got these.'

'If you have been buying scents made by Monsieur Patou,' said Ragwort, 'you may count on your bank manager to remember the transaction. Have you any idea what's in the envelope?'

Julia shook her head.

Comfortably established at one of the round oak tables in the Corkscrew, and with a reassuring glass of Niersteiner in her hand, she none the less continued for some time to gaze at the envelope with bewildered apprehension, turning it this way and that, as if fearing that its contents might prove inimical to her welfare. At last, however, she was prevailed upon to open it. It contained photographs: some two dozen, all in colour, of about the same dimensions as a postcard.

'Julia,' said Ragwort with some severity, 'these are not the sort of photographs which one expects to find in the possession of a member of the English Bar—except, possibly, for the purposes of a prosecution for obscenity. How in the world do you come to have them?'

'I haven't the least idea,' said Julia. 'Oh look,' she added, with every sign of pleasure, 'there's one of Selena and me.'

The picture showed them sitting side by side on a sofa: Selena, with a look of judicial detachment, seemed to be appraising the quality of her champagne; Julia was smiling with sleepy and bemused benevolence at two other persons—one male, the other female, both naked, in an attitude of greater intimacy than I would wish to describe in detail to my readers: though Selena and Julia were fully dressed, the photograph was taken at such an angle as somehow to suggest that all four figures were part of a single tableau. The background I recognized without difficulty, having seen it less than two hours earlier—it was the drawing-room of Rupert Galloway's flat. It required but little scholarship to infer that the photographs had been taken at the gathering attended by Selena and Julia in the previous November; and it seemed not over-adventurous to surmise that the film from which they were made had been in the camera appropriated by the spurious policemen.

'Julia,' I said gently, 'is that the coat which Selena found for you in the cupboard at Rupert's flat?' She nodded. 'And are you,' I continued, 'quite, quite sure that it's yours?'

She turned the coat this way and that, inside out and upside down, searching, I suppose, for some winestain or cigarette burn which would identify it as unquestionably hers. Eventually, at Ragwort's suggestion, she looked inside the collar and found sewn there a small name-tape. On reading it, she became rather pale.

'Oh dear,' she said, 'it seems to be Deirdre's. Do you think it's been there ever since—?'

'Undoubtedly.' I said. 'She would have put it in the cupboard when she arrived for the Boat Race party and no one has since thought to move it. I don't quite know how she came by the photographs, but I fear we may easily guess how she hoped to use them. And that, my dear Julia, solves the last of the mysteries.'

Ragwort raised an eyebrow.

'Deirdre's letter. I think we may safely assume that what Julia construed as an appeal for help was in truth a prelude to blackmail. It would be not inconsistent with the impression we have been given of Deirdre's character; and she would no doubt have thought—she was very young, after all—that this picture was sufficiently compromising for Julia to pay money for it. You had better give the photographs to me—if you keep them, Julia, you will mix them up with some set of papers you are dealing with and cause alarm to your instructing solicitors.'

We were afterwards joined by Timothy and Cantrip and in their company spent an agreeable evening, at the end of which Timothy kindly offered me the hospitality of his flat. I rose late and breakfasted at leisure, reflecting with some complacency on the successful conclusion of my inquiry. I thought myself a trifle at fault in directing my mind too little to the point mentioned by Selena—that a person murderously resolved to secure possession of the Remington-Fiske estates, being more remote in the succession than both Deirdre and Camilla, would not necessarily have disposed of them in order of seniority; but since Deirdre's death had not been achieved by malice, the point seemed an academic one.

Towards noon—Selena, I supposed, was by then already under sail on the blue waters of the Ionian—I went out into Middle Temple Lane and turned my steps towards Fleet Street. The news-vendor on the corner of these two thoroughfares was already offering for sale the earliest edition of the evening paper. I paused to glance at the placard proclaiming the latest news:

HEIRESS FEARED DROWNED
IN SAILING ACCIDENT

I purchased a copy of the paper and looked for the 'Stop Press' column; but for some reason I scarcely needed to read it to feel certain that the headline referred to Camilla Galloway.

CHAPTER 11

There is a sense in which my inquiry had been successful. Its purpose, as my readers will recall, had been to stop Julia talking about Sir Thomas More: in this it had succeeded. It is right, however, to confess immediately that my conclusions were entirely erroneous. In reaching them, I had too uncritically accepted a view of Deirdre's death which accorded with my own preconceived opinion, banishing from my mind those curious features of the unhappy incident which were left unexplained: an error all the more culpable in that the facts were already known to me which should have led to a virtual certainty of the truth, requiring only a trivial piece of commonplace research to be confirmed beyond question. I blame myself much for my failure of judgement; though I could hardly have foreseen how dangerous it would prove to persons whom I held in affection.

The news of Camilla's sailing accident did not persuade me, for more than a moment or two, to reconsider my opinion. Dismissing as irrational my sense of uneasiness, I concluded merely that the descendants of the late Sir James Remington-Fiske were peculiarly inclined to misadventure. Fuller and more accurate accounts of the incident appeared in due course in the English newspapers. I refrain, however, from setting out any of these *in extenso*, since there is nothing in them which is not also related in Selena's letters to Julia: these, being most material to my narrative, must be placed before my readers in their entirety.

The first arrived some ten days later, on a day when I happened again to find myself in London. Looking into the Corkscrew at an early hour of the evening, I discovered Julia on the point of reading it, and willingly accepted her offer to do so aloud.

SV *Kymothoe* at anchor in
the bay of Mourtos.
Sunday afternoon.

Dear Julia,

I have been obliged to put in here by unrest among the crew, namely Sebastian. I had meant to take advantage of a nice westerly breeze to press on northwards to Corfu; but the crew claimed the sea was too rough for sailing on and threatened strike action. I pointed out that lying in the cockpit and reading aloud from the *Odyssey*—these being his principal duties—did not actually constitute an essential contribution to the smooth running of the vessel. It was further represented to me, however, that it would be wrong to pass by Mourtos without a second glance, since it was the scene of the great sea-battle which marked the outbreak of the Peloponnesian War and changed the history of the Western world; and had a taverna where we could eat grilled prawns. I yielded to these arguments against my better judgement.

I must tell you a most extraordinary story I have heard about Camilla Galloway. It may perhaps have been mentioned in the English newspapers; but I don't imagine they would have thought it worth reporting in detail.

The first I heard of it was at Preveza.

Preveza is on the west coast of mainland Greece, on the north side of the Gulf of Amvrakikos. We arrived there on Friday morning, collected the necessary papers from the shipping office and took possession of the *Kymothoe*. She is a 25-foot Snapdragon, small enough to be handled by two people, but with plenty of space below decks and everything one needs to be comfortable—a well-designed little galley and a proper lavatory and shower, quite separate and private, with room to stand upright there as well as in the cabin. I really think, Julia, that even you—well, no, perhaps not.

Our destination is Ithaca, but by a roundabout route: northwards between Corfu and the mainland coast until we round the northern end of Corfu, then southwards again. This is a longish voyage under sail in a fortnight, and of course I don't want to motor any more than I have to: it seemed to me that if we were going to see anything of Ithaca we should waste no time, but set sail as soon as we were properly provisioned.

I could see no reason for lingering in Preveza—it looked like a very ordinary fishing port, all whitewash and cobble-stones, such as one might see anywhere on the Mediterranean, and distinguished only by the unusually pungent smell from the harbour. I was told by the crew, however, that in ancient and mediæval times it had been a place of great strategic importance and that in the surrounding waters a battle had been fought which had changed the history of the world; I was also reminded that it was nearly lunch-time. (It's rather extraordinary that whenever the crew wants to stop for lunch we find ourselves at the scene of a battle which has changed the history of the world—there are judges I know who would think it a most remarkable coincidence.)

We accordingly went ashore and ate moussaka and Greek salad at a taverna overlooking the Gulf, while the crew told me all about the battle. It appears that Aktion, on the south side of the Gulf, is the same place as Actium, where Octavian defeated Antony and Cleopatra and started the Roman Empire—the Greeks, as is their custom, have changed the name to confuse foreign visitors. (Attempts were made to persuade me that it had really been called Aktion all along; but Shakespeare calls it Actium, so I dismissed these as subversive.)

After this it was too late to make any serious start on our voyage—we could not have been sure of making a safe harbour before nightfall. We spent the afternoon dawdling about inside the Gulf, getting used to the foibles of the *Kymothoe* and from time to time stopping for a swim. The sky was clear and the winds very light, so much so that I eventually had to use the motor to take us back to Preveza. The water, however, was a good deal choppier than one would expect in such weather. I began to wonder why, and what conditions would be like outside the Gulf. While we were drinking our first ouzo at a bar by the quayside, I instructed the crew (whose duties include those of interpreter) to engage the barman in conversation about the weather.

This was how we came to hear that on the previous night there had been a violent storm, in which a yacht owned by an Englishwoman had been lost and all those on board her drowned. Or almost drowned. Or one drowned, and the others almost—our informant was rather vague about the details. Of course I didn't know, at that stage, that it had anything to do with Camilla.

We put to sea early on the following morning, having taken such steps as we respectively thought prudent to ensure a safe voyage: that is to say, I had listened to the weather forecast and checked that the engine was working, and the crew had poured a glass of retsina over the bows as a libation to Poseidon.

'Sebastian,' I said, 'you have always told me that you are a dialectical materialist, and do not believe in gods of any kind.'

'I don't,' he said. 'But it does no harm to be on the safe side.'

The gods seemed to show less gratitude than they might have done for these attentions—a brisk west wind and the after-effects of the storm combined to produce in the sea outside the Gulf a distinct bumpiness, which caused the crew to feel not quite well. He lay in the cockpit, groaning, and unable to attend to the duties previously mentioned—namely, the reading aloud of the *Odyssey*. I tried to divert his mind by asking why Homer always speaks of the wine-dark sea, when the Mediterranean is such a striking shade of blue, and whether this meant that the Greeks of that period drank some kind of dark blue wine. The crew, however, showed no enthusiasm for this interesting question, but continued to lie in the cockpit and groan.

You will perhaps think it heartless of me, but I was enjoying myself more than if the sea had been entirely smooth. I don't know how to describe to you, Julia, how splendid it is being at the helm of a sailing-boat in a firm wind on the open sea—there's nothing like it in the world. I suppose one might compare it to having a very good day in court—I don't mean when it all goes well from the start, but the sort of day when the judge begins by thinking your witnesses are liars and there's a House of Lords decision against you, and you bring him round gradually to taking a more sensible view and finding in your favour: well, it's something like that, but better.

★

'I didn't know,' said Julia, amazed at understanding her friend so little, 'that Selena thought anything was better than that.'

★

We made reasonable progress, close-reaching at a speed of about five knots on a course almost due north and parallel to the coast of Epirus: this is what the books on navigation would call 'an aggressive littoral'—an almost unbroken line of oatmeal-coloured cliffs dropping straight down into the sea, with occasional clumps of dark green scrub, like undernourished spinach, trying to scrape a living from the cracks in the limestone. I intended at first to press straight on to Parga; but seeing that there was no prospect of the crew making lunch, still less eating it, while we were still under sail, I decided to put in at Ayios Ioannis, a little harbour some twenty miles north of Preveza. When the crew was sufficiently recovered to take an interest in things, I showed him that according to the chart we were at the mouth of a river called the Akheron.

★

Julia turned pale and lit a Gauloise.

★

This was thought to be news of most sinister significance: the Akheron, it seems, is really the Acheron, known to all students of classical mythology to have its source in Hades, the Kingdom of the Dead: further libations were insisted on, this time to the gods of the Underworld. (It is the duty of a ship's captain to respect the religious sensibilities of the crew, though I did think it rather a pity to waste so much retsina.)

All this reminded me that there was a temple nearby which the crew had expressed a wish to see—a place called the Necromantion, dedicated in ancient times to the cult of the Underworld. Although we had meant to visit it by bus or car from Parga, it occurred to me that it might be even easier to reach it from Ayios Ioannis. With this in mind we went ashore, and were supplied by the local grocery not only with retsina and goat's milk cheese, but also with the services of a boatman—the son-in-law of the grocer's cousin—who was willing, for a modest consideration, to row us up the Acheron.

The crew read to me, as we were rowed along between banks of willow trees, from Book XI of the *Odyssey*, which describes the voyage of Odysseus into the Underworld. With a following wind and some rather vague sailing directions from Circe, it seems to have taken him only twenty-four hours; but one of his men still managed to arrive before him, having fallen when drunk from the roof of Circe's palace and so found a much shorter way to Hades.

Everyone thinks, says the crew—and you, having had a classical education, will no doubt be included in his concept of 'everyone'—everyone thinks that Odysseus sailed westwards to reach the Underworld, and that the Kingdom of Hades can accordingly be located somewhere in the area of Manhattan Island; but that is on the strength of what Odysseus told the Phaecians. It is to be noted (says the crew) that all the really unlikely stories in the *Odyssey*—the magic and monsters and giants and wizards and impressionable goddesses living alone on islands—all these stories are the ones told by Odysseus himself at the fireside of King Alcinous, when invited by the Phaecians to sing for his supper by telling them of his travels: under such conditions, the most truthful of travellers might embroider a little. To others he gives a less colourful account of his adventures; and I was called on to notice that on such occasions, though he says nothing about Hades, he often mentions having spent some time in Thesprotia—the region where the cult of the Underworld was practised and through which we were at that moment travelling.

This doesn't mean that I can claim to have made the same journey as Odysseus. Ah no—the crew remembered just in time that he is a serious classical scholar and that it would not be respectable for him to believe that anything in Homer ever actually happened. The most he will let me say is that in Homer's time there would have been a temple on the same site as the Necromantion, dedicated to the same cult, which people would have visited to hear prophecies from the ghosts of the dead; and that Book XI of the *Odyssey* may be regarded as a fanciful and poetic account of such a pilgrimage.

I was rather baffled by the business about prophecies: I couldn't see why the ghosts of the dead should know any more about the future than anyone else—rather less, I would have thought. The crew, admitting the force of my objection, suggested that the oracle might have been used to reveal the truth about any mysterious death, especially where murder was suspected:

'For it must be supposed,' he said, forgetting again about being a classical scholar, 'that it is those who have died young, or by violence, or by the treachery of those who should have protected them, whose unquiet ghosts would gather closest to the banks of the Acheron, pale with the thirst for blood and wailing to be avenged.'

We picnicked beside the Acheron on bread and goat's milk cheese washed down with retsina, and afterwards climbed up to the Necromantion: a temple built of polygonal blocks of stone, of massive size and irregular in shape, which are fitted together without cement or mortar to produce something like a cartwheel pattern. The chief attraction is to clamber down a rickety iron staircase to a sort of underground chamber, its roof formed by a series of rough stone arches, which is said to be the place where the prophecies were made. The only lighting is from a dim electric light bulb at the far end from the staircase: very sinister and atmospheric, but in view of the uneven floor also rather hazardous. Three-quarters of the way along one comes without warning to a shallow trench— no more ancient, I dare say, than the staircase or the electric light bulb, but supposed to have been used for sacrifices: I managed to avoid it; but the crew stumbled on the edge and scraped his wrist quite badly. I bathed the wound in retsina, however, which I suppose from its taste to have strong disinfectant qualities, and there seem to be no ill-effects.

★

Julia, pausing to refill her glass, looked troubled. I saw that she thought it an ominous thing that Sebastian had stumbled and suffered injury in the Temple of the Dead.

'My dear Julia,' I said kindly, 'it is simply a minor accident, such as might happen anywhere. It does not mean that something bad is going to happen to Sebastian. It is not a sign or an omen, you see, or anything of that kind. Not in the same way, for example, that leaving the pan on the stove for an hour is a sign that your supper will be burnt or that drinking wine after whisky is an omen that you will have a headache next morning—nothing like that at all.'

She continued to look anxious, however, and I saw that the distinction was beyond her understanding.

★

In spite of this diversion we reached Parga well before nightfall, having had to motor only a short part of the way, and berthed in the western harbour.

The accident of having a long sandy beach has turned Parga from a fishing village into a cosmopolitan little tourist resort, especially popular with sailing people. It has two or three hotels and several open-air fish restaurants, in one of which we sat down for dinner. At the table next to us there was a group of English people whom at first we felt inclined to avoid: rather hearty and brick-coloured and laughing uproariously at jokes I had heard quite often before, mostly from Cantrip. When I heard them mention the name of Camilla Galloway, however, I felt curious enough to engage them in conversation. There was no difficulty in persuading them to repeat the story—no one in Parga is talking of anything else, at least in sailing circles.

On Thursday, presumably just after saying goodbye to Rupert and Jocasta, Camilla and her cousins sailed down from Corfu to Preveza, where friends of theirs were holding a party. When it was over they decided not to wait until morning but to sail back by night as far as Paxos. They had all, it was thought, had a good deal to drink. A few miles south of Parga they were overtaken by the storm of which we

129

had already heard, and Camilla was swept overboard from the deck.

You may be under the impression that the deck of a sailing-boat is much the same as the deck of a Channel steamer—a broad expanse of solid timber, with good stout railings round it. This is not the case: on a boat such as Camilla's—I gather it was a Sadler 32—the deck consists of the cabin-top and a strip of timber, about eighteen inches wide and slightly sloping, on each side of it. There is a wire safety rail, of the same thickness as a washing-line, at about knee height.

You will understand, then, that if you were on the deck of a sailing-boat in a heavy sea with a gale blowing—and I think, Julia, that you should avoid the contingency—it would not be at all difficult to be swept off. In such conditions it is customary to wear a safety-harness—a webbing contraption with a lifeline shackled to it: the lifeline should be clipped to some secure point on the boat, so that if you do go over you have some chance of getting back. No one knew whether Camilla had been wearing such a thing: if she had, she had still been unable to get aboard again.

And that, in any ordinary sailing story, given the visibility and weather conditions, would have been the last of Camilla.

Beauty and riches, however, are not the only attributes which she shares with the heroine of a romantic novel: she has also, it seems, the same indestructible quality. In the early hours of Friday morning she was discovered by a fisherman somewhere on the seashore between Parga and Ayios Ioannis, wearing only a black silk negligée—by some accounts, indeed, entirely naked, but the black negligée version is preferred by connoisseurs. After going overboard she had simply struck out for the shore and kept swimming until she reached it—a distance, it was thought, of about three miles. She was bruised and fairly exhausted, naturally, but otherwise (said the sailing men, leering) in perfect condition. It really is a remarkable achievement: three miles may not sound far, but in pitch darkness with a heavy sea running, and without a mask or wetsuit—well, I suppose one might do it if one had to.

Such was the public interest in the notion of Camilla in her black negligée that I could learn little of what had happened to the others, though they too apparently spent an adventurous night. They were eventually taken off by a fishing vessel and the Sadler broke up on the rocks a mile or two from Parga—it seems very hard on Camilla, to be almost drowned and then find her boat was lost. I can give you, however, no further details.

It will soon be too dark to go on writing. The sun has gathered itself into a compact red circle and is slipping neatly down the sky behind Sivota Island. The bay where we are anchored looks rather pretty by this light, like a lake in Arcadia—almost encircled by mountains, with olive groves coming right down to the water's edge and no sound except the tinkling of goat bells: Hilary would see nymphs and satyrs at every turn.

Further unrest among the crew, who complains of hunger and thirst and wants to go ashore for dinner. He instructs me to send you his love and to tell you of his sufferings and hardships—you will agree that I have done so in almost unseemly detail.

                    SV *Kymothoe*—at the same anchorage.
                    Monday morning.

By a coincidence less remarkable than you might think—the Ionian Sea is really a very small place—I have more news of Camilla.

The only other customers in the taverna where we had dinner were three Greeks of villainous appearance, all looking as if they were born with cutlasses between their teeth. After a while the oldest of them—a man about five foot square, with a huge walrus moustache—asked us in quite a friendly manner where we were from, and seemed very pleased when the crew replied in Greek. There followed an amiable conversation, which from time to time was translated to me in summary.

In the course of this the crew made some remark which gave rise to great hilarity, with much stamping of feet and

131

banging of fists on the table: he had mentioned the story we had heard in Parga on the previous evening, and so put everyone in mind of Camilla's black silk negligée.

It had been a friend of theirs who found her—a fellow-fisherman by the name of Stavros. Their friend Stavros was always lucky, they said, too lucky to come to any good end. It was therefore typical of him to have spent the night of the storm safe and comfortable in his bed and gone out in the morning to fish up an heiress, while the rest of them had been out on the rough sea and got nothing but the small fry—two boys and one girl only between the three of them, and her not an heiress. It was they who had taken the other three off the Sadler.

They had gone out with their nets as usual on Thursday night, not quite trusting the weather but unwilling to lose a night's work and meaning to make for Parga if it looked like breaking. The storm, however, blew up more suddenly than they had expected, and overtook them a few miles south of Parga at about three o'clock in the morning—a force eight gale, gusting nine, and blowing from the south. Parga is at the centre of a stretch of rock-bound coast running west to east for about twelve miles, almost at right-angles to the main coastline—when the wind is from the south, an absolute lee shore: a dangerous harbour to run for in a southerly gale. The skipper accordingly decided to ride out the storm at sea. They had just settled down comfortably for the night—I tell the story as it was told to me—when a distress flare went up somewhere on the starboard bow.

They motored towards the place where it had seemed to come from and after a few minutes the light of their storm-lantern picked up a small sailing vessel. She was carrying far too much sail and looked to be shipping a good deal of water. She was also moving fast towards the Parga shore. It seemed a pretty even chance whether she sank or broke up on the rocks, but certain that she must do one or the other.

Given the weather conditions, there was no possibility of salvaging the yacht, but the skipper thought they might manage something to help the people on board: he could see three of them above decks, and he didn't think he needed to ask if they wanted to be taken off. He took the fishing-boat round to windward of the yacht and on to a parallel course, trying to bring her close enough, without a collision, for the two decks to be within leaping distance. The erratic progress of the yacht made it a difficult manœuvre and it took him longer than he had hoped—all the time, you see, they were moving closer to the Parga shore. At last there were a few seconds when the two vessels were within six feet of each other, with the fishermen all shouting to those on the yacht to jump. One of them did and landed neatly enough on the deck of the fishing-boat: but the others couldn't or wouldn't.

At this stage the skipper was inclined (he said) to give himself no more trouble about the matter, and to leave the other two in the good hands of God. At the last moment, however, when the boats were moving apart, young Andreas jumped the other way—from the fishing-boat on to the deck of the yacht. This (said his shipmates) was because he had noticed that one of those left on the yacht was a girl, and he thought this would be a fine opportunity to cuddle her. (Great laughter and much digging of Andreas in the ribs—he was a large, placid-looking young man, who bore it all with fortitude.) They were in two minds (said the skipper) about going back for him; but he was the son of the skipper's youngest sister, who had said he must be kept out of trouble, and probably meant that they shouldn't let him cuddle strange women on sailing-boats. So the whole manœuvre had to be repeated, with the Parga shore coming closer all the time.

This time it went better. Andreas threw the girl across to his shipmates and then jumped back himself, carrying the second boy in his arms. The three from the sailing-boat had survived their tossing about without much serious damage. They were tired and bruised, and the older boy had a broken arm—this had made him unable to balance for the jump when the boats were first alongside each other, and his sister had refused to leave him; but otherwise they were well enough. They were all in great distress, however, about another girl who had been on board the yacht and had been

133

swept overboard about twenty minutes earlier. The skipper knew that by this time she must certainly have drowned; but he put out a call on the radio, asking any shipping in the area to be on the lookout for her. When at last they put in at Parga he reported her missing, with no idea that she was tucked up safe in bed at the house of their friend Stavros—safe from drowning, at any rate, said the skipper, leering horribly over his walrus moustache.

The story, as you will gather, was related by the fishermen in a very casual and light-hearted manner, as if it were the sort of trifling adventure that happens to everyone once a month or so. I should make it clear, however, that what they had done was nothing at all of that kind, but a most remarkable piece of seamanship, such as one rarely hears of, and involving greater risk to all of them than one would readily undertake, especially for a stranger and with small hope of success. I accordingly asked the crew, to show that this was our opinion, to invite them to have a round of Metaxa with us, seven star if possible. After this—I don't know why, you will think I must already have drunk too much retsina—after this I burst into tears.

There was no seven star Metaxa to be had in the taverna— it was a very simple place; but we ordered a bottle of five star and drank it between us.

At some stage when we were talking of Camilla's remarkable escape I asked whether anyone knew if she had been wearing a safety-harness. Andreas became suddenly very angry, spat on the floor, and began calling someone (according to the crew's translation) 'a pack of bloody murderers'.

It turned out that he was referring to the manufacturers of Camilla's safety-harness. She had indeed been wearing one (over the black silk negligée) when she went overboard; but the shackle had snapped. There was, said Andreas, no question about it: he had seen the broken shackle with his own eyes—Stavros still had the harness and had shown it to him that morning. I felt some sympathy with his view of the manufacturers: one doesn't often have to depend on a safety-harness, but when one does it's probably for one's life, so a faulty shackle is something worse than careless.

It was late, I need hardly say, when we returned to the *Kymothoe*, and the crew is now recalcitrant about rising from his berth to set sail for Corfu. Well, I am the most indulgent of skippers, and have refrained from throwing buckets of cold water over him—but let no one say that it's my fault if we don't reach Ithaca.

It's very odd about Camilla's safety-harness—they don't usually break. I'm glad we resolved our doubts over the other business—one might otherwise feel inclined to find the whole thing rather sinister.

With very much love,
Selena.

CHAPTER 12

The suggestion had been made by some of my colleagues that I should participate in the marking of the summer examinations which in Oxford we refer to as Schools. Much as I was honoured by the proposal, I had felt obliged to decline: who am I to sit in judgement on the young? Moreover, the marking of examination scripts is among the most tedious of occupations. I had accordingly explained that the demands of Scholarship—that is to say, of my researches into the concept of *causa* in the early Common Law—precluded any other commitment of my time and energies.

The effect of this, I now discovered, was to make life in Oxford quite impossible during the first weeks of the summer vacation. I could not absent myself for five minutes from my desk in the Bodleian Library without meeting reproachful and accusing glances from other members of the Law faculty. It was more than could be endured: I sought refuge in London and Timothy's hospitality while I considered my plans for the summer.

It was thus that I found myself again in the Corkscrew an evening or two later, when Julia opened a letter bearing at its head the address of Dorothea Demetriou and her distinguished husband.

Villa Miranda,
Near Casiope,
Corfu.
Tuesday morning.

Dear Julia,

Please note with suitable astonishment the address from which I write. Be patient and I will tell you how we come to be here.

The sea was smooth and the sky cloudless when we weighed anchor for Corfu; but after so many stories of shipwreck and disaster we were careful to see that everything was in good order and the *Kymothoe* fully prepared for any emergency. The crew showed great diligence in making sure that all moveable objects which in rough weather might fall about and cause damage were securely stowed—a very seamanlike precaution, not to be thought less so merely because he happened to stow the transistor radio on the shelf behind the compass: it wasn't his fault, as he rather indignantly said afterwards, if the idiotic compass couldn't tell the difference between a transistor radio and the magnetic North.

We came without further misadventure to the island which I call Corfu, which its inhabitants call Kerkira, which ancient historians call Corcyra, and which Homer calls Scheria, the land of the Phaecians—never try to tell me that the Greeks don't do this on purpose. It is roughly the shape of a tadpole, with a broadish head to the north and a long tail wriggling southwards parallel to the mainland coast. The landscape is one of curves and soft contours, with olive-covered hills rising over gently rounded bays. There are also a great many flowers, very colourful and highly-scented.

The principal town of the island is on the east coast, approximately at the point where the head of the tadpole joins the tail. We did not put in there, but continued northwards, running goose-winged before a light south-easterly breeze and going so smoothly that we hardly seemed to be moving, though in fact I think we were making about three knots. The crew, very pleased with these conditions, lay in the cockpit and read me the passage in Homer which tells of

Odysseus arriving shipwrecked on the coast of Corfu: it is at this point (said the crew) that Odysseus emerges from the world of myths and magic and stumbles, naked and destitute, into the world of reality.

Our own landing had no such traumatic qualities. We anchored at Casiope, at the northern end of the island, a little before six o'clock, and went ashore to drink ouzo in one of the pavement cafés.

I noticed that not far away some boys were playing street cricket, with a wicket marked in chalk on the wall behind the batsman, and was gratified by this sign of enduring British influence. (Corfu, as I dare say you know, was under British rule for a period of about fifty years in the nineteenth century: here, as in other parts of our Empire, it was our enlightened policy to prepare the inhabitants for self-government by teaching them to play cricket.) I was unable, however, to attend closely to the game, since the crew thought this a suitable moment to make a certain suggestion—namely, that I should marry him.

'Sebastian,' I said, 'you have said in public, and on several occasions written, that marriage is a bourgeois and degrading institution designed to reduce women to the status of mere chattels.'

'So it is,' he said. 'But with you and me it would be different.'

I could not help thinking this a rather unprincipled attitude in a man well regarded in feminist circles for the soundness of his views on the question. Moreover, 'With you and me it would be different' is tempting to believe; but we do have several friends, don't we, who yielded to similar persuasion and found afterwards that it wasn't quite different enough? Still, a measure of tact is needed when rejecting such a suggestion: I took care to explain that my reluctance was due to the idyllic perfection of our existing arrangements, which made me feel that any change must inevitably be for the worse. I wondered if it might not be sensible, in the hope of avoiding further argument, to be a little hurt that Sebastian was not of the same view.

Before I had reached a decision on this point, my attention

was again drawn by the cricket match—to be specific, by the discovery that the cricket ball was now moving in my direction at a speed which gave me the choice of (i) catching it or (ii) allowing it to strike me a sharp blow in the midriff. I chose the first alternative. 'Ah,' I thought, as one of the players, rather slender and elegant of figure, strolled towards me to retrieve it, 'that looks like the sort of thing that Julia might fancy.' I saw, as he drew closer, that I had been right in my judgement: it was Leonidas Demetriou.

'Well caught,' said Leonidas. 'Oh—it's Miss Jardine, isn't it? Miss Jardine of Lincoln's Inn?'

I introduced him to Sebastian, to the great satisfaction of both: Leonidas clearly had in mind the advice of his Classics master that a boy hoping to go up to Oxford in the next academic year should miss no chance to make a favourable impression on a senior member of the University; while Sebastian, on learning that this was the son of the distinguished poet Constantine Demetriou, was as pleased and interested as if I had given him a personal introduction to Homer's great-grandmother.

Apparently content to abandon his part in the match, Leonidas sat down at our table. At some stage he went away to make a telephone call—as it turned out, to his parents: he represented them, on his return, as yearning for our company at dinner and scarcely to be consoled should we refuse. Well, there was no question of that: Sebastian had been daydreaming for ten minutes of meeting personally the man he so much admired. A little before dusk we found ourselves at the Villa Miranda, in a garden looking out across the sea to Albania.

Since you have not enjoyed the remarkable privilege of meeting Constantine Demetriou, I must try to make up for your loss by giving you a full account of the great poet's manner and appearance. He is tall, rather thin for his height, but fairly muscular, and with features which put one in mind (it is not for me to suggest he cultivates the impression) of one of the older gods of Olympus, as depicted in painting and sculpture—Poseidon, say, or even Zeus himself: dark eyes set deep under a high sloping forehead; an aquiline nose; and a spade-shaped black beard, slightly curly and streaked with grey. He has also the quality, which one sees in successful advocates, of holding the attention of those about him even when he has nothing in particular to say.

The Zeus-like effect was heightened, when we first saw him, by the fact of his being surrounded by the younger members of the Remington-Fiske family—all of whom, as you know, are very tall and splendid to look at, admirably suited to supporting roles in a dramatic tableau of family life on Mount Olympus. Lucinda, with her copper-coloured hair and abundance of curves, would make an excellent stand-in for the goddess Aphrodite; and her brother Lucian is very good-looking, and has literary ambitions—I think he can be cast as Apollo. As for Camilla—well, I'm not sure that the qualities of a romantic heroine include the intellectual attributes of Pallas Athene; but she is certainly athletic enough to do for Artemis, and said to be suitably virginal. Leonidas would be Hermes, I suppose; or perhaps Ganymede—he was very diligent about keeping everyone's glass filled. None of them seemed to have suffered any serious harm from their misadventures on Thursday night: Lucian had his arm in a sling, and I noticed later that Camilla still has some bruises; but apart from that they all seem to have recovered remarkably well.

Dolly, of course, does not fit in at all with the Mount Olympus picture. You would have to imagine that Zeus and Hera had been divorced—from what Homer says of their domestic life this seems not at all unlikely—and that Zeus had taken up with some less formidable goddess, with untidy hair and paint under her fingernails. It was Dolly, when we arrived at the Villa Miranda, who first came running across the garden to meet us; but her husband followed and overtook her, seized Sebastian by the hand, embraced him, and asked if he was indeed Sebastian Verity, the translator of Theocritus.

Oh joy—the great poet had read Sebastian's translation of the *Idylls*. Oh honour undreamt of—not merely read, but admired.

I do not in fact see why Sebastian should have been so

surprised. His translation of the *Idylls* may not have had a great commercial success; but it was favourably reviewed by all the critics whose opinion is worth having, and *The Times* called it essential reading for anyone with pretensions to a liberal education: our host might have been expected to have read and admired it.

Dolly went to great lengths to make sure I did not think myself the less honoured guest, introducing me without a blush to her husband as one of the most brilliant advocates of my generation. I ventured to remind her that she had never heard me open my mouth in court—when we varied the trusts of her father's will, you remember, I was led by Basil Ptarmigan; but she was not at all disconcerted.

'I know,' she said. 'I thought it was a shame you weren't allowed to say anything. I'm sure you'd have done it just as nicely as Mr Ptarmigan, and it wouldn't have been so expensive, would it?' Do by all means report this to Basil when you next see him. 'But I do know you're brilliant, because Ronnie Tancred told me so.'

I am bound to admit that I was rather pleased. Without believing that Tancred would have said anything so exaggerated, I thought I could infer that he had said something pleasant about me, and it is always gratifying to be well spoken of by one's instructing solicitors.

I had hoped during dinner to hear about the events of Thursday night from the point of view of those on the sailing-boat. Dolly, however, could not bear to hear the subject spoken of: she had spent all Friday thinking that Camilla was drowned; she had afterwards learned that they could all have been drowned; it had been, she said, the most horrible day of her life, and she never wanted to think about it again.

Her husband and Sebastian, as was to be expected, fell into a discussion of poetry and politics—subjects which neither of them seemed readily able to distinguish, so that one might have gathered from listening to them that the main objection to the Colonels was their unsoundness on matters of poetic diction.

I began to be embarrassed at the thought that everyone

was talking English entirely for my benefit, since all the others at the table understood Greek: even Camilla and the twins seem to speak it quite fluently. After dinner, when we adjourned to the garden for coffee, I thought it tactful to attach myself to the younger members of the family (who were not passionately interested in questions of poetic diction), leaving Sebastian and our host to continue their conversation in Greek. Since Dolly remained with them, I now felt free to ask again about what had happened on Thursday night. I said that I had heard about it in Parga, but did not mention the fishermen at Mourtos.

'I suppose,' said Camilla, 'that they told you I was washed up on the shore wearing a black negligée. That's what all those rotters in Parga are saying, and it's an absolute lie—it was the top half of my black silk pyjamas.'

'And if she hadn't lost the bottom half somewhere in the Mediterranean,' said Lucian, 'she'd have been perfectly respectable, wouldn't you, Millie?'

In accordance with the established convention in sailing circles, they spoke off-handedly of their adventure, saying modestly that there really wasn't much to tell. In accordance with the corresponding convention, I took no notice of this, but continued to press them for a full account.

On Thursday they had sailed down to Preveza in Camilla's yacht, the *Sycorax*, for a dinner party with friends. The gathering, however, had been less convivial than they expected, and by eleven o'clock they were back on board. A south wind had sprung up, which Camilla and Leonidas thought it a pity to waste: they both enjoy night sailing, and it would have been annoying to wait at Preveza until morning and then find that the wind had dropped.

'And Lucian and I didn't mind much either way,' said Lucinda. 'There was plenty of booze on board, and as long as no one expected us to do anything energetic in the sailing line we didn't care whether we drank it moving or standing still.'

The sky at this stage was clear, and it did not occur to anyone to listen to the weather forecast. Camilla took the first watch, having laid a course for Port Gaio on the island of

Paxos and expecting to arrive there in the early hours of the morning. Leonidas took over at about two o'clock, with instructions to keep on a compass heading of 295 degrees. By this time it was very dark, the sky having clouded over, and the wind had freshened to something like a force five. There was some discussion about whether they should hoist the storm jib instead of the genoa. Leonidas thought he could handle the boat without any change of sail, and Camilla agreed in the end that it would be enough to take a reef in the mainsail.

'So I told Leon to give me a yell if he had any problems,' said Camilla, 'and went off to the forecabin to get my beauty sleep. The twins, of course, were sprawled out all over the main cabin in a newt-like condition, snoring their heads off. And that's when Leon decided, for reasons best known to himself, to point the boat north a bit.'

Well, Leonidas still maintains that he kept on a heading of 295 degrees, as Camilla had told him to; but from what happened afterwards it seems that he can't have done. I wondered at first if it might be Camilla who had made a mistake, by not making the right adjustment for compass error. The rest of them, however, had all sailed often enough on the *Sycorax* to know pretty well by heart what adjustment would be needed on any particular heading, and they all agreed that 295 degrees would have been right for the course that Camilla meant to take. There seems no doubt, therefore, that Leonidas must somehow have misread the compass—perhaps by mistaking north-west for west-north-west. Whatever the reason, he was about fifteen degrees off course.

The wind rose steadily during the first hour of his watch, until it approached gale force. He realized that he was carrying far too much sail, but he also knew he could not reduce sail single-handed, and he was reluctant to rouse Camilla so soon after she had gone off watch. I think that his judgement may also have been affected by the absolute darkness all round him, which can be unsettling. The darkness of a night at sea with no moon and no stars isn't like being in a room with the light shut out: the sea is black and the sky is black, so that there is no horizon, and the darkness has no limits to it. With the sea running high and the boat heeling over at an angle which brought her deck within inches of the water, he had the sense to reach for a line and lash himself to the stern rail. He did not, however, call out for anyone to help him, but stayed alone at the tiller while the *Sycorax* went careering through the night at a speed he had never sailed at before—God knows how none of the rigging snapped—with the black waves towering over her and the gale screaming into her canvas. It was like sailing, he said, 'from nowhere into Hades'.

'It must have been very frightening,' I said.

'Oh no,' said Leonidas. 'No, it was marvellous.'

One can see, of course, that it would have been.

The thing that at last made him call out to Camilla was seeing lights on the starboard bow—the first sign he had that the boat was not on her intended course. He had expected that eventually he would see the lights of Paxos on the port bow, but lights to starboard were inexplicable—he could think only that he had somehow sailed straight past Paxos without seeing the lights there and was now running up the west coast of Corfu.

'Actually,' said Camilla, 'I was awake already, or I don't think I'd have heard him over the racket the wind was making. But I'd woken up and noticed we were moving a bit smartly for a 32-footer in nil visibility, and I'd just decided to go up on deck to find out what was doing. So when I heard Leon calling out I nipped straight up through the forehatch. Well, it was pretty obvious we were carrying too much sail, so I yelled out to Leon to put her into the wind so I could get the genoa down. I wasn't sure he'd heard me, so I was getting ready to yell again when put her into the wind he duly did. The rigging screamed like all the devils in hell and the *Sycorax* lurched like a drunken chorus girl and over I went. I was just thinking what a good thing it was I'd remembered to clip on my safety-harness as I climbed out of the forehatch when the damned shackle snapped. So I just had to swim for it.'

A conversation followed, of a sort common in sailing circles, about the relative merits of different kinds of safety-harness. Camilla, it seems, has always favoured the sort which incorporates a life-jacket. The others all think this too cumbersome, but in spite of the defect in her particular harness she looks on the night's events as confirming her view. She would never have taken the time, she said, to put on a separate life-jacket, and without one she would certainly have drowned.

'Even with it,' I said, 'you must have had a fairly rough time.'

'Well,' said Camilla, 'the swim itself wasn't too bad—I could see lights, so I knew I was heading for land, though I hadn't an earthly what it was or how far. The worst part was coming ashore—I thought I was going to get smashed to bits on the rocks. But eventually I managed it, and got collected up by a passing fisherman—all frightfully embarrassing, of course, what with having lost the bottom half of my pyjamas. Anyway, he took me home to his mother and about six aunts—I bet they didn't tell you that in Parga—and they put me straight to bed. When I came round again I found there'd been a tremendous tizzwozz and messages were flying about all over the place saying I'd been drowned. Actually, it sounds as if life was a jolly sight more dangerous back on board the poor old *Sycorax*.'

It took Leonidas two or three minutes to realize that his cousin had gone overboard: the lights of the boat were not enough for him to see clearly from the cockpit what was happening on the foredeck, and he was struggling to regain control of the steering. When it became clear to him that Camilla was no longer on board, he shouted to his brother and sister for help, though with not much hope of waking them. He couldn't reach the starting-handle of the engine; but he tried to go about under sail to return to the place where Camilla had last called out to him. This proved to be a mistake: struck amidships by the full force of the gale, the *Sycorax* was simply knocked flat; her mast-top dipped under the water and her cockpit was entirely submerged. After what seemed to Leonidas a very long time the boat righted herself, and rewarded his foresight in lashing himself to the rail by putting him back at the tiller only three-quarters drowned.

'The effect of this interesting manoeuvre,' said Lucian, 'was to remove Cindy and myself from our comfortable bunks and to throw us against the ceiling of the main cabin. That was how I broke my arm. At the same time, various objects lying about in the main cabin suddenly got all spiteful and began to attack us—there was a bottle, I remember, which had formerly contained Nuits St Georges and which definitely seemed to have something personal against Cindy.'

'And there was a lot of wetness about,' said his sister. 'One expects things to get fairly damp on a sailing-boat, but three inches of water in the main cabin is a bit much. So we thought we'd better go upstairs and help chuck some of it back where it came from.'

Their first thought, on learning that Camilla was missing, was to start the engine, with the object of returning under power to the place where she had gone overboard. The engine behaved as any true sailing man would expect a first-class engine, properly maintained, to behave in an emergency—it refused to start.

Recognizing the futility of looking for Camilla on their own, they decided to send up a distress flare, in the hope that there might be some more powerful vessel in the area which would assist them. It was little more than a pious gesture: the chances were minimal of the flare being seen, and almost non-existent of anyone finding Camilla—by this time, after all, she had been missing for seven or eight minutes.

'I did my best to look on the bright side,' said Lucian, 'by reminding myself that if I'd lost a cousin I'd gained several thousand acres of agricultural land in an area ripe for development—if Millie snuffs it before Grandmama, you know, I'm next in line for Grandfather's estate. But even so—'

'Honestly, Lucian,' said Camilla, not seeming at all put out by this remark, 'you really are the most frightful rotter.'

'—even so, this didn't comfort me as much as you might expect, not only because I'm quite fond of Millie but because I started thinking the prospects for the rest of us weren't too healthy, either. The *Sycorax* was still bucketing along at about

145

twice the speed intended by the designer and shipping so much water we didn't dare stop baling long enough to reduce sail. Mind you, we probably couldn't have got any of the sails down anyway—conditions on the foredeck were fairly rumbustious, and we wouldn't have wanted any more of us going overboard.'

'Another thing that was a pity,' said Lucinda, 'was not knowing where we were. Leon said we must be somewhere off the west coast of Corfu, but he couldn't think how we'd got there.'

'Still,' said Lucian, 'we were quite pleased at the idea that that was where we were. We thought that with any luck, as long as the *Sycorax* didn't simply fall to bits, we could just keep running north until the gale blew itself out—there'd have been quite a long way to go before we bumped into any land.'

'Which was sound thinking,' said Lucinda, 'while there were only lights on the starboard side.'

'Yes, absolutely sound. But then we saw that there were lights ahead of us—ahead and to the left. The lights of Parga, as it turned out. And that's when we started feeling a bit despondent.'

Under the heading 'What to do when running on to a lee shore without power in a gale' the advice given by the better sailing manuals is 'Do not allow such a situation to occur.' Bearing in mind the savagery of the Parga coastline, one would have described the *Sycorax* as being at this juncture on a very direct course for Hades.

'And then this lovely fishing-boat turned up,' said Lucian.

'With this lovely fisherman on board,' said Lucinda.

Their account of the rescue was substantially the same as that I had heard at Mourtos. They spoke of the fishermen with the warmest admiration—Lucian for their seamanship, Lucinda for the personal attractions of young Andreas. He had made her, she said, feel small and vulnerable—for a girl of five foot ten, amply proportioned, it would no doubt be a novel experience.

Soon after this Dolly joined us, and we talked of other matters; but her husband and Sebastian continued their

146

conversation until an hour at which she easily persuaded me that it would be 'simply too ridiculous' to go back to the *Kymothoe* when a spare room and a comfortable bed were available at the Villa Miranda. They were still talking when the rest of us went to bed, and I have no idea when they adjourned—late enough for Sebastian still to be sleeping at half past nine this morning.

I, on the other hand, woke early and could not get to sleep again—I would not otherwise be writing at such length. We shall spend the day, I suppose, looking at the art and antiquities of Corfu—I will give you in due course a full and instructive account.

★

Lighting a cigarette is one of those simple tasks which even Julia can usually perform with moderate competence. I perceived, however, that she was now making her fourth attempt to light her Gauloise with one of the spent matches which it is her custom, in an attempt at tidiness, to return after use to their box.

'My dear Julia,' I said, gently taking the matchbox from her and selecting from it one better suited to her purpose, 'is something troubling you?'

'I was just thinking—oh, thank you, Hilary.' She seemed pleased, though baffled, by the superiority of the new match over its predecessor. 'I was just thinking about Leonidas. He is an adorable creature and one would not willingly believe ill of him.' She drew deeply on her Gauloise. 'But I was thinking—I was thinking of him alone there at the tiller of the *Sycorax*. Quite wide awake, I suppose, and in control of things, while his brother and sister and cousin were all fast asleep in their bunks. And steering them through the night on a course quite different from the one they were supposed to be on—on what Selena describes as a direct course for Hades.'

'Himself along with the rest.'

'An agile boy with sound nerves would no doubt calculate that he could swim clear, with the advantage of knowing where he was and what was going on.' She drew again on her Gauloise. 'If Leonidas wanted to inherit the Remington-

Fiske estate, he would have to dispose of both Camilla and Lucian. If we weren't quite sure about Deirdre—'

'But we are quite sure about Deirdre,' I said a trifle peevishly. 'Do stop talking nonsense, Julia, and buy another bottle of wine.'

She did as I suggested, for she is a docile creature; but it was still with an anxious expression that she resumed her reading of Selena's letter.

CHAPTER 13

Same place.
Tuesday evening.

No art, no antiquities—our host will hardly admit, indeed, that there are any worth visiting: 'If you see something in Corfu which looks like a Greek temple,' he says, 'you'll find it's a church built by the British.'

I thought it reflected rather well on us, when we came across a Greek island with no Greek temples on it, to have tried to make good the deficiency; but the great poet's smile of Olympian melancholy indicated that he did not share this view.

When I asked if there was nothing at all of historical or artistic interest, he answered vaguely that we must go to the Archæological Museum to see the famous Gorgon, and some inscriptions which would interest Sebastian—yes, certainly; and we must not miss visiting Corfu Castle—no, of course not; but we could do these things at any time, someone would drive us to the town whenever we liked.

It seemed to be understood, however, that 'whenever you like' was not exactly to be taken to mean 'now'; and to have been settled, I don't quite know how, that we would be spending a further night at the Villa Miranda.

I am beginning to have an odd feeling of—it would be absurd to call it uneasiness: a sense of disorientation, and of not knowing what is going on around me—or rather, of *thinking* that I know but not being sure that I do. There is no good reason for it: one or two things have happened which have disconcerted me, but of a very trivial kind. Perhaps I am developing some interesting neurosis.

I suppose it's due to the heat, and too much retsina, and everyone talking a language I don't understand. It may also have something to do with our misgivings about Deirdre: it's difficult to be altogether at ease with people of whom one has entertained such disagreeable suspicions. I don't quite like to say anything about this to Sebastian: I never happened to mention to him our doubts about Deirdre's death, and now they have been resolved it seems unfair to cast any sort of shadow over his friendship with the Demetriou family.

Sebastian, you see, is in a state of rapture—starry-eyed and walking several feet above solid ground. He has been invited to become the English translator of the work of Constantine Demetriou: this (he says) is the most extraordinary and wonderful honour that could possibly be imagined. I do not think myself that the honour is all on one side; but it is no use saying so to Sebastian. You see how unkind it would be of me to spoil things.

Apart from the impression he has made on our host, Sebastian has also become an object of interest to Lucinda and Camilla: he is, after all, the only young man within range who is not related to them. After breakfast, therefore, they did not go away to paint pictures (as Lucinda was supposed to be doing) or to read Salmond on Torts (as Camilla was supposed to be doing) but remained in the garden to assist in our entertainment. They naturally proposed those forms of amusement which would show them to best advantage: Camilla, who looks splendid in a tennis dress, suggested tennis; Lucinda, who looks magnificent in a bikini, suggested a swim.

I rather enjoyed the tennis and swimming: a long time ago, you may remember—when I was first at Oxford, and before I was corrupted by left-wing intellectuals like you and Sebastian into drinking coffee all night and not bothering to keep fit—I used to be rather keen on that sort of thing. Sebastian, however, took no part in either, and from the

149

point of view of Camilla and Lucinda making an impression on him it was rather a waste of effort.

They would have done better to see if they couldn't dash off a swift elegy or two for translation from Greek to English, for so far as I could judge there was nothing else which might have distracted Sebastian from his conversation with Constantine Demetriou. They had begun talking about Homer, and a passionate discussion had developed of the historical accuracy of the *Iliad* and the *Odyssey*. Sebastian, as a respectable classical scholar, felt obliged to maintain that hardly a word of them was true, and that Homer had invented the whole thing. Our host is of the opposite school of thought:

'Yes, yes, yes, Sebastian, my dear friend, I know what the archæologists say. Because they can't find a tin hat with the name of King Agamemnon on it, they say that King Agamemnon did not exist and the Greeks never came to Troy and that Homer made it all up—the whole city of Troy and all the ships and armies of the Greeks—just like that, out of his imagination. But you, Sebastian, who are not an archæologist but a poet, and know how difficult it is to imagine anything—even a small thing, like a bird or a flower or a fold in a girl's dress—how can you think such a thing is possible? Our poor Homer of all people, who one would swear was worse than any of us, worse than your Shakespeare even, and could only describe things just as he saw and heard them, because he had no imagination at all. So that even when he is talking about the immortal gods he doesn't know how to give them a proper dignity and mysteri-ousness, but makes them sound like some farmer and his wife that one met last week in the taverna. Do you think such a person could invent whole cities and armies and systems of government? Po-po-po-poh.' This is what the Greeks say when they wish to express great astonishment and disbelief.

Sebastian, listening to this, looked like an atheist hoping for conversion.

'And when it comes to the kings and the great heroes he is even worse,' went on our host. 'He has to pretend that they behave like his own friends and acquaintances—fellow poets, probably, and other riff-raff of that sort—and would drink and tell lies and sulk and quarrel over women and prize money. But everyone knows, of course, that kings and heroes and the leaders of great nations could not possibly behave like that. That is how Homer has given us poets a bad name, Sebastian. People think we are all slanderers and blasphemers, who have no respect for anything and do not understand the difference between great men and everyone else. No one sees how unfair this is on respectable, well-behaved poets like you and me.'

The discussion of Homer led to the first thing which disconcerted me. The sun had risen high enough, by this time, to discourage any strenuous activity, and Lucian and Leonidas had joined the rest of us in the garden to drink retsina and eat olives. With the flattering implication that Camilla and I would be especially qualified to comment on the question, our host asked us how one would translate in English the Homeric expression *themis*—which seems to mean something like law, justice and general good behaviour.

Camilla adopted a robustly positivist approach, saying breezily that law had nothing to do with justice, but was simply whatever Parliament told one to do, whether it was right or wrong. Feeling that I was expected to present the other side of the case, I trotted out the argument about 'just' not simply meaning 'good' but referring specifically to the virtue of treating like cases alike; this (I said rather pompously) is also an essential feature of the concept of law, and any law or legal system which lacks this quality is not only capricious and oppressive but cannot properly be termed law at all. I have had a good deal of practice with this argument—it comes in useful when you have a judge who doesn't want to follow a precedent in your favour—and it went down extremely well with our host: he clapped his hands and said 'Bravo!'

'And if you agree,' I went on, 'that there is that sort of necessary connection between law and justice, and if you think that that's what Homer would have meant by *themis*, I

151

suppose it's expressed in English by the phrase "the rule of law".'

'Ah no,' said Constantine Demetriou, disappointed in me. 'No, surely that can't be right. That is the phrase used by people like Millie's father—if you will forgive me saying so, Millie—to mean that people dressed up as policemen can do what they like and everyone else must do as they're told.'

At this point Lucian, who had not so far seemed much interested in the discussion, looked up from his wineglass and said, 'Oh, I think you're wrong about that, Costas. I don't think Uncle Rupert would approve of people who *dressed up* as policemen. Do you think he would, Cindy?'

'Oh no,' said his sister, making her eyes very wide and gooseberry-like, 'I don't think he would at all.'

They were both then overcome by merriment, chortling and gurgling as if at some brilliant piece of wit. The rest of the family, though mildly perplexed, seemed accustomed to the twins having private jokes which were meaningless to any-one else. To me, however, when I came to think about it, it was far from meaningless: I saw that if Lucian and Lucinda had somehow heard of the raid on Rupert's flat by the spurious policemen, their mirth was not at all unaccount-able.

Then Lucian looked at me, and winked.

This, as I have said, I found disconcerting. It must mean, mustn't it, that the twins had heard not only about the spurious police raid but also of our presence when it took place? Well, it's not a secret exactly—the story is known to several people in Lincoln's Inn; but it's a little disturbing, don't you think, to find it so widespread as to be known to the twins?

★

'How in the world,' said Julia, 'could Lucian and Lucinda have known about our being at Rupert's party?'

'My dear Julia,' I said kindly, 'when any mildly scandal-ous story is known to several people in Lincoln's Inn, it is known to the rest of London within a week. I am not much

surprised to find that it is known to the rest of Western
Europe within a month or two.'

★

I have sometimes suggested, I think, that when your fancy
is taken by a young man of slender figure and pleasing profile
you should not disclose at too early a stage the true nature of
your interest. Young men, I seem to remember saying, like to
be thought of as people, not as mere physical objects: you
should therefore begin by seeming to admire their fine souls
and splendid intellects and showing a warm interest in their
hopes, dreams and aspirations.

It looks as if someone has given the same advice to Camilla
and Lucinda. Seeing that Sebastian was not to be drawn
away from the company of Constantine Demetriou, they
settled down on the grass close by and arranged themselves
in attitudes of attentive admiration, designed to suggest that
there was nothing they found quite so fascinating as the
theory and technique of translating Greek verse. When our
host made some reference to a recent article of Sebastian's
published in one of the learned journals, they went so far as to
ask what it was about.

I am now obliged to mention a slight pitfall in the
approach I have recommended: the young man may actually
tell you about his hopes, dreams and aspirations. Fascinating though he believes the subject to be, Sebastian is not the
sort of man to lecture anyone against their will on the errors
in the P Codex of Euripides' *Helena*; but Camilla and
Lucinda—to quote any common law judge in almost
any rape case—were asking for what they got. They had led
Sebastian on to believe that they were the sort of women who
would be willing, even eager, to listen to a learned exposition
of the finer points of textual criticism: if they didn't like it, as
appeared from their glazed looks and blank expressions to be
the case, they had no one to blame but themselves, and it
should have been a lesson to them not to go about admiring
the souls and intellects of other people's young men.

I did at last try to create a diversion by talking about our
previous three days' sailing, which I thought would be a

topic of more general interest. I cannot claim, however, that this was a great success. Sebastian was reminded of his theory about the Necromanteion and Book XI of the *Odyssey*; Camilla and Lucinda continued to look bemused; Constantine Demetriou was moved to warm enthusiasm; and the conversation, as was to be expected in these circumstances, again lapsed into Greek.

★

'At least Sebastian is enjoying himself,' said Julia with a touch of disapproval.

So it seemed. By what curious quirk of the subconscious, then, did the thought of my gentle young colleague in the garden of the Villa Miranda, surrounded by charming and beautiful people, for a moment put me in mind of a victim garlanded for sacrifice?

★

I have done what I can, by the way, to further your interest with young Leonidas. He seems to be quite a sensible boy really, though rather precocious, having been encouraged by people like you and Hilary to think himself interesting on account of his looks; and at least he doesn't tower over me, like everyone else here apart from Dolly, as if I were Gulliver in Brobdingnag. He is thinking of coming to the Bar when he has done his degree and would like to specialize in tax matters. I warned him of the difficulty of obtaining a tax pupillage; but suggested that when the time came, if he could persuade you of the seriousness of his interest in Revenue law, you might be willing to take him on as a pupil. I don't know, of course, to what lengths he may be prepared to go to convince you of his seriousness, nor am I to be thought to approve of his going to them, whatever they may be, nor of your encouraging him to do so; but I hope you will feel that I have done my best for you.

★

'Oh,' said Julia, 'what a delicious idea—how very kind of Selena to think of it.'

154

She had forgotten, presumably, that a few minutes earlier she had suspected Leonidas of seeking to contrive the death of three of his close relatives.

★

The second thing which disconcerted me happened in the afternoon.

Dolly had been telling me at lunch about pottery-making—she is part-owner, you may remember, of a small ceramics business near here, for which she designs plates and things. When I said I would like very much to see how it was done, she invited me to her studio, where she keeps some examples of her work and a potter's wheel for trying out her designs. She showed me how to use it, and I managed eventually to make quite a respectable sort of bowl, hardly lopsided at all.

The pottery I liked best was of a kind apparently traditional in Corfu—a black or deep blue glaze decorated in gold with scenes from Greek mythology and so forth. When I admired it, she insisted on making me a present of a pair of little jugs in this style—shaped like ancient amphorae, with a picture on one of Penelope weaving her web and on the other of Odysseus sailing his ship. Since she said that it was a joint present to Sebastian and myself, I asked which one she thought he should have.

'Oh,' she said, with a matchmaking look in her eye, 'it would be a shame to separate them.'

She has made her mind up, it seems, to marry me off to Sebastian, and was at pains to persuade me of the attractions of the married state: 'It's lovely,' she said, 'it's so comfortable.' She did concede, however—rather wistfully, I thought—that it was not quite as exhilarating as other possible arrangements.

'You can't expect your husband to spend the whole day thinking how wonderful it is that he's going to have dinner with you—he usually does have dinner with you, so there's nothing special about it. One does rather miss that sort of thing—it makes one feel so cheerful, doesn't it, and so good-tempered and energetic? But men don't understand that, they like being married—it makes them feel safe and secure. You wouldn't want poor Sebastian to feel insecure, would you?'

I suggested that the ideal arrangement might be to have both a husband and an admirer—that being the correct term, I believe, for a man who looks forward to having dinner with one.

'Oh, it is,' she said, with more enthusiasm than you might expect from a respectable married woman. 'But you can't make it last, you see. The admirer always wants to marry you and be safe and secure, so you end up with complications and unpleasantness.' I suppose she was thinking of her divorce from George Fairfax.

It was silly of me, in such a light-hearted conversation, to make any mention of Deirdre's death. It seemed heartless to have said nothing at all about it, and I thought this a suitable opportunity to offer some sort of condolence; but I ought to have guessed that Dolly would find it upsetting.

'Poor Deirdre,' she said. 'And the awful thing is, I hardly notice she isn't here—it's as if she never existed. I tried to love her as much as the others, but I couldn't quite—I did try, but it wasn't enough. She must have been so unhappy—oh, poor Deirdre.'

She buried her nose in a paint-stained handkerchief. I found myself reminding her that Deirdre's death had been an accident and had nothing to do with her being unhappy. 'You were with her, weren't you,' I said, 'just before it happened, and she seemed quite cheerful?'

'Yes,' said Dolly. 'Yes, that's true—I was with her on the roof terrace just a minute or two before, and she seemed in very good spirits—quite excited about something. I told them that at the inquest.'

But the thing is, you see—

You know how it is, Julia, when one is cross-examining a witness, that sometimes there is something about the way they answer a particular question which means they are not telling the truth? Well, the thing is—it would be absurd, of course, to think oneself infallible—but if we had been in court when Dolly told me about being with Deirdre on the roof terrace, and if she had said it in the same tone and manner—well, the thing is, Julia, I'd have staked my reputation that she was lying.

Even if I'm right, it's nothing to make a great fuss about: if Deirdre was not in such good spirits as Dolly led the Coroner to believe, one can hardly blame her for doing what she could to avoid a verdict of suicide. Still, I felt slightly uncomfortable: I left the studio as soon as I could, and came into the garden to continue writing to you.

After telling you about the things which disconcerted me, I see they are even more trivial, and my sense of uneasiness even less reasonable, than I thought when I began. There is no more to it, I suppose, than this: Sebastian would evidently be quite happy to stay at the Villa Miranda for as long as our welcome lasts, whereas I would prefer to go on sailing round the Ionian Islands. You will say that if I insisted—

Oh yes, I dare say, if I insisted on leaving Sebastian would not insist on staying. Things, however, are not as simple as that. When Henry disrupted my plans for Easter and then again for Whitsun he also disrupted Sebastian's; and Sebastian, it is fair to say, behaved rather well about it—there are men who would claim that their holiday arrangements are more important than my brief in the Court of Appeal, even in a leading case on equitable estoppel. If translating the work of Constantine Demetriou is Sebastian's equivalent of a brief in the Court of Appeal, I should not like to do anything to interrupt the progress of their friendship: it would make me feel selfish and ill-natured and see myself in a bad light. I do not at all want to spend ten days sailing round the Ionian seeing myself in a bad light.

There is also the matter of the cricket match—no, Julia, your eyes do not deceive you, we are involved in a cricket match: the annual fixture between the Writers of Corfu on one side and the Artists on the other, the former under the captaincy of Constantine Demetriou. Lucian, though unpublished, is considered eligible to play for the Writers and was to have done so; but his broken arm has put him out of action. Sebastian has been invited to take his place; he regards this, I need hardly say, as a most extraordinary honour, and there could be no question of his refusing. Fortunately, it isn't feasible to remain in Corfu until this event takes place: the terms of my charter require me to re-deliver the *Kymothoe* at Preveza on Friday week, and the match is to be played on the following day, so that whatever happens we shall have to sail back to the mainland at some stage before the match and return to Corfu by ferry. But if Sebastian gets the idea that he ought to have some batting practice—

It seems unreasonable and ungrateful of me to object to remaining at the Villa Miranda: I expect you would think it a perfect Paradise. Somehow, though, it is not quite my sort of place. Besides, having meant to go to Ithaca, it seems a pity not to.

> With very much love,
> Selena.

Having an Opinion to write on the construction of the Taxes Act, Julia felt unable to join me for dinner. It was perhaps fortunate that I could not share with her the disquieting reflection which found its way into my mind in the course of the meal—namely, that with the exception of Tancred all those who had been present on the occasion of Deirdre's death would also have had the opportunity to tamper with Camilla's safety-harness.

Even Rupert and Jocasta had been in Corfu in the fortnight preceding the storm and would presumably have had access to the *Sycorax*; though it seemed to me that Rupert, quite apart from any considerations of paternal affection, must have every reason to hope that his daughter would survive to enjoy her inheritance; and there was no reason for the girl's grandmother to wish any harm to her. Her cousins, however, would have had the plainest motives; so also, by the same token, would Dolly and her distinguished husband, since it is natural for parents to seek the advantage of their children.

If Camilla's harness had been indistinguishable from those worn by the others aboard the *Sycorax*, I might have dismissed these tiresome notions; but hers, it appeared, had been the only one which incorporated a life-jacket. I reminded myself that tampering with it would none the less have been a haphazard and uncertain means of achieving any sinister objective. The storm could not have been contrived: even Demetriou, however magical the power of his Muse, could not to that extent clothe himself in the mantle of a Prospero or an Aeolus. If an adventurous and athletic young woman spends three months sailing the Mediterranean there is a possibility, but no more than that, that she will at some point depend for her life on her safety-harness. An attractive possibility, no doubt, to a person wishing malice to seem like accident: I thought, however, that such a person would not rely on a single hazard, but would arrange to place in Camilla's path a sufficient number of similar traps and pitfalls to multiply risk into certainty. There was nothing to suggest that this had occurred.

Not until the next letter arrived.

CHAPTER 14

Spare room at the Villa Miranda.
Wednesday morning.

Dear Julia,

A rather disagreeable thing has happened to Sebastian—I almost hesitate to write to you about it.

It occurred to our host during dinner yesterday evening that we should on no account miss seeing Palaeocastritsa, a village some twenty miles away on the north-western coast of the island; it was, he said, a place of great magnificence and natural beauty; also, by tradition, the site of the palace of King Alcinous, who gave hospitality to Odysseus on his way home to Ithaca.

'Ah, Sebastian, my dear friend, I know that you don't believe King Alcinous ever existed—you think that Homer imagined him, him and his palace and his wife and his daughter and his daughter's washing. Wouldn't you think,

159

though, with all that imagining, that he could imagine some better reason for a princess to go down to the seashore in the morning? Something sublime and majestic and suitable to be mentioned in a great epic? But no, it's to do her washing, just like a peasant girl. Oh, he's hopeless, poor fellow—just fancy thinking a princess would ever make her clothes dirty.' He sighed and looked very satirical. 'But who knows? Perhaps if you go to Palaeocastritsa and search carefully you'll find the Princess Nausicaa's laundry-list, and be able to tell your archæologist friends that she existed after all. Or perhaps, when you stand alone on the seashore at Palaeocastritsa, and see the great cliffs rising above you and the dark sea foaming against the rocks, perhaps you will believe in the Princess Nausicaa even without her laundry-list.'

'Alone?' said Camilla at this point, rather lowering the tone of the conversation. 'Alone? On the seashore at Palaeocastritsa? Honestly, Costas, you must be thinking of it the way it was thirty years ago. Nowadays it's all high-rise hotels and hamburgers—you might as well talk about standing alone on the beach at Blackpool on August Bank Holiday.'

'It's true that nowadays it's very crowded,' said our host sadly. He was plainly having difficulty, as so often happens with you left-wing intellectuals, in reconciling his political principles with his dislike of crowds and hamburgers. 'But it's right that it should be—it's right that so many people should wish to see the city of King Alcinous.'

'They don't go to see the city of King Alcinous,' said Camilla. 'They go for a booze and a bathe and a bit of slap and tickle. The only time it's bearable is first thing in the morning.'

'Ah yes,' cried our host, 'yes, that's the time to see it. At dawn, with the sun rising behind Mount Pantocrator—ah yes, Sebastian, if you could see it then—'

This inevitably led—inevitably, that is, given Sebastian's reverence for the lightest word of Constantine Demetriou—to a discussion of how we might reach Palaeocastritsa by sunrise on the following morning. There were practical objections to our borrowing Dolly's car, on which the family

160

are largely dependent for transport; but Camilla has a motor-scooter, which she claimed was ideal for quick journeys from one part of the island to another, and offered us the use of it. Sebastian, who has been riding round Oxford on a motor-scooter for years and prides himself on his expertise, accepted immediately.

Waking up this morning well before daybreak—I don't sleep as well here as on board the *Kymothoe*—I had the following sequence of thoughts: (1) that no one except myself now seemed to have any notion of our continuing our voyage round the Ionian Islands—this slightly depressed me; (2) that even if we didn't, we could still have a reasonable amount of sailing in the waters around Corfu—this cheered me up a little; (3) that since Camilla had lost her own boat we couldn't very well go sailing without inviting her and her cousins to join us. This I found so dispiriting that when Sebastian also woke up (which he always does quite easily when he wants to) I said grumpily that I didn't feel like bumping across the hills of Corfu on the back of a motor-scooter and proposed to go back to sleep again.

After he had gone I failed to go back to sleep, but lay in bed thinking how unfair it was that he should be seeing interesting things in Palaeocastritsa, and looking for Nausicaa's laundry-list, while I was left stranded at the Villa Miranda in the company of people who towered over me in the Brobdingnagian fashion previously objected to. Without the stimulus of coffee, however, I could work out no way of regarding this as Sebastian's fault rather than mine, and so was prevented from sympathizing with myself as fully as I would have wished. After about twenty minutes, I dressed and went downstairs.

Dolly was already up, drifting about the kitchen in a housecoat, trying simultaneously to make coffee and to read a letter which she had evidently just opened. She gave the impression of being upset by it, though as if at news of a minor rather than a major misfortune. I asked her if anything was the matter.

'Oh no, it's nothing really,' she said. 'Just a silly letter from my solicitor. Oh dear, don't people make things difficult?

One does one's best to do the right thing, but it doesn't do any good.'

I wondered for a moment whether it might have something to do with Rupert's investment plans for the Remington-Fiske funds; but I remembered that Dolly's interest had been extinguished by the variation, so that there would now be no reason for anyone to write to her about it.

'Solicitors,' I said, 'often write silly letters. Is it anything that I could help with?'

I didn't discover whether it was or not, because at that moment there was a ring at the doorbell. Seeing that Dolly was at a crucial stage in her coffee-making, I went to answer it. On the doorstep was Sebastian, with his clothes torn and blood all over him.

It wasn't, when we had cleaned and tidied and disinfected him, as bad as it looked at first sight, but still disagreeable. We learnt, in the course of our ministrations, that a goat had run out into the road in front of him on the way down to Casiope: he had swerved to avoid it, lost control of the motor-scooter and landed in the ditch at the roadside. In spite of protests that he was only shaken and there was nothing to worry about, we had no difficulty in persuading him to return to bed.

Discreetly left by Dolly to attend alone at the bedside—the matchmaking look was in her eye again—I poured him a medicinal dose of Metaxa and made some adverse comments on the character and ancestry of the goat.

'Oh no, don't say that,' he said, 'it was a lovely goat. I won't hear a word against it.'

Rather alarmed at this—I could think of no rational explanation for such saintly benevolence—I expressed a desire to know what on earth he was talking about.

'The brakes on the motor-scooter weren't working,' he said. 'If it hadn't been for the goat, I wouldn't have known until the hairpin bend.'

The Villa Miranda is on a side road, narrow and not well surfaced, which runs along the cliffs for about half a mile before joining the main road to Casiope. The first occasion one would normally have to brake after leaving the Villa is just before the junction, where the road begins to descend more steeply and twists sharply back on itself. At this point one has a sheer cliff face on one's right and on one's left an unbroken drop of about a hundred feet to some fairly jagged rocks: not a good place to discover unexpectedly that one's brakes were out of order. I decided that I too needed a medicinal Metaxa.

'You won't mention it to anyone, will you?' said Sebastian. 'Camilla might feel embarrassed about lending us the scooter.' He then went peacefully off to sleep, apparently not in the least troubled, nor expecting me to be, by the thought of how close he had come to falling over a hundred-foot cliff.

So here am I at his bedside with all sorts of sinister notions running through my mind which common sense tells me are altogether absurd. I don't go so far as to imagine that anyone intended any harm to Sebastian: they have known him, after all, for only two days, during which the worst he has done is to talk a little too much about Book XI of the *Odyssey* and the transmission of the texts of Euripides—even someone not much interested in these subjects would hardly try to murder him for that.

But it was Camilla's motor-scooter, and I suppose that in the normal course of events she would have been the next person to ride it.

No, this is all nonsense. I am suffering, as previously supposed, from an interesting neurosis—Henry's fault, I expect, for disrupting my holiday arrangements.

With very much love,
Selena.

During the week that I had been his guest, I had hardly seen Timothy for five minutes together—the members of Lincoln's Inn, in the weeks which lead up to the Long Vacation, become tediously over-occupied with the concerns of their profession. On the Friday, however, in recompense for his unsociable conduct, he had undertaken to buy me lunch at one of the better restaurants in Chancery Lane.

My confidence in the arrangement was not unqualified: I knew all too well how characteristic it would be of Henry to conjure up in the course of the morning some obstacle to Timothy's lunching at leisure or at all. I judged it prudent, therefore, before proceeding to the restaurant, to seek confirmation at 62 New Square that our plans were unchanged.

Entering the Clerks' Room with a certain diffidence—Henry does not quite approve of me—I perceived that the only occupants were the temporary typist and the solicitor Tancred: he was seeking to persuade her of the urgency of an Opinion, to be written by Timothy in the course of the weekend, which would be entrusted to her for typing on Monday morning.

'So you see, Muriel, my dear,' said the solicitor, reinforcing the persuasiveness of his tone with an avuncular pat on her shoulder, 'if you would be so kind as to give it your immediate attention, I should really be most grateful.'

'I'll do my best, Mr Tancred,' said the temporary typist, unimpressed by the mellow tone and avuncular manner, 'but I've only one pair of hands, and you're not the only one that wants things urgently, you know.'

I gave a discreet cough to draw attention to my presence. The solicitor turned towards me and nodded coldly: he had again forgotten, I gathered, how he had made my acquaintance, but remembered that he did not much want to renew it.

'If you're looking for Mr Shepherd,' said the temporary typist with dark satisfaction, 'you've missed him. He's gone to lunch and I don't know when he'll be back.'

In the restaurant in Chancery Lane, Timothy was seeking the views of Ragwort and Cantrip on one of those fine questions of professional propriety which are so dear to the Chancery Bar.

'Suppose,' said Timothy, 'that your instructing solicitor is one of the trustees of a settlement. He is being urged by his co-trustee to concur in the investment of trust funds in a manner not authorized by the provisions of the settlement or by the Trustee Investments Act. The consent has been

164

obtained both of the income beneficiary and of the person presumptively entitled to capital, but your client wishes to know what steps, if any, he should take to ensure that it is an informed and genuine consent: that is to say, that the beneficiaries understand the nature of the transaction and are aware that they are not obliged to agree to it.'

'I suppose,' said Ragwort, 'that the life tenant is a person of advanced years, whose intellectual powers have for some time been failing and who is now—' He paused and sighed.

'Completely round the twist,' and Cantrip, perceiving his friend at a loss for the *mot juste*. 'Too nutty to tell the difference between a letter of consent and an old bus ticket.'

'As it happens,' said Timothy, 'the difficulty is not with the life tenant. Although she is in her eighties and not, alas, in the best of health, her mental faculties are unimpaired. No, the difficulty is with her great-granddaughter, who is entitled to capital contingently on surviving her. She is a sensible, well-educated girl, and could normally be counted on to take care of herself. It so happens, however, that she is the daughter of the importunate co-trustee: your client fears that filial respect and affection may prevent her from exercising an independent judgement. She is at present abroad, and he is unable to discuss the matter with her in person. Still, he has been presented with a letter of authority bearing her signature, and he would find it embarrassing to refuse to act on it unless firmly so advised by Counsel.'

'I can see,' said Ragwort, 'that it is a somewhat delicate matter. I don't see, though, that it presents Counsel with any problem of professional propriety.'

'Not even,' said Timothy, looking at the ceiling, 'if Counsel has reason to believe, on the basis of information from an entirely different source, that the beneficiary has in fact declined to sign the letter and that there is therefore a strong possibility that the signature is forged?'

'My dear Timothy,' I said, 'do you mean to tell us that Rupert Galloway—?'

'I don't mean to tell you anything,' said Timothy, directing his gaze towards some point in the middle distance beyond my left shoulder. 'That is to say, I don't mean to tell

165

you anything which would involve a breach of professional confidence. The problem, as I have said, is a hypothetical one.'

Before I could comment further, the sound of coatstands being knocked over and handbags being dropped on the floor proclaimed the arrival of Julia. She was clutching, but too agitated by its contents to read aloud, another letter from Selena. While she restored herself with gin and tonic, we passed it round the table.

> SV *Kymothoe* at anchor off Paxos.
> Friday morning.

Dear Julia,

As you will see, I have cut and run for it. The Remington-Fiske family may be free of any homicidal tendencies; but they are remarkably accident-prone, and it seems to be catching.

On Wednesday evening, when Sebastian seemed fully recovered from his misadventure with the motor-scooter, I ventured to suggest that we might be outstaying our welcome: we had, after all, only been invited to dinner. It appeared that the same thought had already occurred to him, and he had said something to Dolly about not wishing to impose on her hospitality; this had brought down on him many reproaches for even thinking of such a thing, and assurances that neither she nor her husband would willingly see us leave any sooner than we had to.

'But I do see,' said Sebastian, 'that you may not be getting as much sailing as you'd like. You will say, won't you, when you want us to be on our way?'

He looked so downcast, however, at the idea of leaving that I could not have accepted the offer without feeling selfish and mean-spirited, and seeing myself in a bad light: this, as I have said, is something I wish to avoid. I proposed by way of compromise that on the following day we might sail down to Gouvia, and from there visit Corfu town to see the Museum and the Castle; if there was not enough time to sail back to Casiope, we could leave the boat at Gouvia and return by bus or taxi to the Villa Miranda.

When during dinner we told the others of these plans, I felt obliged to say that if any of them would like to join us they would of course be very welcome. Dolly's children all declined; but Camilla said that she would be delighted to come with us. I tried fairly hard to persuade myself that I would enjoy having on board a girl of forceful personality who knew more than I did about sailing in these waters and would probably expect to take the helm all the way to Gouvia.

As it turned out, the effort was unnecessary. After breakfast, when Dolly was preparing to drive us down into Casiope, Camilla said that she was feeling 'a bit fragile' and thought she had better stay at home.

I had a feeling, as we went aboard the *Kymothoe*, that something was not quite as it should be; but decided, seeing nothing to account for it, that this must be another example of my interesting neurosis. Still, I opened the after-hatch with caution and peered suspiciously down into the cabin as if expecting it to be full of armed desperadoes. Having satisfied myself that it wasn't—the cabin is only eight feet by six and they would have been conspicuous—I went below, leaving the crew on deck to make ready to weigh anchor. I looked round carefully to make sure that everything was in order, and could see nothing out of place apart from a dead wasp on the floor beside the stove: this I swept up and disposed of.

I found, as I began to go back up the companionway, that I was rather worried about the wasp. I thought it had chosen an eccentric place to expire: wasps, it seemed to me, do not make a habit of dropping dead on the floor; they usually try to escape from a confined space through a window or porthole; when exhausted, they breathe their last somewhere near the window-frame. I decided, feeling rather foolish, to take a closer look at the stove.

The fuel supply to the stove is from a cylinder of bottled gas, connected by a pressure valve to the pipes which lead to the burners. I noticed that although the taps had been turned off the valve was still in the 'on' position. Well—a safety expert might have raised an eyebrow, but many people leave the pressure valve on the whole time: it ought not to matter provided the pipes are sound. I tested them with soapy water and saw no ominous bubbles. Thinking, however, that if I was going to do a safety check I might as well be thorough, I lifted up the burners and examined the pipes underneath the grill: there was no need to make any more soapy water tests—at the junction between the pipe and the pressure valve there was a clearly visible crack, nearly an eighth of an inch wide.

The gas cylinder had been full when we went aboard at Preveza and we had made comparatively little use of the stove. Since bottled gas is heavier than air and therefore sinks, I concluded that most of its contents would by now have settled down peacefully in the bilges.

At this point the crew called down the after-hatch saying that all was now ready above decks and offering to make coffee while I started the engine.

'No,' I said. 'Don't let's do either of those things for a little while. Let's pump the bilges instead.'

It is wrong for a ship's captain to spread unnecessary alarm among the crew. I therefore thought it better not to mention that the *Kymothoe* was at present not so much a sailing-boat as a floating bomb and liable, if the engine were started or a match struck, to disperse herself rather messily all over the harbour.

'Sebastian,' I said, when we had been pumping for ten minutes or so, 'it is one of the duties of a ship's captain to prevent the crew from falling into the clutches of sirens.'

'Sirens,' said the crew, 'are predatory birds with the voices of women, who lure men on to the rocks and devour them alive.'

'That seems to me,' I said, 'a very fair description of Camilla and Lucinda. I have been observing them closely, and they both look at you as if you were something savoury on the breakfast menu.'

'Skipper,' he said, with an astonishment understandable in a man who for three days has paid no attention to anyone but a middle-aged Greek poet, 'you don't seriously think—?'

'No,' I said, in a tone not designed to carry much conviction, 'no, not exactly, but if you continue to find Corfu a more attractive anchorage than Ithaca—'

A touch of plain, straightforward jealousy seemed to me to provide a flattering and persuasive pretext for wishing to resume our voyage immediately, without returning to the Villa Miranda. I was unlikely, I thought, to be suspected of duplicity in admitting to feelings so unbecoming to a reasonable, civilized woman; and despite the convention that jealousy is to be resented, I have met few people who are not just a little pleased to be its object and do not at all enjoy the sense of magnanimity which comes from indulging it. The crew did not prove to be one of them—though it is fair to say that he behaved very well, and was not nearly as insufferable as many men would have been about being magnanimous and indulgent.

Before setting sail I went ashore again and found Dolly still bargaining for eggs and aubergines in one of the village shops. I accounted for our change of plan on sentimental grounds, explaining apologetically that Sebastian and I had few opportunities to be alone together and that I had been overtaken by a fit of possessiveness. She thought she understood perfectly, and assured me that neither she nor her husband would take offence at our abrupt departure. This was on condition that I brought Sebastian back to Corfu in time for the cricket match between the Writers and Artists: foreseeing that nothing I could say would keep him away from it, I promised that I would.

I allowed her to think that we still meant to sail first to Gouvia, on the east side of the island, and take a look at Corfu town; but once out of harbour I headed westwards. It was absurd, of course, but I somehow found it more comfortable to think that no one at the Villa Miranda, not even Dolly, would know our exact whereabouts. I continued on a westerly course until we reached Cape Cefali and then made all speed south, using the engine when the wind slackened and not stopping for anything until we reached Paxos.

I am slightly anxious about Camilla, but can't see what to do about it. One can hardly suggest to her, can one, that until her inheritance vests in possession she would be wise to avoid the company of her relatives? It's a monstrous suggestion, and there's no real evidence for it. Indeed, seeing things from an objective distance, you may already have decided that I am making much out of nothing, with the subconscious motive, perhaps, of finding a respectable reason to leave the Villa Miranda. Very well, Julia—if you choose to have such a low opinion of my subconscious, I won't argue with you. It's true that the pipe could have broken by accident, though I checked it at Preveza and it looked sound enough. On the other hand . . .

On the other hand, Julia, when one has been sailing for a number of years, there are various safety precautions which one takes more or less instinctively and without needing to think about them any more than cleaning one's teeth in the morning; and whatever you may say about my subconscious, one thing I don't think I would forget is to turn off the pressure valve of the gas cylinder before going ashore.

I will send you postcards from Ithaca, but expect to be back in London before them.

With very much love,
Selena.

Soothed by gin, and the thought that Selena was now at a safe distance from any persons of homicidal tendency residing at the Villa Miranda, Julia was restored to her usual cheerful spirits and displayed a healthy appetite for lunch. I refrained from any comment which might reverse these happy consequences; but I could no longer deflect my thoughts from a chain of disquieting speculations which my conscious mind at least had hitherto managed to exclude.

'What's got into you, Hilary, old thing?' asked Cantrip, observing my abstraction. 'You've been moaning all week about us being too busy to gossip and buy you drinks, and now we're taking you out to lunch you sit there looking like a wombat that wishes it was somewhere else. What's up? Was something wrong with the lobster?'

'No indeed,' I answered, touched by the boy's solicitude. 'The lobster was excellent. I was reflecting—I was reflecting on the familiarity between the solicitor and the temporary typist.'

There is a sense in which this was entirely true.

CHAPTER 15

It was not until the others had left us and Timothy was settling our account that I mentioned my need to borrow a rather substantial sum of money: the holiday season being at its height, I feared that it would only be by tendering the first-class fare that I could persuade any airline to convey me to Corfu by the following morning. Unfortunately, since the rewards of Scholarship are not of a material nature . . .

'Yes,' said Timothy, seeming perplexed, 'yes, Hilary, I know about the indifference of the Scholar to worldly wealth, you've told me about it before. But why have you suddenly decided that you want to be in Corfu by tomorrow morning?'

'Because tomorrow is the day of the cricket match between the Writers and the Artists, and Sebastian is not a young man to default on such an obligation. He and Selena will therefore return to Corfu tomorrow. There is little doubt that they will receive an invitation to spend tomorrow night at the Villa Miranda; and I am concerned for their safety.'

'My dear Hilary,' said Timothy, 'you can't possibly be serious.'

It took me several minutes to persuade him that I was in earnest.

'Well,' he said at last, 'if you really think there's going to be some sort of unpleasantness, I suppose it would be better if I went. God knows what Henry will say.'

'There is no need,' I said, 'to disrupt your professional engagements. My dear Timothy, you cannot imagine that I propose to engage in any adventure of a physical nature—it is simply a matter of persuading Selena and Sebastian not to return to the Villa Miranda.'

Eventually, though not without doubtful looks and anxious murmurs, he agreed that it was I who should go—only, perhaps, because he still did not altogether believe that the matter was a serious one.

'I can understand,' he said, 'that Camilla might be in danger. But what earthly reason could anyone have for doing any harm to Sebastian and Selena?'

'I think,' I said, 'because Sebastian talked too much about Book XI of the *Odyssey* and the transmission of the texts of Euripides.'

The Esplanade at Corfu, if considered as a public park, is not particularly extensive. The Corfiots, however, do not choose so to regard it, but boast instead that it is the largest public square in Europe. An elliptical space of ground lying between the town and the Citadel, encircled and traversed by avenues of chestnut and acacia, it beguiles the memory into recalling it as green—a varied and luxuriant green; though the truth is that the grass does not flourish there, and much of its area is a bare and sunburnt brown. From a table on the pavement in the Liston, the arcade of shops and cafés which occupies the north-western quarter of its circumference, I sat looking across at the more westerly of the two peaks of rock on which the Citadel is built, trying in vain—so precipitous is the rock and so massive its fortification—to distinguish the work of Nature from the work of man. The eastern summit, though hardly less formidable, is hidden by its companion from the view of spectators in the Liston.

Corfu has the charm of a place which reminds one of other places—which and for what reason one is not altogether certain. The deviousness of the narrow streets, winding in and out of small, unexpected squares; the elaborate little balconies tête-à-tête above long flights of marble steps; the bazaar-like profusion of merchandise outside obscure shopfronts; the noises of seafaring; the occasional smell of drains mingling with the scent of flowers—these things, I suppose, remind one chiefly of Venice, especially of those things in Venice which remind one of Istanbul. The Liston, however, has a certain Parisian flavour; and there is something about the Esplanade—the neo-Classical architecture and the

172

circular bandstand—which irresistibly recalls Cheltenham or Bath. A town, one can hardly deny it, in every sense provincial; but with the faded, rather sluttish elegance of a provincial beauty who a long time ago spent a season in the capital.

I had lunched at the Aiglou restaurant, thinking it the probable rendezvous for those engaged to play cricket on the Esplanade in the afternoon. Two or three of those who passed by were known to me from previous visits, and paused to exchange greetings; but of those concerned in the matter which brought me there there was no sign.

I removed, having eaten, to the adjoining café, where the purchase of a small black coffee and a Metaxa would secure me the undisturbed occupation of a table for the rest of the afternoon. I chose a position from which I could observe both ends of the Liston and the far side of the Esplanade, supposing that if anyone approached it would be from one of those directions. I had forgotten that the shops and cafés of the Liston have entrances also on Capodistria Street, and that a new arrival at the table behind me might escape my notice.

'If I see an Oxford don being ravished by my sister,' said a cheerful English voice, 'is it my duty to interpose myself between them?'

Looking round in some alarm, I saw that the occupants of the table were the copper-haired Fairfax twins. Their attention, however, not being directed towards me, I concluded that I was not the imagined victim of the hypothetical outrage.

'Chance,' said Lucinda, 'would be a fine thing. I do think it's mean of Selena to keep Sebastian away until the last moment—she might at least have brought him back to Corfu in time to have lunch with us. Didn't anyone ever tell her that she ought to let other little girls play with her nice toys?'

'The toy doesn't want to be played with,' said Lucian. 'Take the advice of a brother who has your best interests at heart—forget this man and stick to Greek fishermen. Sebastian doesn't fancy anyone but Selena.'

'I don't see why,' said his sister plaintively. 'What's she got that I haven't got?'

'Absolutely nothing, sweetheart, lots less of practically everything. But that's how it is—*le cœur a ses raisins*, as the French say, which the raisins know nothing about. You might as well ask why men go overboard about Mama.'

'I've given up trying to explain that,' said his sister. 'I just watch out for the signs and stand by to help with the debris.'

They both sighed, overtaken by that indulgent despair so often induced in children by reflecting on the conduct of their parents—closely resembling that induced in parents by reflecting on the conduct of their children.

The news that Sebastian and Selena were not as yet in the company of the Demetriou family filled me with a relief little short of euphoria. Moreover, it occurred to me that the circumstances afforded a happy opportunity to verify my opinion concerning a particular aspect of the matter under investigation.

I had still in my possession the photographs which Julia had found in the pocket of Deirdre's coat. I took them out and put them down on my table, in the manner, as I hoped, of the conscientious tourist preparing to write postcards to family and friends. When next the waiter came hurrying past me I contrived a slight collision between us, in apparent consequence of which the photographs went flying in a colourful cascade across the space of ground between myself and the Fairfax twins. The two young people jumped up in good-natured haste to set about retrieving them.

'Thank you,' I said extending my hand, 'that is most kind.'

They made no attempt, however, to restore my property to me, but stood as if rooted to the pavement under the sunlit arcade, staring at the photographs, then at each other, then at me, then again at the photographs.

'Where—?' said Lucian.

'How—?' said Lucinda.

'I must apologize,' I said, 'for their rather indelicate nature. They were not intended for public display.'

'It's not that,' said Lucian. 'It's just—it's just that we'd awfully like to know where you got them.'

'Yes,' said his sister. 'Yes, we would. Can we offer you a Metaxa or anything?'

174

I accepted the invitation and joined them at their table.

'It would be indiscreet of me,' I said, 'to explain exactly how the photographs which engage your interest come to be in my hands. I may say, however, that they were formerly in the possession of a young woman—now, sadly, no longer living—who had acquired them by rather dubious means from two cousins of hers. I believe, not to put too fine a point on it, that she had stolen them.'

'It was Deirdre,' exclaimed Lucinda. 'I always said it was Deirdre—the little beast. Oh dear,' she added, biting her knuckles, 'I shouldn't say that now she's dead. Oh dear, poor Deirdre.' The difficulty seemed almost universal of remembering, in relation to Deirdre, the maxim *de mortuis nil nisi bonum*.

'I perceive,' I said, 'that you have some knowledge of the matter.'

'It's an extraordinary coincidence,' said Lucian, 'but we think that this girl's cousins are people who are friends of ours. Quite close friends, actually.'

'So you see,' said Lucinda, 'if we keep the photographs and promise to give them back to these friends of ours, it will all be all right, won't it?' She made this suggestion with such lively enthusiasm that I hardly had the heart to disappoint her.

'I am afraid,' I said, 'that that will not quite serve. Your friends, you see, had also acquired them by means not entirely orthodox—their title to them is by no means clear. Your friends, as you may know, have a relative whom they rather dislike—I will call him their uncle, though that is not the precise relationship. In recent years they have had few personal dealings with him; but there are certain points of contact between the circles in which they move. Their uncle has seen fit to interest himself in their activities and to inform their father of matters which he thought to merit disapproval. What especially infuriates your friends—a young man and a young woman, I believe, of similar age to yourselves—what especially infuriates them is that their uncle, in his own private life—but perhaps they have told you all this, and I trespass on your patience by repeating it?'

Shaking their coppery heads, they mutely reassured me that my narrative still held their interest.

'—that their uncle, in his own private life, is himself accustomed to indulge in practices which would cause a raised eyebrow among the strictly conventional. Last autumn, finding themselves in London, they saw an opportunity to be innocently revenged. Having learnt from some mutual acquaintance that their uncle had invited several of his friends to join him on a particular evening in certain idiosyncratic diversions, they intruded on the gathering in the guise of members of the police force, conducting what is known as a raid.'

'I say,' said Lucinda, resolutely ingenuous, 'how awful of them. Weren't they afraid they'd be recognized?'

'Evidently not. Their uncle had not seen them since they left school, and they made liberal use of wigs and false moustaches. You may perhaps think, knowing them as you do, that the girl would have had some difficulty in disguising her strikingly feminine appearance; but it is surprising—I have had a little experience with amateur theatricals—how easily a young woman of voluptuous figure may, with suitable padding, pass as a substantially built young man, provided that she does not open her mouth. Well, the enterprise succeeded beyond their expectations—not only did they embarrass their uncle, but they also secured possession of his camera, with which he and his friends had been photographing one another in various interesting poses. They developed the film, and the photographs which you are holding are the result. Your friends, I gather, made no immediate use of them, though they were comforted by the thought that if their uncle made any further attempt to interfere in their private lives material was at hand to discredit his opinion. Meanwhile, they kept the photographs in a place which they fondly imagined to be secure and private, taking them out from time to time merely for their personal amusement.'

'Deirdre didn't know about all this,' said Lucian, 'you can't have heard about it from Deirdre.'

'No,' I said. 'No, it wasn't from Deirdre—though she

176

evidently had a certain talent for knowing things she was not supposed to know and finding things she was not supposed to find. Certainly she found these photographs, on some occasion when she was visiting her cousins, and decided—I say nothing of her motives—to take possession of them. When her cousins discovered the loss they were, I rather think, more than a little perturbed: much as they disliked their uncle, they had never intended that such damaging photographs should pass into general circulation. Still, there was nothing to be done: they had almost forgotten the incident, until a few months later the photographs were scattered on the ground before them on the Esplanade at Corfu.'

'Oh,' said Lucinda despondently, 'you know it's us.'

They sat gazing at me with bewildered apprehension. Lucinda sought or offered reassurance by surreptitiously clasping her brother's hand.

'I don't understand how you know all this,' said Lucian. 'You seem to know things that no one could know except us.'

'It's as if you could see into people's minds,' said his sister. 'Who are you? How do you know all these things?'

'I am a scholar,' I said. 'Few mysteries are impenetrable to the trained mind.'

They continued, however, to gaze at me with a sort of superstitious dread, as if supposing me studied in some darker and more secret learning than is to be found in the statutes of Edward I or the books of Glanvil and Bracton. My heart warmed to these delightful young people: it was such a different response from any I could have hoped for in Lincoln's Inn, where my carefully reasoned deductions would have been described as mere guesswork, or else as so childishly simple that the members of the Nursery, had they not been occupied with more important matters, could have worked them out for themselves in half the time.

'There is no need,' I said kindly, 'to look so anxious. Your conduct is quite understandable: the interference of your relative in your affairs must have been most irritating.'

'We wouldn't have minded,' said Lucian, 'but it's so beastly for Mama. Rupert writes to Father saying we're behaving badly and Father writes to Mama and says she can't have brought us up properly and Mama gets all upset. It's terribly unfair, because she has brought us up properly—well, she's tried.'

'You may think,' said Lucinda, 'that we're not terribly well brought up. But it isn't Mama's fault.'

'I believe,' I said, 'that you are very fond of your mother, and would go to great lengths to protect her from any distress?'

To this they both vigorously assented.

'And we didn't keep the camera,' said Lucinda. 'We gave it to Oxfam.'

There was a further question which I should have liked to ask them; but I thought, despite the impression I had made on them, that they would not have given me a truthful answer. With the photographs again in my possession, I left the Fairfax twins and made my way, by a discreetly circuitous route, to another café further down the Liston, where I sat at a table shaded from the sun by a wide blue canopy.

Men in white had begun to gather beside the Esplanade, some young, some middle-aged. The older men—these, presumably, were the Writers and Artists—were dressed in conventional white flannels; the younger ones—those qualified, I supposed, by ties of blood rather than personal accomplishment to play for one or other of the two sides—had preferred to wear shorts. They hoped, perhaps, to impress with the shapeliness of their legs those tourists of the female sex who were now beginning to take afternoon refreshments at the tables in the Liston; though Julia, most susceptible of tourists, has been heard to say that the traditional cricketing costume, if worn by a young man of graceful figure, is of all forms of masculine dress the one most conducive to desire. (But that, I seem to remember, was under the influence of some particular attachment.)

Looking across to the far side of the Esplanade, I observed a motor-car draw up there, of moderate size and rather shabby, and a tall, dark man emerge from the door nearest to the driving seat. Though I had not the privilege of any personal acquaintance with Constantine Demetriou, I thought that I would instantly have known him, even had he not been accompanied by Camilla and his wife and son. I would not have doubted, even at such a distance, that this was a man of no ordinary sort, but one marked out by some kind of greatness. I cannot say precisely what it was that produced this effect: though tall, he was not in truth so much above average height as to account for the impression he gave of Olympian stature: but he walked across the Esplanade like a man who treads an immortal path, in the footsteps of Homer and Aeschylus.

The Writers and Artists welcomed him with enthusiasm. With a certain air of ceremony, he settled Dolly at a table close by the edge of the cricket pitch, in the shade of a thick-leaved acacia tree, with Camilla and Leonidas on either side of her; the group was completed by the Fairfax twins, who strolled across from the Liston to join them. The poet himself continued to go to and fro among the players, no doubt with words of encouragement and exhortation for his team.

There was as yet no sign of Sebastian and Selena, and Constantine seemed once or twice to look anxiously at his watch. At last, however, I saw them hurrying towards the cricket pitch from the southern end of the Esplanade, Selena every few yards or so giving a little skip to keep pace with Sebastian's longer stride. She was wearing the dress of sky-blue cotton which I had admired on a previous occasion, and Sebastian had somehow provided himself with clothing of suitable whiteness for the activities of the afternoon. Constantine waved, and went a little way to meet them.

They joined the group at the edge of the cricket pitch, Leonidas yielding to Selena his place beside his mother. The reunion seemed an occasion for much laughter and many embraces: I could hardly think it a suitable moment to break in on the gathering with dark warnings of malice and danger. Which might, after all, be quite unfounded: the theory which in London I had held with such conviction had begun, in the sunlit warmth of Corfu, to seem like a morbid and improbable fancy. Moreover, I was persuaded that there was nothing to fear until they all returned to the Villa

179

Miranda. I accordingly resolved to remain where I was, awaiting an opportunity to speak privately to Selena.

The twenty-three-yard strip of coconut matting which is the island's substitute for the carefully tended green wickets of England was rolled out in the centre of the pitch and secured to the bare brown earth. Though too far away to be certain which side had won the toss, I supposed that it must have been the Artists, since they went in to bat first: on the Corfu ground, I am told by those who understand such matters, this is almost always an advantage, obliging the other side to waste their energies in the field in the hotter part of the day and to face the bowling when the deceptive shadows of evening have begun to reach towards the wicket.

Constantine, however, gave no impression of feeling that luck was against him, but set his field in the bold and heroic style which shows confidence in the favour of the gods: the majority of his team were gathered closely round the batsman, hopeful of catches, and those left to wander in the outfield had an exiled, solitary look. I gathered that Constantine was not of that school of thought which holds that in limited over matches, such as are played in Corfu, the primary object of the fielding side should be to contain the scoring rate rather than to take wickets.

His strategy seemed at first to be vindicated by success, for the opening batsmen were swiftly and inexpensively dismissed. The Artists had scored fourteen runs for two wickets when their captain took his place at the crease—a bushy-bearded, barrel-shaped man, with whom I had a slight acquaintance. The vigour and panache of his painting had earned him, if not an international reputation, one which at any rate extended beyond the shores of his native island. He brought the same qualities to his batsmanship: if, as he notoriously believed, the true function of the brush was to transfer as large a quantity of paint as possible to the canvas, the function of the bat was by the same token to hit every ball bowled, of whatever speed or length, as hard as possible towards the boundary. This technique, if there were any justice in the game, would have cost him his wicket half a dozen times before he reached double figures; but there is none, and he survived.

Constantine began to look anxious. In spite of bowling changes and the reluctant withdrawal of fielders to the depopulated outfield, the painter could not be dislodged and continued to score freely. He did manage, in his eagerness to score at the end of each over the single run required to retain the bowling, to run out two of his partners; but it was plainly too much to hope that the whole team would be similarly disposed of. At the end of the seventeenth over, when the Artists' score had reached the eighties, Constantine shrugged his shoulders, as if willing to try anything once, and threw the ball to his son.

Not following the fashion of his contemporaries, Leonidas was dressed in flannels, but with a shirt slashed like a tunic from arm to waist: a design intended, no doubt, to give greater ease of movement, but also affording to the on-lookers, when he ran up to bowl, a tantalizing glimpse of bare brown flesh. I thought how fortunate it was that Julia was not with me.

The first ball he bowled was what an *aficionado* would have described, I believe, as being of a good length and pitching on the off stump: the painter hit it for four runs, finding a gap in what is termed the leg side field. Anticipating a similar stroke, Constantine moved a fieldsman ten yards to the right. The second ball was again of good length and pitching on the off stump: again the batsman hit it for four—through the space left vacant by the fieldsman. Looking dejected, the boy turned and went back to begin his run-up for a third time: once more he bowled a ball well pitched up on the off stump. The batsman, seeing how closely it resembled its prede-cessors, stepped forward to deal with it in a similar manner; but on this occasion it turned shyly, almost coquettishly, away, leaving the bat to pass through empty air; and then moved back again to continue on its way towards the off stump. The painter, as he walked back to the Liston, shook his head sadly at Leonidas, as if deploring that one so young should be capable of such duplicity.

The Artists were in due course dismissed for a total of a

hundred and thirty-one runs—a respectable score for the ground, but by no means invincible, requiring the Writers to score at a rate of precisely four runs an over in order to secure victory. Leonidas had taken four wickets. Sebastian had done nothing in particular to distinguish himself or bring glory on the name of his College and University; on the other hand, he had done nothing to bring them into disrepute, which is more than can always be said of my colleagues travelling abroad.

Tea was taken. I use the expression in a conventional sense, to signify the interval between one innings and the next, since players and spectators alike preferred for the most part to refresh themselves with lager. I felt for a moment a certain uneasiness at the thought of Sebastian and Selena taking food or drink in the midst of the Demetriou family; but the waiter brought a number of bottles and glasses on the same tray, and there seemed no way of anyone foreseeing who would drink from which.

Whether from a fixed regard for the quality of English batsmanship or because he thought it an honour proper to be accorded to a guest, Constantine selected Sebastian to be one of the opening batsmen. His partner was a dark man of saturnine appearance, whom I recognized with a slight effort of memory as an amateur historian of the Byzantine era and the author of a despondent epic novel set in that period: he batted cautiously, guarding his wicket as carefully as his sister's honour from the brutal onslaughts of the bowler, but betraying no consciousness that the game was one which involved the scoring of runs. In spite of his caution, however, he was caught at square leg off the first ball of the fifth over. The spectators observed his departure with not un-mixed regret; and Sebastian was joined at the crease by his captain.

Though I profess no expertise in the subtleties of the game, I had sufficiently often been persuaded to lend the encouragement of my presence at College and University matches at once to recognize the high quality of Constantine's batmanship. He played with a fluency and majestic elegance I had seldom seen equalled. His eye and speed, no doubt, were not what they had been in his youth; but I thought that in his prime he could hardly have found himself outclassed in any side he chose to play for.

Sebastian also, as if inspired by his example, began to play with a sparkle and stylishness I had not known him to possess. It commonly happens, I have seen it often, that two batsmen playing together for the first time are unable, whatever their individual talents, to score with much rapidity: one calls for a run; his partner hesitates; the first retreats; the second sets forth down the wicket; the first shouts 'No'; the second, according to temperament, goes back cursing under his breath or forward cursing at the top of his voice; at best there is no run, at worst there is a run-out. With Constantine and Sebastian there was none of this: between them there seemed to be so perfect a sympathy as to preclude such misunderstandings; and despite a defensive field they maintained a scoring rate approaching six runs an over.

It may be that some of my readers would wish me to give a full description of this agreeable interlude, relating in detail the particular attributes of each ball bowled and each stroke played. Regretfully, I must disappoint them: such an account would not be germane to my narrative, nor is mine the pen to undertake such a task. The partnership ended in the nineteenth over, when Sebastian fell victim to an interesting and original interpretation of the leg before wicket rule on the part of one of the umpires—who was, I now remembered, a cousin of the barrel-chested painter. Sebastian, being a well-brought-up young man, walked back without argument or reproach to rejoin the group gathered round Dolly at the edge of the cricket pitch.

I had hoped that when his innings was concluded Selena might be tempted to pay less attention to the game—perhaps to wander about a little, looking at the shop windows of the Liston, and so providing me with an opportunity of private conversation with her. She chose, however—whether from motives of politeness, or because the game had reached a sufficiently dramatic stage to engage her interest—to remain in her place beside Dolly. I resigned myself to making, if I could not speak to her before the match was concluded, a less discreet approach than I had hoped.

Aristotle, I suppose, would have approved of cricket—a game which peculiarly demonstrates how a moment's error may bring down the protagonist from the heights of prosperity to the depths of disaster. At ten minutes past six o'clock the Writers seemed in an enviable position: a mere forty runs needed for victory; thirteen overs in which to make them; eight wickets standing; and their captain still at the crease in apparently invincible form. By half past the hour matters were very different.

The two batsmen who succeeded Sebastian (a minor poet and the nephew, I believe, of the epic novelist) were out of form or out of luck; their wickets fell before the score reached a hundred. Leonidas played a charming little innings, giving signs of having inherited something of his father's talents; but he played at a ball which his father would have left to its own devices, and was caught behind the wicket with only a dozen runs to his credit. Four further batsmen (of whose literary achievements or connections I am unable to give particulars) came and went without making much contribution to the total; and the Writers, at the fall of their penultimate wicket, still needed six runs to win.

The influential critic and belles-lettriste who occupied eleventh place in the batting order, though undoubtedly familiar with Aristotelian principles, had assumed at some much earlier stage that his services would not be called on and that there was no reason to reject the generous offers of lager made by those anxious for his goodwill. After an unsteady progress to the wicket he stood leaning heavily on his bat, evidently grateful for its support, and smiled with hazy benevolence at those about him. When the bowler began to hurl projectiles in his direction, he took no offence at this unfriendly conduct but gently waved his bat in the air in what seemed to be a gesture of forgiveness and good fellowship. By some dispensation of Providence his wicket survived the three balls which remained of the over.

It could not be supposed that such a miracle would be repeated. Unless Constantine were able to make the necessary runs during the next over, the Artists would be assured of victory: it was merely a question—since his partner was clearly in no condition to participate in any running between the wickets—of ensuring that the ball never reached the boundary. The Artists accordingly set a defensive field.

Constantine, with Homeric calm, prepared to receive the bowling, looking carefully about him for any vulnerable space between the fieldsmen. The first four deliveries, however, all rather wide outside the leg stump, gave him no opportunity for any scoring stroke. It seemed to me—I suppose this cannot actually have occurred—but it seemed to me that all those in the Liston held their breath as he waited for the fifth ball of the over. It was slightly short of a length, and he took two majestic paces down the wicket to meet it. The sunlight gleamed on his bat as he drove the ball high over deep mid-on.

I heard a cry and a crash of breaking glass; I felt rather than saw a massive figure hurtling towards me; and I was enveloped in darkness.

CHAPTER 16

I looked up into eyes the colour of lapis lazuli.

'My dear Professor Tamar,' said Leonidas Demetriou, 'I do hope you haven't hurt yourself.'

'I feel,' I said, 'no pain.' I feared this might signify that my injuries were unusually grave; but I accepted the boy's assistance in rising from the undignified position in which I found myself. 'Would you,' I continued, 'be kind enough to tell me what has happened? Was I struck by the cricket ball?'

'Oh no,' said Leonidas, with his slightly malicious Byzantine smile. 'Oh no, Professor Tamar, the ball was going far too high to have hit you. It went through the window of the café over there. The man who owns the café was rather put out about it—my parents are busy saying soothing things to him. But the lunatic fielding at mid-on thought it might be a catch—idiotic of him really, it was six all the way. He was running so hard to get to it, and not looking where he was going, that he went straight into your table and knocked your canopy down on top of you. And he's quite a big chap, I'm afraid. I'm really extremely sorry.'

I considered his explanation and found it consistent with the evidence.

'Well,' I said, 'I am glad at any rate that the Writers have been victorious. You are not, as it happens, my only acquaintance in the side. Sebastian Verity—'

'Oh yes, of course, Sebastian is a colleague of yours, isn't he? And Selena—Miss Jardine—who is also a friend of yours, is here with him. Have you seen them yet? Do they know you're here?'

'No,' I said. 'My coming to Corfu was a matter of impulse and will be a surprise to them.' I looked towards the place where Selena and Sebastian had been sitting; but they were no longer there, nor could I see them elsewhere in the Liston. Indeed, although it could hardly have been for more than a minute or two that I had lain dazed and helpless under the wreckage of the canopy, the whole Demetriou family, with the exception of Leonidas himself, had somehow managed in that time to disappear from view. 'I was meaning,' I went on, 'to have a word with them when the match was over, but I seem to have lost sight of them. Do you know where they might have gone?'

'They've gone up to the Citadel,' said Leonidas. 'My father said it was unthinkable for them to leave Corfu without seeing the view from the eastern summit, so they had to promise to go straight up there as soon as the match was finished. Do you want to follow them, or would you rather wait to see them when they come down again?'

My uneasiness returned. I did not imagine, certainly, that the Citadel would be deserted: on a fine evening in the height of summer, it would be surprising if my friends ever found themselves out of sight and earshot of at least half a dozen fellow tourists engaged on a similar exploration. Thinking, however, of its precipitous battlements; of the massive blocks of stonework poised above its narrow pathways; and of the inscriptions which one finds there commemorative of de-

186

struction and violent death—thinking of these things, and the apprehensions which had brought me to Corfu—

'I think I should prefer,' I said, 'to follow them up to the Citadel.'

The boy appeared to assume that he should come with me. Reflecting that it was some time since I had last visited the Citadel and that unguided I might not strike on the most direct route to the eastern summit, I was not displeased to have his company. We set forth together across the Esplanade.

A narrow, steep-sided channel, deep enough for small sailing-boats to bob about in it, divides the town of Corfu from the projection of rock which by some irony of Nature makes the gentlest of islands one of the most powerful naval strongholds in the Mediterranean, impregnable save by guile for almost a millennium. The Citadel, I remembered, had not always been completely encircled by sea; but in the sixteenth century, perceiving the slender connecting isthmus as a weak point in the defences, the Venetians had slit it as neatly and efficiently as if it had been the throat of some inconvenient diplomat.

'It occurs to me,' I said, when we had crossed the bridge over the channel and were approaching the great gateway, 'that you were not surprised to find me beside the Esplanade.'

'My brother and sister told me you were here. They didn't remember who you were, of course, but I recognized the description. What *have* you been saying to them, Professor Tamar? They're off buying crucifixes at this very moment in case they meet you again.'

'That,' I said, 'is most gratifying. But I fear that you, my dear boy, are less easily impressed.'

'I don't think,' he said, with the same malicious and satirical smile, 'that I believe in necromancy. But you do find things out, don't you? Things that one wouldn't expect.'

'It is by way,' I said, not ungratified, 'of being my profession. The Scholar is dedicated to the pursuit of Truth, most of all when she is hidden and elusive.'

'Isn't the pursuit sometimes fruitless?'

'Where nothing at all is known, even Scholarship is helpless; but even a small amount of information, perhaps of little
apparent relevance, will enable the Scholar to detect the
minute inconsistencies which betray the boundary between
truth and falsehood. It is logically impossible, you see, for a
lie to be perfectly consistent with truth: in order to tell an
undetectable lie, it would be necessary to invent an alternative universe.'

Having passed through the barbican, the visitor appears to
be presented with a choice of three routes by which to explore
the Citadel. The choice, however, is to some extent illusory.
The broad, even-surfaced roadway to the right is no more
than a digression, affording a closer look at the Doric façade
of St George's Church before winding back though the pine
trees to rejoin the central pathway on its ascent to the plateau
known nowadays as the Square of Heroes. Turning to the
left, the visitor may follow the outer line of battlements along
the base of the western summit and round the eastern, but is
eventually obliged, if wishing to explore further, to undertake the climb up to the plateau. From there, there is only one
way up to the eastern summit. The western, having been
appropriated to the purposes of local government or television or something of that sort, is not open to the public.

Despite its less inviting gradient, we took the route which
leads most directly to the plateau, a marble-flagged roadway
wide enough even to allow the passage of a small motor
vehicle. I rather hoped, since I could not suppose that Selena
and Sebastian were more than a few minutes ahead of us,
that with haste we might overtake them by the time they
reached the plateau.

'I should not have thought,' said Leonidas, as we continued on our upward path, 'that the activities of my brother
and sister were a very likely subject of scholarly investigation—how did you come to know about them?'

'For various reasons,' I said, 'I have felt for some time a
certain curiosity about the affairs of your family.'

'I thought perhaps you had. It did occur to me, after you

came to Godmansworth, that you had shown a more flattering interest in my conversation that it quite deserved.'

'My dear boy,' I said, 'you are too modest.'

'Thank you, Professor Tamar—people don't often say
so.'

The Square of Heroes is dominated by the barracks which
the British built there in the nineteenth century—an unpre-
possessing building and now derelict. From the open space in
front of it there is admittedly a very fine view across to the
island of Vido; and part of the area has been at some time laid
out as a formal garden, shaded by trelliswork, with an
ornamental pond and two circular stone dance-floors: I
could imagine it having once been a charming setting for
women in evening dress and officers in brightly coloured
uniforms to drink champagne and eat water-ices; but there
seemed to me now to be something melancholy about the
place. Selena and Sebastian were nowhere to be seen.

'They must already be at the top,' said Leonidas. 'Never
mind, Professor Tamar, it isn't far.'

I resigned myself to climbing the haphazard and irregular
steps, providing an often treacherous foothold, which rise in
a steep diagonal from the north-eastern corner of the Square:
the evening was still too warm for such an exertion to be
pleasurably undertaken. Moreover, it seemed when ac-
complished to have been undertaken in vain: arriving at the
entrance to the stairway which leads upwards through solid
rock to the top of the eastern summit, we were confronted
with a notice announcing in Greek and English that excavations were in progress and entrance was forbidden.

'Oh,' said Leonidas, 'don't worry about that. Millie was
saying at tea-time that some idiot had put a "No Entry"
notice up here, but it's a mistake or a joke or something. All
the excavations are down by the main gateway.'

He stooped to go through the low doorway and I followed
him with misgiving. The first few steps of the stairway were
lit, though dimly so, by the light from the doorway; after that
there was total darkness. Proceeding cautiously up the worn

and uneven stairs, I drew some comfort from the prospect of a reunion with friends. Sebastian, I supposed, would be taking the opportunity to explain to Selena that the Citadel had been the scene of events which changed the history of the world—it may fairly be claimed that if the Turkish siege of 1537 had been successful, Western Europe would have become part of the Ottoman Empire. I hoped he would remember that it was the western summit, not the eastern, which was so heroically and momentously defended—the Venetians had grudged the expense of fortifying the latter.

We emerged at last into daylight to stand on the crest of the eastern summit. The fortifications which Venice was at last persuaded to build there have crumbled again into ruin, and broom and wild sage grow rife among the stones; but the view of the island northwards and southwards and across the sea to the jagged mountains of Epirus remains commanding and majestic. It had deservedly been recommended by Constantine to the admiration of Selena and Sebastian—who were, however, notable by their absence.

'I know,' said Leonidas. 'They must be down in the catacomb. I'll go and find them and tell them you're here.'

Paying no heed to my suggestion that we might simply call out and see if they answered, he scrambled with great agility down an opening very similar to the one from which we had just emerged, but enclosing a staircase in an even more alarming state of dilapidation. It led, I recalled, to a tunnel-shaped chamber, hollowed out of the rock, and having no other means of entry or exit. Two embrasures—one at the eastern end, beside the staircase, the other at the centre of the south-facing wall, each high enough and deep enough for a tall man to stand or lie full-length without discomfort there—opened on to an almost sheer cliff-face and looked down to the rocks some hundreds of feet below. The boy was quite wrong, of course, in referring to it as a catacomb; but the thought crossed my mind that it must be curiously similar in size and shape to the sacrificial chamber in the Temple of the Dead, where Sebastian had stumbled and grazed his wrist. I called out to inquire of Leonidas whether Sebastian and Selena were indeed there.

'No.' His voice was blurred by its own echo. 'No, they're not here—I can't think where they are. But I've found something rather extraordinary—do come down and see, Professor Tamar.'

Looking at the dilapidated staircase, I asked if he could not come above ground again, bringing with him whatever it was he thought might engage my interest.

'No, Professor Tamar, I can't do that—it's sort of attached. It isn't really difficult to get down here, you know—if you sit on the edge, you have your feet on quite a solid bit of the stairway, and after that it's all right.'

There are few hardships, as I have written elsewhere, which the Scholar is unwilling to endure in pursuit of knowledge. Following his advice, I managed to lower myself without misadventure into the underground chamber; but wondered, as I tried to accustom my eyes to the gloom, whether the ascent would be equally straightforward. The boy stood in the dark angle between the wall and the staircase with something in his hand which seemed to glitter in the remnants of light penetrating the embrasures: I drew closer, intending to study it.

'I'm really very sorry about this, Professor Tamar,' said Leonidas, holding me by the shoulder and the knife against my throat.

By declining the duties of examiner I had hoped to avoid this sort of treatment on the part of the young. I now saw that I had, on the contrary, deprived myself of the specialized experience required to deal with such contingencies. I also saw how much better it would have been to allow Timothy to come to Corfu in my stead.

'My dear boy,' I said, 'you are making a grave mistake.'

'No,' said Leonidas, 'no, Professor Tamar, I don't think so. I understand now what you meant when you said you didn't believe that Deirdre had killed herself. I was never quite sure that you meant you thought she had died by accident—and now I know you didn't.' The blade of the knife seemed to draw even closer to my throat.

There appeared to be some misunderstanding. I had long discarded the notion of Leonidas having any responsibility for his cousin's death; and if the view I now held were well-founded, nothing could be more absurd than any attempt on his part to protect the person culpable. The prospect, however, of having one's throat cut has a remarkably stimulating effect on the mental processes: after only an instant or two of bewilderment, there came to me some notion of what was troubling him. He had thought again about the events of Boat Race Day; and he *knew* there had not been time for Dolly to have left the roof before Deirdre fell or was thrown from it.

'My dear boy,' I said again, striving with some difficulty to maintain that evenness of tone which is desirable when dissuading the young from behaviour they may afterwards regret, 'my dear boy, you don't imagine that I believe your *mother* had any hand in Deirdre's death?'

He seemed to relax a little, and the knife blade receded by about a millimetre; but then he grew tense again, as if fearing that I spoke from expedience rather than from conviction.

'If she was there when Tancred did it and didn't say anything, she'd be an accessory, wouldn't she?'

It was in the abstract sense a not unattractive theory, which under happier conditions I would have commended for its ingenuity. I had no doubt that the solicitor had formed for Dolly a passionate attachment of the kind which she was accustomed to inspire, and to encourage, perhaps, to an extent which might be misunderstood by both admirer and husband. If Deirdre had become aware of it—and to do so would have been not uncharacteristic of her; if she had seen an opportunity for profit or malevolence—and again, it would have been not uncharacteristic; if all three of them had been gathered together on the roof of Rupert's flat . . . psychologically, however, it was inconceivable; besides—

'It is,' I said, 'an ingenious suggestion. But it won't do. It does not explain, you see, the most curious aspect of the whole episode. It does not explain how it happened that Deirdre fell to her death while your brother Lucian was still attentively watching the race from the balcony—and your brother did not see her fall.'

From above came the sound of voices: I was able to

identify them, with some relief, as those of Selena and Sebastian.

'Professor Tamar,' said Leonidas very quickly, still holding me pinned at knife-point in the dark corner between the wall and the staircase, 'you wouldn't be so foolish, I hope, as to call out.' His lapis lazuli eyes shone like a cat's in the darkness. I believed, however, that he would not wish to cut my throat without knowing my explanation for the curious circumstance to which I had just referred.

Then there was another voice, seeming to come from much closer at hand: a voice of great beauty and resonance, which I had never heard before but had no doubt was that of Constantine Demetriou. He spoke as if ill or injured, in halting and disjointed phrases which I could not think to be characteristic of him; though in his actual tone I could detect no note of alarm or anxiety.

'Is that you? . . . Sebastian? . . . I'm down here . . . Can you help me? . . . Sebastian . . . I'm down here.'

I tried in vain to imagine where he could be. His voice had seemed to come from within the underground chamber of which I supposed Leonidas and myself to be the only occupants. Although the further end of the room was in shadow, the darkness was not so impenetrable as to have concealed his presence; besides, it did not seem to me that his voice came from that direction. I could only suppose that he had descended the staircase unheard by Leonidas and myself, had stumbled perhaps on the last step, and was now lying hidden from our view by the projection of the supporting wall.

'Sebastian . . . I'm down here . . . Can you help?' The same disjointed phrases in the same even and unagitated tone.

'Constantine? Is that you? Don't worry, I'll be down in a few seconds.' I could hear Sebastian's voice sufficiently clearly to know that he had already begun the descent. There followed a slithering of stones, the sound of a fall and of the mild imprecations to be expected from a young man of gentle and poetic disposition who has missed his footing and been thrown headlong on to a hard, uneven surface.

I must have made some involuntary movement as if to go to the assistance of my unfortunate young colleague: a slight increase in the pressure of the boy's hand on my shoulder and the pricking of the knife point against my skin suggested that this would be imprudent.

'Sebastian, what's happened? Are you all right?' Selena's voice also was now clearly audible.

'More or less—I've tripped over some kind of netting and I can't get free. And I can't see Constantine—Constantine, are you there?'

He was answered by silence. My perplexity deepened, since he was now in the only part of the chamber which was hidden from my own view.

Not doubting that Selena would accomplish the descent with her customary elegant agility, I was astonished, a few seconds later, to hear further sounds of stumbling and a cry of vexation which suggested that she also had fallen.

I became conscious that one of the meagre sources of light had been partially obscured. A tall, dark figure, holding what seemed to be a spear, stood in the embrasure nearer to the stairway: not Constantine: Camilla.

'Amazing how easy it is to trip on those stairs, isn't it?' said Camilla. 'Specially if someone's chucked a bit of old fishing-net over the bottom step. Don't try to move, by the way—Sebastian's tummy's just nicely in line with the point of this fishing-spear, and it's sharp enough to go straight through.'

'Camilla,' said Sebastian, 'what on earth do you think you're doing? And where's Constantine? We heard him calling out from here less than a minute ago.'

'Oh,' said the girl, 'you don't need to worry about Constantine. That was just a sort of selection of the great man's conversation put together on my dinky little tape-recorder. I didn't think you'd come down here if it was me you heard calling, so I spent a day last week getting it ready. Quite clever, don't you think?'

'Most ingenious,' said Selena. 'You have evidently been to some trouble to arrange this little gathering. And to some risk, if you got up there from the pathway. It's quite a precipitous climb, and a long way down to the rocks.'

'Oh,' said Camilla, as if deprecating any praise for her athletic accomplishments, 'that wasn't difficult. I left a rope hanging down there earlier this afternoon, the same time I fixed up the "No Entry" sign to make sure we weren't disturbed. So when I was certain you were on your way up here, I just came round the other side and shinned up it.'

'Did you,' asked Sebastian, 'have any particular purpose in making these arrangements?'

'So that I could kill you, of course,' said Camilla.

The boy and I remained equally motionless: I had hardly noticed, so entirely was my attention held by Camilla, the moment when he ceased to hold the knife to my throat; but when he drew breath as if to speak, I had put my hand to his mouth. My friend Sebastian, a glimmering patch of white in the shadows at the foot of the staircase, lay helpless at the mercy of Camilla's spear; and I did not doubt, as Leonidas may have done, that she was wholly in earnest. I thought that it would require no little circumspection to ensure that any of us left the chamber alive.

'Are you sure,' asked Selena at last, in a pleasantly conversational tone, 'that that is a very good idea? The consequences, if you happened to be found out, would be rather disagreeable; and it is not immediately clear what advantage you hope to obtain.'

'You must be joking,' said the other girl. 'You don't think I'm going to spend the rest of my days letting you two blackmail me, do you? I suppose you thought you'd have a meal-ticket for life, once my great-grandmother died and I came into the money. Well, you've picked the wrong woman for that game—I know what to do about blackmailers.'

'What on earth makes you think—?' Some warning movement by Selena, I supposed, discouraged Sebastian from completing the question.

'Oh, don't start trying to pretend you weren't going to blackmail me, I know what you were up to. It makes it absolutely justifiable to get rid of you in any way I can— every one agrees that blackmail's worse than murder. And no one's going to find out about it. You're going to have a nasty accident due to fooling about too close to the edge of

195

that opening.' She pointed towards the embrasure facing southwards.

'Rather like Deirdre,' said Selena, sounding interested. 'You don't feel that people may begin to make unpleasant remarks about the inflationary effect of your presence on the fatal accident figures?'

'Why should they? When Deirdre fell off the roof of Daddy's flat I was down in the drawing-room, with half a dozen witnesses to prove it.'

'Ah yes, so you were,' said Selena thoughtfully. 'How did you manage it? It sounds rather clever.'

'Yes, it was rather, though I says it as shouldn't. Specially as I didn't have time to plan anything properly—I didn't know I was going to kill her, you see, I'm not even sure I really meant to. Afterwards, of course, I saw it was the only thing I could have done. She'd been all excited and pleased with herself all through lunch, but I didn't know why. And then afterwards, when we were alone on the roof, she told me she'd found out—well, the same thing as you two, of course. She was gloating and crowing over me fit to burst, you'd have thought she *wanted* to get herself murdered. Anyway, I got so riled I just went for her, and before I knew what had happened there she was with her neck broken, silly little beast. So I had to think pretty quickly what to do about it. The first thing I thought of was chucking her straight over on to the pavement, but then I thought it might mean some embarrassing questions. So I pitched her over the side on to the bedroom balcony—it sticks out a bit further than the roof—and went downstairs to watch the Boat Race on television. When it got to the exciting bit and everyone was concentrating on it, I muttered something about going to the loo, and went and tipped her over on to the pavement—from the end of the balcony, of course, so it would look as if she'd fallen from the front of the building. It didn't take a minute, I don't think anyone even noticed I was gone. Not bad for the spur of the moment, don't you think?'

'Extremely quick-witted,' said Selena. 'But how did you persuade Dolly to say that Deirdre was still on the roof when she went up there again?'

'Oh, Dolly didn't go back on to the roof. She was having a touching farewell scene in the study with old Tanks—she'd let him squire her about for a few weeks before Costas came over to London and he'd fallen for her in a big way. The twins were covering for her, the way they always do. So when Dolly came back into the drawing-room, she pretended she'd come down from the roof—and of course she thought Deirdre was still up there.'

'From your point of view,' said Selena, 'a rather fortunate combination of circumstances.'

'Yes, it was rather, because it meant no one twigged that I was the last person who'd been alone with Deirdre. Mind you, it's a good thing I wasn't counting on it—Costas got the idea it was his fault Dolly hadn't been on the roof at the right time to stop Deirdre falling off it, and she got in a tizzwozz and started thinking she ought to set his mind at rest by saying where she really was. But I managed to persuade her he'd be happier feeling bad about Deirdre than knowing about the little fling with Tancred.'

Looking at the boy Leonidas, I noted that his expression was one of relief. His satisfaction in being assured of his mother's innocence was no doubt very commendable; I hoped it would not render him for too long impervious to the danger of our present position.

'The sailing accident,' said Selena, 'was also most ingenious. You arranged a suitable compass deviation, I suppose, with the assistance of a transistor radio or some other magnetic object, and left Leonidas obediently steering straight for the rocks of Parga. So when you went overboard, you knew just where you were and what point to swim for. You were wearing a wetsuit, I expect, under the famous black pyjamas, and I suppose you had a face mask and flippers and so forth—it would have been too dark for Leonidas to see what you were wearing. You'd have had to dispose of them, of course, before you went ashore—that must have been rather nerve-racking. How disappointing, after so much risk and effort, to find that your cousins had all survived.'

'I had the rottenest luck,' said Camilla. 'It was a super plan, and the conditions were simply perfect. That's the important thing—seeing one's opportunities and making the most of them. Well, that's what I did, and if it hadn't been for those damned fishermen it would have worked perfectly.'

'Still, as you say, it was an excellent plan—with the particular merit that whatever happened no suspicion could possibly attach to yourself. That's why I'm surprised at your putting yourself in this awkward position so far as Sebastian and I are concerned.'

'I wouldn't say I was the one who's in an awkward position,' said Camilla.

'Oh, don't you think so?' Selena seemed to find this a novel and interesting point of view. 'I thought the idea was that we would appear to have fallen by accident. That means, surely, that you have to persuade us to go close enough to the edge to be pushed over; and your only means of persuasion is that fishing-spear.'

'I think,' said Camilla, 'it'll be quite an efficient form of persuasion.'

'Do you think so? But if we're supposed to have died by accident, you see, it really won't do for us to be found with spear-wounds: all sorts of questions would be asked, and you can't risk that, can you? That's what I mean by your being in an awkward position: you can't expect to achieve much by threatening us with a weapon which we both know you can't afford to use.'

'Don't kid yourselves,' said Camilla. 'I'll use it if I have to.'

'I find it hard to believe,' said Selena, with a smoothness which she generally reserved for the Court of Appeal, 'that you would do anything so . . . unintelligent. Do you really prefer the prospect of twenty years in a Greek prison to paying Sebastian and myself a modest retainer in exchange for our continued discretion?'

'Ah,' said the other girl triumphantly, 'you admit you were going to blackmail me.'

'In the circumstances, it would clearly be useless to deny it. But what makes you think it would be so very unpleasant? You don't imagine, surely, that we would make demands which would reduce you to unaccountable penury or raise ourselves to unaccountable affluence? Anything on that scale would lead inevitably to our exposure, and we don't share this taste of yours for spending long periods in prison. We would content ourselves, in our own interest, with a very trifling proportion of your total income, such as you would happily expend on services of far less value. Moreover, since you are the only potential purchaser of our discretion, we would naturally have your welfare very much at heart: our own safety and prosperity would depend on yours, and we could be expected, in our own interests, to use for your advantage whatever talents and influence either of us may possess.' A wistful note came into her voice. 'It's still very difficult, you know, for a woman to achieve recognition at the Bar, whatever her abilities. It makes all the difference if one has someone whose help and support can be absolutely relied on—not simply for the sake of friendship, which may be capricious and half-hearted, but because there is a genuine identity of interest.'

'My God,' said Camilla, 'you make it sound as if you'd be doing me a favour.' She stood gazing at Selena with fascinated amazement; and the spearpoint wavered forgetfully from its menacing direction.

There was perhaps no need for haste. I have known Selena, when negotiating a compromise of Chancery litigation, to divert the attention of far abler lawyers than Camilla with arguments no less specious for considerably longer than five seconds. It took no more than that, however, for Sebastian to rise from the darkness and leap for the embrasure.

The struggle might have been brief if both participants had been of equally murderous intention, each content to send the other on the swift and deadly journey from the edge of the embrasure to the jagged rocks below. It could not be expected, however, that Sebastian would so easily set aside the constraints of temperament, education and principle: he fought only for possession of the spear, and any advantage he may have had in strength was cancelled out by his care for the safety of his antagonist. She drew him, as they struggled in the confined space of the narrow aperture, ever closer to the edge; and it seemed to me that none of us who watched had any power to prevent her.

199

But the boy Leonidas stepped out of the shadows and called to her by name. When she saw him she released her grip on the spear; without resisting further, she allowed Sebastian to take it from her and step back to the safety of the chamber. If she had chosen to follow him, I scarcely know what we would have done: it would have been a hard thing, when it came to it, to consign so splendid a creature to long years of dark imprisonment.

She chose instead to retreat as she had come—by the rope hanging down the precipitous rockface: she was still confident, it seemed, that her athletic skills would assure her a safe descent; but on this occasion they failed her.

CHAPTER 17

Thinking it absurd after travelling so far to return immediately to the uncertain skies of London, I spent some further weeks on the shores of the Mediterranean in diversions not material to my present narrative. It was not until September that I again found myself at a candlelit table in the Corkscrew, in the company of those members of Lincoln's Inn whom I accounted particular friends.

In view of the part I had played in penetrating the mystery of Deirdre's death and in frustrating, at no small personal risk, a murderous attack on Selena and Sebastian, I rather expected my arrival at this first reunion to be greeted with a certain amount of congratulation and admiring comment, and was ready to answer a stream of eager questions as to the process of reasoning by which I had reached my conclusions. I should have remembered that the events which I have described, having occurred some weeks before, would by now have been displaced in the interest of my friends by matters of greater weight and consequence.

Timothy and Selena were attempting to negotiate an equitable compromise, on behalf of their respective clients, of a dispute concerning rights of drainage. Cantrip was complaining of a decision given against him that morning in a possession action in Little Piddlecombe County Court. Julia was relating to an unsympathetic Ragwort her disappointment in what she was pleased to term an affair of the heart: the rejection of her advances, now freely admitted to have been over-precipitate, by a graceful and elegant young man met on her recent holiday.

Eventually, however, I found an opportunity, while Timothy was acquiring another bottle, to remark to Selena that I hoped she was fully recovered from the disagreeable experience of a few weeks before. Remembering after scarcely a moment's thought the events to which I referred, she assured me that she was.

'Though at the time, I must admit, I found it all most disconcerting. Especially since Camilla was the only member of the family I'd never suspected of any homicidal tendencies—I always thought of her as the prospective victim. I wish we knew,' she added absent-mindedly, 'what she thought we were blackmailing her about.'

This observation surprised me. It was true that the circumstances in which we had last met had not seemed appropriate to a detailed explanation: I had judged it tactful, so soon as decorum permitted, to take an unobtrusive farewell, leaving Selena to devise with Sebastian and Leonidas such account of Camilla's death as would cause least distress to the surviving members of the family. I had supposed, however, since she knew so much of the truth, that subsequent reflection would have made clear the remainder.

'I say, Hilary,' said Cantrip, 'you don't mean you know what it was?'

'My dear Cantrip,' I said, 'how otherwise could I have foreseen her attempt on the lives of Selena and Sebastian?'

'Oh,' said Cantrip, looking mildly surprised. 'We didn't really think you expected anything like that—we thought it was just a coincidence. The way we saw it was that you'd got a bit fed up hanging around in London and wanted to touch Timothy for the first-class fare to Corfu.'

Waiting in vain for the others to disclaim this outrageous opinion, I was tempted to preserve a dignified silence and leave them to perplexity. They refilled my glass, however,

201

and begged for enlightenment; and it is not in the nature of the Scholar to refuse Knowledge to those who seek it.

'I said at the outset,' I began, 'that if a murder were to take place in the Remington-Fiske family it would be the heiress who was murdered. My view has been vindicated by events.'

They became, as sometimes happens, rather cross with me, accusing me of talking in riddles and paradoxes; but after a little while they allowed me to continue.

'I will begin,' I said, 'with something that happened last summer, though the true starting-point of the story is much longer ago than that. In the summer of last year, as Cantrip discovered on his excursion to Cambridge, Camilla obtained employment in a lawyer's office—not, of course, because she needed money, but to acquire practical experience of the English legal system. The services which she offered, since she had as yet no professional qualification, were presumably of a secretarial nature. We know that she had sometimes done work of that kind for her father—you mentioned it, Selena, in connection with your case about the lease of Rupert's flat.'

'With all her faults,' said Selena with a sigh, 'I can imagine that Camilla might have been a very competent typist—a good deal better than Muriel, I dare say. If you could see the Statement of Claim she did for me this morning—oh, I'm sorry, Hilary, do go on with your story.'

'How,' I asked, 'would you expect a young woman in Camilla's position to go about obtaining such employment as I have mentioned?'

'I suppose,' said Selena, 'that if there were any solicitors whom she knew personally, she would ask them if they could find a place for her for a few weeks during the summer. I suppose she might have asked Tancred.'

'Quite so. In view of the long-established connection with her family it is probable that she would have asked him; and in view of his desire that the connection should continue, it is improbable that he would have refused. I was much at fault in overlooking the significance of Tancred's addressing her as 'Camilla, my dear', though he punctiliously referred to

Deirdre as 'Miss Robinson'—I should have asked myself how he came to be on more familiar terms with the heiress than with her cousin. The explanation was simple: she had been his temporary typist. Once one knew that, the truth was not far to seek.'

'It is perhaps not quite proper,' said Ragwort, 'for a person intending to practise at the Bar to accept employment with a solicitor. But in these permissive times, I would not regard it as the first step on a path leading inevitably to murder.'

'In the present case, my dear Ragwort, your tolerance is misplaced. Imagine yourself in Camilla's position—working in the office of the solicitors who drew up her great-grandfather's Will, the Will under which she is a great heiress, and who administer the estate which she is to inherit—what do you think you would do in such circumstances?'

'I think I might be tempted,' said Ragwort, frowning a little, 'to neglect my proper duties for a minute or two and have a small peep at the Will.'

'And what you would want to look at would be not merely the draft, used for everyday reference purposes, but the Probate, kept carefully in the safe and never actually read by anyone. It is, you will remember, a long and rather tedious document. The late Sir James had six children, and his Will contained elaborate and repetitive dispositions in favour of each of them in turn and their respective issue. All this, when the Will was prepared, would have had to be copied from the draft in a fair copperplate by some unfortunate clerk in the solicitor's office. How his eyes and wrist must have ached, poor fellow, by the time he reached the dispositions in favour of the fourth child—is it any wonder if he paused to rest for a moment, or allowed his attention to be briefly distracted? And when he went back to his task to copy yet again the words "and with remainders over", is it any wonder if he resumed his task at a point in the draft a few lines beyond the point at which he had broken off?'

'No,' said Selena, 'it couldn't really happen.'

'My dear Selena, it is extremely common—it is the form of error known to students of textual criticism as haplography.

So that when Camilla, succumbing to temptation, searches in the Probate for the magic words which make her an heiress—which make her interesting and desirable, which make her an object of envy, admiration and love, which make her the person she is and has always been—when she looks for them, they simply aren't there. It is Deirdre who is the heiress.'

About us there was still the convivial hum of journalists and lawyers exchanging secrets and scandal; but those with whom I shared a table gazed at me in unaccustomed silence. Timothy refilled my glass.

'She would have known, of course, that the Probate copy was not the original. Her first step would have been to bespeak a photocopy of the original from the Probate Registry, in the hope that it was there that the error had occurred, rather than in the making of the Will. That failing, she instigated the application under the Variation of Trusts Act. No doubt she was genuinely concerned about the tax liability; but she would not solely on that account have taken the appalling risk that the judge might actually read the Probate copy. The chief purpose was to seize the opportunity offered by her position as temporary typist—she wanted a pretext for bringing into existence a number of neatly typed copies of the Will, remedying the unfortunate omission, whose authenticity would never afterwards be questioned. At the same time, she intended to contrive an occasion on which the Probate might appear accidentally to have gone astray.'

'Do you mean,' said Julia, with astonishment, 'that it really wasn't my fault?'

'Of course it wasn't, Julia,' said Selena, 'we always said it wasn't.'

'It might all have turned out as she hoped if Deirdre had not been the kind of girl she was—an inquisitive and rather malicious girl, who found things out that she wasn't supposed to know. Somehow or other—perhaps out of mere curiosity she applied to the Probate Registry for a copy of the Will—she discovered the truth. I wronged her in thinking that her letter to you, Julia, was a prelude to blackmail: she

204

wanted your professional advice on establishing her claim. But the secret was too much for her to keep: on the day of the Boat Race she told Camilla what she had learnt, you know with what consequences.'

'So the way you see it,' said Cantrip, 'Camilla didn't start off meaning to do in the whole family?'

'No, I think not—I think that Deirdre's murder was, as she said, a matter of impulse. But people who have found murder a convenient solution to their difficulties have a tendency to make a habit of it. And what had happened with Deirdre made her realize, I dare say, the precariousness of her position—it entirely depended on no one asking the right question at the Probate Registry. She would be secure in her inheritance only if all her cousins were to die without attaining a vested interest—that is to say, in the lifetime of her great-grandmother. In that event, as you will remember, there was an ultimate remainder to the estate of her deceased uncle, of whom she was the sole heir.'

'It would have been a matter then,' said Selena, 'of some urgency—Lady Remington-Fiske is always referred to as being in her eighties and not, alas, in the best of health, though she seems to have a remarkable capacity for surviving her descendants. But I still don't see how Camilla got the idea that Sebastian and I were going to blackmail her.'

'Don't you? You arrived at the Villa Miranda, and on your first day there Sebastian talked about his article on the transmission of the texts of Euripides. The central argument, as I believe I mentioned once before, turns on a rather striking instance in the text of the *Helena* of the mistake of haplography. So Sebastian sits in the garden of the Villa Miranda, earnestly addressing Camilla on that subject. He smiles, no doubt, as he does so, his usual engaging smile—or so you or I would think it; but would it seem so to a person whose most carefully guarded secret was the existence in a particular document of precisely such an error?'

'You mean,' said Selena, 'that she thought he was telling her that we knew about the Will? Oh really, didn't it occur to the silly woman that it might be a coincidence?'

'It would have seemed from her point of view an improbable one. She had met you, after all, because you were instructed on the variation: she would not think of you as a person unconnected with the matter of her inheritance, but on the contrary as someone who had been closely concerned with it. If she had any doubts, they would have been resolved when Sebastian began talking, a few minutes later, about Book XI of the *Odyssey*: describing vividly, I expect, how the ghosts of the young who have died by violence or treachery gather on the banks of the Acheron to cry out for vengeance. My dear Selena, what would *you* have thought?'

In a work of fiction it would be customary and elegant to conclude the narrative with a brief summary of the subsequent lives and fortunes of those who had figured in it. The historian of Truth is, alas, denied this attractive expedient: the events which I have described are too recent for those concerned to have progressed much further in their careers; and, if they had, I am not so well acquainted with the family as to make it certain that I would know of it.

I did read in *The Times* some weeks ago of the death of Lady Remington-Fiske: it was mentioned that Lucian would inherit the family estates. I have also seen a moderately favourable review of his first novel, and his sister's marriage to a Greek fisherman has attracted some attention in the gossip column of the *Scuttle*.

Following an investigation by the Department of Trade into the affairs of Galloway Opportunities Limited, there was talk of a prosecution; but it was decided, I am told, that in view of his tragic bereavement Rupert should be treated with lenience.

It proved unnecessary for Sebastian or myself to put ourselves to any trouble on behalf of Leonidas: he submitted excellent papers in the entrance examinations and is now reading Law at Balliol. I do my best, when he comes to me for tutorials in legal history, to forget how close he came to cutting my throat. He intends, when he is qualified, to accept Julia's offer of a pupillage: it is to be hoped that by then the passage of time will have qualified the beauty of his profile or the warmth of Julia's ardour, but at present I am bound to say that there is no sign of it.

Sebastian is working with enthusiasm on his translation of the work of Constantine Demetriou, and they correspond a good deal. He seems to think, however, that it will be some time before they meet again: Selena prefers to sail in other waters than the Ionian Sea.